EARL
Driftwood: St

MW00526725

"In *Driftwood,* Joseph Conrad collides with Jimmy Buffett in a journey through the dark heart of Mexico's Riviera Maya. Weaving together the tales of American expats fleeing their mundane lives in the States for crystal-blue Caribbean water—and far too many pitchers of margaritas—author Anthony Lee Head makes it all so real because he has lived that life."

~ Bob Calhoun, bestselling author

Anthony Lee Head's delightful book *Driftwood* ... snuck up on me like a stealthy lover, seized me and carried me away on every page. Life in Mexico is perceived with a sense of compassion and clarity. Don't miss it."

~ Peter Coyote, author, actor, Emmy award winner

"As someone with an innate wanderlust and many extended years in faraway lands, this book completely transported me into the notion of, "what if I REALLY stayed? The romance and repose of an idyllic beach, the camaraderie with fellow expats, the complexities of leaving all things familiar—and the harsh truths of living in the third world. These captivating characters, on their Margarita Road, intimately escorted me beyond my own return flights. Great read."

~ Adam Briles, producer/director of Survivor

"The setting for these sunlit, beguiling stories is Playa Paraiso, a Mexican beach town not yet overrun by high-rise resorts and franchise restaurants, and its characters are the wide range of people who come there seeking an earthly paradise. These tales of human foibles range from funny to touching, memorable to unforgettable."

~ Cyra McFadden, bestselling author

"This debut collection of short stories features an exotic location populated by believable people ... Some stories are humorous; some are poignant; some defy description ... There are also "Margaritaville"-type reflections and paeans to life off the middle-class, money-grubbing grid ... The author is at his best with tales that may be rooted in the local milieu but are really universal. Truly wonderful and moving tales; the author is a writer to watch."

~ Kirkus Reviews (starred review)

Driftwood

Stories from the Margarita Road

Anthony Lee Head

Luna Blue Books

This book is not about you. Neither is it about anyone you know. You will not find your friends, roommates, coworkers, traveling companions, or mother in these pages. Nothing in this novel actually happened. The places and people referenced in this book are not the places and people you know. It is entirely a work of fiction, and any perceived similarity to actual individuals, events, or locations is either a result of coincidence or your own overly active imagination.

Published by
Luna Blue Books
www.lunabluebooks.com

ISBN 978-1-7352781-0-0 print book

eISBN 978-1-7352781-1-7 ebook

Publisher's Cataloging-in-Publication Data

Names: Head, Anthony Lee, author.
Title: Driftwood : stories from the margarita road / Anthony Lee Head.
Description: San Rafael, CA: Luna Blue Books, 2021.
Identifiers: ISBN 978-1-7352781-0-0 (pbk.) | 978-1-7352781-1-7 (ebook)
Subjects: LCSH Mexico--Fiction. | Adventure and adventurers--Fiction.
| Short stories. | BISAC FICTION / Action & Adventure | FICTION /
Short Stories
Classification: LCC PS3608.E227 D75 2021 | DDC 813.6--dc23

Design and Layout by Val Sherer, Personalized Publishing Services
Cover Design by Sarah Bursey Infante, Graphicos Design

PRINTED IN THE UNITED STATES OF AMERICA

For Cheri

Like a plank of driftwood
Tossed on the watery main,
Another plank encountered,
Meets, touches, parts again;
So tossed and drifting ever,
On Life's unresting sea.

~ *from the Hitopadesa (Book of Good Fortune)*
by Narayan Pandit (1300-1400)

Translated from the original Sanskrit
by Edwin Arnold (1832-1904)

Contents

1 Poppa's Story 1

2 The Great Beer Commercial War . . . 18

3 Lenny's Second Coming 38

4 Moto Marty Finds His Purpose In Life . . 58

5 The Fairer Sex 83

6 Part Time Paradise 94

7 One of Our Own 114

8 The Sexiest Man In Mexico 135

9 Mrs. Timmons Gets a Tan 157

10 Letting Go 178

11 Jackie Boy Starts a New Life 204

12 The Old Man In the Sea 221

13 Storm Warnings 233

14 Heading Out 246

Acknowledgments 259

The Author 263

1
Poppa's Story

I call it the Margarita Road. It's the course your heart sets when you want to leave the past behind and start over someplace new and warm. Usually the path heads south to blue water and white sand, with any bumps along the way smoothed over by rum and tequila. It's not for everyone. This is a highway traveled mostly by runaways and drifters. I know, because I'm one of them.

"I think I'd like a piña colada for breakfast." The hammock swayed slightly as Nicole leaned over and whispered in my ear. Her breath tickled.

I pried one eye open and saw the sun reflecting off the sand. It seemed awfully early to be waking up. It wasn't even noon. But who was I to say no to a pretty lady wanting an umbrella drink? "Okay," I said with a yawn, reluctantly opening the other eye.

We had fallen asleep the night before in a hammock strung between two palm trees just outside the thatched-roof cabaña where I lived. Nicole rolled to the edge and stood up. I saw a flash of dark eyes and a swirl of black curls as she bent over, kissed me, and pulled away. "I'm going to get dressed," she announced brightly.

Lifting my head, I watched her walk toward the nearby outhouse that served as my bathroom. Along the way, she stopped and took her bikini from the hook on the outside wall of the cabaña. I groaned and stretched my arms out. "Then I guess I should, too."

I got up carefully, knowing from experience that falling out of a hammock can ruin your whole day. I reached for the shorts that lay crumpled nearby on the beach where they were dropped the night before. I shook off the sand and pulled them on, standing a little unsteadily to look out at the sea's blue water.

I had been living on a small harbor carved out of Mexico's Caribbean shoreline for the past year. It was called Playa Paraiso. Paradise Beach. Corny but true, I was officially living in paradise.

It was little more than a fishing village, with a main cobblestone promenade running parallel to the shore. Along narrow side streets were small, open-air restaurants where freshly caught fish and slabs of marinated flank steak sizzled on grills. Nearby markets sold the necessities of life such as rice, beans, and beer. Thankfully, there was no big resort scene, although the buses from Cancun occasionally brought day-tripper tourists who wanted to see the 'real' Mexico. A few small posada-style hotels catered to the divers and sports fisherman who visited in the summer months.

And there was the beach—with white talcum-powder sand bordering a sea made up of every color blue you ever heard of and a few that hadn't been named yet. Coconut palms lined the shore, and little fishing boats painted with names like Maria were anchored in the surf. Here and there you could stumble across a beach bar or hostel, but mostly it was beautifully wide open. It wasn't called Paradise without good reason.

I was admiring the view as I did every day, when Nicole returned from the washroom dressed in her bikini. "Are you ready, Poppa?"

That's me: Poppa. Or Poppi. I answer to either. No, it isn't some Hemingway fetish or anything weird like that. It's just a nickname I picked up from some of the local working girls in town. They started calling me that back when I first came to this part of the coast.

"Oh Poppi, you are so good to us," they would laughingly call out when I would occasionally splurge on a round for the house at a local cantina. They were probably just teasing, since I wasn't one to indulge in their regular services. Or maybe they just thought of me as an old man. Not that I'm a geezer. I was still in my thirties when I first landed on Paradise Beach, but even that may have seemed ancient to some of those girls.

Whatever the reason, the name stuck. It wasn't long before everyone called me that. I didn't mind. If I were going to start a new life, I figured I might as well have a new name.

Now that Nicole and I were dressed, or as dressed as life on the beach requires, we started walking along the shore toward the El Capitan for our liquid brunch. The tropical sun was already high and fierce. As we pushed our feet through the sand, Nicole gave me a sideways glance. "Are you still thinking about my idea?"

I told her I was. How many times does someone offer you a do-over at life? When that happens, you give it some serious thought.

"You're running out of time," she reminded me.

It didn't take us long to reach El Capitan, a ramshackle dive bar not far from my cabaña. The ground floor consisted of a large, three-sided room open to the ocean. Inside was a bar against the back wall, and out front a palm-thatch-covered deck stretched over the sand.

Wooden stools lined the bar, and a few plastic tables and chairs filled the room. In one corner, a small bandstand rose up about a foot off the floor. Out on the deck, a few faded lounge chairs sat near an old oil drum grill used to cook burgers and tacos. An impossibly narrow stairway hidden behind the bar's back wall led to a couple of rooms on the second floor.

El Capitan offered everything I always dreamed of: cheap food, good drinks, and a spectacular beach. That dream seemed to be a problem for some people I knew. They thought I should want more from life. I was beginning to worry they might be right.

"Jorge!" I called, as we walked up the steps from the sand onto El Capitan's deck.

Jorge smiled broadly from behind the bar. "Hola, Poppa. Hola, Nicole."

Jorge was one of my favorite people in town. A few years younger than I, he was thin with dark brown skin from a life in the sun. Like many Mexicans, he spoke perfect English whenever other gringos were around. We spoke Spanish when we were alone, and he was always kind enough not to laugh at my often miserable attempts to master the language.

He had been a guiding light when I first hit the beach, offering advice on such important matters as which hustlers to avoid, the going rate to bribe local cops, and where to get the best barbacoa tacos. He even helped arrange for me to rent my little hut.

"How are you, my friend?" I asked, as Nicole and I sat on a couple of stools.

"Bien bien, Poppa." He gestured out toward the cold grill. "I'm sorry, but if you want food, I haven't started cooking yet."

"No problema," I assured him. "We're going to drink our breakfast today. Dos piña coladas, por favor."

"Perfecto," he replied with a laugh.

"Just remember, you won't get this type of service stateside," I said to Nicole as Jorge began to mix our drinks.

"No, I sure won't," she said. "Rum for breakfast is frowned on in most places back home."

As we watched Jorge construct our cocktails with care, we shouted our hellos down the bar to Patrick, who sat on a stool at the far end. Pat was the elderly owner of the El Capitan. A short, round American with thinning white hair and a flowing white beard, he gave us a smile and a wave.

When Jorge finished the drinks, he placed a glass of frozen, alcohol-laden pineapple and coconut slush in front of each of us. Nicole and I both had a taste. "Ooh, that's good," she said and flashed a grin at Jorge. Then the smile faded as she looked around. "I'm really going to miss this place."

Nicole first walked into my life at the beginning of the summer season. I had been sitting on the sand with a freshly opened bottle of tequila—contemplating life—when I saw her strolling along the shore, splashing her feet at the water's edge. "I have enough for two," I yelled, holding the bottle up high.

She stopped in her tracks and gave me a long look, as if

considering all the possibilities at hand. "I'm not sure you do," she shouted back as she walked toward me. "I can drink a lot."

It was tropical lust at first sight, followed by a real friendship that blossomed over the next few months. The first part was not unexpected, but the second was a bit of a surprise. We weren't exactly mirror images of each other.

I was a beach bum, plain and simple. Once upon a time, I used to pour drinks for a living. Now I was even 'retired' from that. My biggest question each day was which palm tree to use for shade at naptime.

Nicole, on the other hand, was one of those people on the fast track to success. She had an Ivy League education with an MBA from Harvard and had just graduated law school. After passing the New York bar exam with flying colors the previous June, she rewarded herself with an extended vacation traveling around the Caribbean before starting her life as a big-time lawyer.

A few nights in Paradise Beach were part of a scuba tour she had joined. The group spent two days exploring the reef offshore. When the tour moved on, Nicole decided to stay and got a small room in town. "How could I leave all this?" she would ask, as we sat on the sand in front of my little place, sharing joints and fresh mango slices.

Sadly, she did have to leave—and soon. Summer was ending, and there was a job waiting with her uncle's Wall Street law firm. It was time for her to return to the real world. I was going to miss her. What I hadn't planned was her inviting me to go along when she left.

We had been cuddling on the bed in my cabaña one night, watching a gecko scamper up the wall in the candlelight, when she suddenly said, "Let's talk seriously for a minute, okay?"

That sounded ominous and not our style at all, but I said, "Okay."

"You used to be a bartender, right?"

"That's no secret. Why do you ask?"

She placed a hand on my chest. "I really like you, Poppa."

Nicole must have seen something in my face because she hurriedly added, "Now don't freak out. I'm not talking anything other than good friends here. Lord knows I have too much ahead of me to even think about getting into a serious relationship."

I involuntarily gave a sigh of relief. She saw it and smiled. "I just think you're a nice guy. A good guy. In fact, I think you are too good of a guy to hide here in Mexico for the rest of your life."

I wasn't sure I liked this turn in the conversation. "Wait a minute. What makes you think I'm hiding from anything?"

"Come on, Poppa. Don't bullshit me. You think I haven't noticed how you never talk about where you came from and how you never make plans for the future? I'm guessing things haven't gone great for you in the past."

I started to say something to change the subject when she stopped me. "I'm not prying. It's really none of my business. I just thought you might want another chance, regardless of what it was that sent you running down here. So I started wondering if you would like to give New York a try."

I told her I didn't know what to say to that.

"Yeah," she said. "This is out of the blue. It's just that I've been thinking about how my uncle's law firm represents a lot of hospitality groups. They own bars and restaurants all over Manhattan. I can almost guarantee we could find you work with one of our clients. Experienced bartenders are like celebrities in New York. Some of them make more money than attorneys do. A good-looking guy with a nice personality like you could clean up. Trust me, there will be no strings attached." She tilted her head back so she could look directly into my eyes. "I thought maybe you might want to go home."

I thanked her, of course, and said it was as nice a thing as anyone had offered me in a very long time. I promised I would think about it and let her know. True to my word, I had thought about her proposal. I had thought about it every day since then. I was still thinking about it as we slurped our breakfast booze at El Capitan.

After we finished the drinks, Jorge cleared the glasses. Nicole said she needed to go back to her room to clean up. She wanted a shower with decent pressure and hot water, neither of which was available at my place. Before she took off, we made plans to meet later to do some snorkeling on the reef. She stood up and gave me a quick peck on the cheek.

"I'm not trying to push you into going to New York, you know."

"I know you're not."

She hesitated for a moment, carefully putting the words together in her mind. "I just think you could do so much more with your life than hanging out on a beach. You have to go back at some point. Why not now?"

After she left, I stayed at the bar. Jorge poured me some seven-year-old Havana Club Cuban rum as I watched the waves break on the reef. So, Nicole thought I should try to go back, settle down, and get a real job. It's not as if I hadn't heard that before. I had heard the same line for most of my life from teachers, family, and well-meaning friends. I heard it just before I ran away from home.

"Don't you ever want to be the boss? You know, have a real career for once instead of one more job?"

My best friend Duane and I were sharing bartending duties at an upscale restaurant and lounge in San Francisco back then. Amante on Russian Hill served an Italian-California fusion menu that had critics using words like *innovative* and *groundbreaking*. As a result, overdressed, self-proclaimed foodies were five deep at the bar every evening as they waited for a table.

It was the end of a typically crazy Saturday night, and the manager had just locked the front door. As we began to clean up, Duane started to bug me once again about how we should buy a bar. "We ought to have our own place." He was on a roll. "No more bullshit jobs and batshit-crazy bosses. We'd be at the top of the food chain." He paused for a moment to wipe at a particularly stubborn stain on the bar top. "And we could hire people to clean up!"

He had been saying the same thing for close to six months. In his opinion, it was time for us to be in charge.

I started tending bar after graduating college. It was a career that took me from Boston to Miami to California. Never in all that time had I given any thought to doing anything other than slinging booze for a living. In the past, I just ignored Duane when he started his spiel, but lately I had begun to listen.

Dad keeled over from a heart attack when I was 18, and mom died not long after I finished college with a major in Business Communications. I had no real family ties, and being a bartender allowed me to go where I wanted whenever I felt like it. I was free and intended to stay that way. The idea of settling down and going into management, or worse yet being an owner, had never been on my radar.

So why was I now considering Duane's pitch about starting my own business? I can't say for sure. Maybe I was just maturing. Maybe it was my father's voice in my head saying I should grow up. Or, maybe it was the girl.

Maripat was part of the Cosmos-and-cocaine, party-hard office crowd that hung out where I worked. They would show up during my happy hour shift wearing Ann Taylor suits and Come-Fuck-Me pumps to debate the morality of the President getting a blowjob in the Oval Office.

With a pixie-cute look and a devilish attitude, Maripat caught my eye right away. Something clicked when we first met, and in no time at all we were a couple. She liked being the girlfriend of a bartender who knew the hip places to hang out, and I liked taking a hot girl to those places. However, shortly after we moved in together, her expectations for the future began to change.

"Wouldn't it be better if you ... " became Maripat's constant refrain in suggesting ways to improve my life. Didn't I want to learn to dress nicer, get to know a new class of people, and start moving up in the world?

In the past, the answer to those questions had always been no. Now I wondered if I should consider it. Maybe it was time to settle down in one place. It would make Maripat happy, and what did I have to lose, other than my freedom of course? How important was that, really? Other people seemed to do just fine without it.

"Okay," I finally said to Duane after several more weeks of listening to his pitch. "Let's open a bar and see what happens." I still remember the cold feeling in the pit of my stomach when I said it. I figured that must be how it felt to be an adult.

Duane and I quit our jobs, got a lawyer to turn us into a

corporation, and signed on the dotted line for more money than we'd ever had. It was the American Dream come true.

We opened in a small space over in Hayes Valley, not far from City Hall. We called the bar Wild Deuces, and it was a smash. Within six months, word of mouth and a few friendly mentions in the newspaper had the place crowded each night. We had fun while working our butts off. The only problem was we didn't seem to be making any money. Despite the nightly crowds, we were often late on our bills and even had to ask the bank for more cash.

Duane was the point man on our accounting, and I wondered aloud about the lack of profit we were showing. "Don't worry," was his reassuring response. "There are always extra costs at the start of a business. We'll be making the big bucks in no time." I had no reason to doubt him. He was my buddy.

It's a funny thing: you can know someone a long time, work with him, drink with him, and even own a business together, and still not have a clue about his gambling addiction. By the time I discovered Duane had been stealing from our bank accounts to cover his bad bets, we were too far gone to survive.

After he skipped town with the last of the bar's money, it turned into a race to see if our creditors or lenders would close us down first. It was pretty much a tie. Between them, they sold off everything that wasn't nailed down.

If I was crushed, Maripat was hysterical. "I thought you were going to make something of yourself. What am I supposed to do now?"

I tried to tell her it wasn't the end of the world. "I still have some cash in my personal savings plus a retirement account and a few investments. Losing the bar doesn't affect that. That will keep me afloat while I look for another job. Once I get a foot in the door someplace, I can pull extra shifts and maybe make up some of the losses."

She was not impressed. She folded her arms, rolled her eyes, and gave a long, exasperated sigh. "Oh great. We'll have less time together, and I'll end up stuck with a guy who still tends bar for a living."

"Well," I asked, "do you have any better ideas?" It turned out she did. She moved out the next day.

I figured that was three strikes—what with losing my girl, my best friend, and my budding career as a businessman all at once. So, while the rest of the country was focused on Bush's hanging chads, I sold my car, subleased my apartment, and left town.

Looking back now, I'm not quite certain why I decided to go. I don't remember having any clear purpose or plan. Maybe I was tired of trying to meet other people's expectations. Or maybe there was just nothing there to tie me down. In my mind, I was thinking of it as a prolonged vacation. Whatever the reason, I took off, leaving San Francisco's endless fog to head south. I thought some sunshine might bake the sadness out of my bones.

Ending up in Jamaica, I applied liquor, ganja, and reggae to my emotional bruises. I slept on the beach and hung with the dreadlocked locals. It didn't take me long to discover a low-grade rum the Rasta boys called "Buzzard's Butt." It is guaranteed to remove the varnish from your tabletop and the memory cells from your brain. I might have overindulged.

After that were more islands. Eventually I made my way to Havana, although I'm still a little foggy about my time there. Then I caught a ride on a charter boat, working as a deck hand on the way to Mexico's Caribbean coast. I was hitchhiking my way south through the Yucatan Peninsula to Belize when I landed on Paradise Beach.

Pushing my toes into the pure white sand that first day, it became clear I would not pull them out again anytime soon. The little bay with the blue water seemed the perfect place to live cheaply while I figured out my next move. The only flaw in the plan was that now I didn't know if I even wanted a next move.

My memories were interrupted as Pat, the bar's owner, came over to take the stool next to me. Pat was kind of the self-appointed mayor of the expats who lived in my beachside neighborhood. He heaved his short, plump body up onto the seat with a sigh of exertion and turned his sun-creased face to me.

"Word around the beach is that you might be heading home to the States for another go at the real world." Before I could respond, he called to Jorge to bring the rum bottle and an extra glass. "So, are you going back?" he asked me, taking the bottle from Jorge.

"I don't know yet," I said. "And I wouldn't be going home. It would be New York. I've never lived there before."

Pat poured each of us a glass of rum. "Hell, son, it's all the same up there—New York, Cleveland, Los Angeles. It's one big city north of the border." He shrugged his shoulders. "But it's your life. Go where you want. That's what I'm going to do."

I gave him a look to see if he was joking. "You're leaving Paradise Beach?"

He nodded. "Yeah, time for me to move on. This place has a future now. More and more tourists startin' to show up." He grimaced at the thought. "I like things a little less crowded. If I can't wake up and wander down the beach buck naked to piss in the ocean without scaring some family from Des Moines, I need to find a new place to live."

"So where are you going?"

Pat gave a snort and then took a swallow of his drink. "I guess I'll just follow the Margarita Road."

"The what?"

Pat gave a phlegmy, booze-soaked growl of a laugh. "You know that urge you have when you just gotta get out of town and you don't care what direction you go, but it always seems to be south?"

I nodded. In fact, I knew exactly what he was talking about.

"Well, that's what I call taking the Margarita Road. That's where I'm headed."

"And where is the Margarita Road going to lead this time?" I asked.

"Who knows? Who cares? I'm like that driftwood out there." He kept looking at me but pointed out to the beach. "I get washed ashore someplace for a while, but eventually the tide's gonna carry me away again." He gave me a sly grin. "Now I *do* have an invite from a rich widow lady to sail with her from Miami down to Cane Garden Bay in the British Virgin Islands. If that happens, I'll probably spend some time down there with my old pal Pooie. He owns a bar on the beach called the Wedding Chapel." Pat burst out with a throaty laugh. "Damn, I hope that name doesn't give the widow any ideas. After that, who knows?"

"What about the bar?"

Pat looked around for a moment. "I guess I'll try and sell

it. It's just some old boards and bricks. It'll probably come down if a really big storm ever hits us. But what the hell, it has been fun." He drained his glass. "Well son, if I don't see you before you leave, I wish you well, even if it's in fucking New York." He shook his head sadly at the thought and wandered out of the bar and down to the beach, taking the bottle with him.

After he left, I sat staring out beyond the bay to deep water where the blues of the sky and the sea mixed together until it was impossible to see where one stopped and the other began. The horizon had disappeared. I thought of Patrick and his footloose ways. Is that what I wanted for myself—a life spent wandering on the Margarita Road? The only other choice seemed to be drinking away the last of my savings before heading back north with Nicole to jump into the same rat race that wrecked my life once already.

I suddenly had a moment of clarity the old hippie gurus in the Sixties called enlightenment. It dawned on me that Nicole was right. I could have my second chance if I really wanted it. But it wouldn't be her idea of what I should do with my life. And it wouldn't be what Maripat had wanted for me. It would be what *I* wanted. And I wanted to be free of the real world—if only for a while longer.

I made my decision right then and called down the bar, "Jorge, if I bought this place, would you be willing to stay and be my bartender?"

His eyes grew large, and his face broke into a wide grin. "You're going to buy this place?" I nodded, surprising us both. Without a word, he filled two shot glasses from a bottle of Herradura Añejo. Carrying them around the bar, he handed one to me and tapped his own glass against mine.

"Salud, Jefe."

I worked things out with Patrick the next day. Within a week, papers were signed. I cashed in my IRA and took the last of the money from my stateside bank account to make the deal. It was all I had, but for some reason it felt right, as if I were starting over with a clean slate.

Jorge and I cleared out a second-floor storage room for me to live in. I bought a used table, dresser, and bed. The space was tiny, but it had a large window with wooden shutters that opened onto the Caribbean Sea.

It didn't take long to haul my things from the cabaña. I only had a few bags, and there wasn't much in them: clothes, some sandals, my old laptop, a plastic envelope filled with papers, and my passport. I also brought my CD collection of rhythm and blues, a journal, and a few books by Alan Watts. I unpacked in about fifteen minutes and went downstairs.

"Everything all right, Jefe?" Jorge asked.

I still wasn't used to him calling me that. "Just fine," I said.

"People are asking if you're going to change the name of the bar." He handed me a cup of Chiapas-grown coffee with a little Cuban rum floating on top.

"Yes, I am. I'm going to call it Poppa's. Poppa's Bar and Grill."

Jorge smiled his approval. I sipped the coffee, welcoming myself to my new life.

Nicole stopped by later that day to say goodbye on her way to the Cancun airport. She was wearing more clothes than I had ever seen on her: a white blouse, black jeans, and sensible flat traveling shoes. She looked different. She looked normal.

We walked out onto the beach, watching the blue of the

water darken in the afternoon light. I had told her of my plans as soon as I made the decision. She took the news well and seemed happy enough for me, if maybe a little envious.

She looked up at me now, her face colored a soft pink by the setting sun, and slipped an arm through mine, squeezing tight.

"So you're really staying? This is going to be your home?"

I watched the blue-green waves of the Caribbean rumble onto the shore, the force sending a smooth sheet of water racing across the sand. Just before reaching our feet, it slowed and then stopped for an instant before pulling away back to the sea.

"Yeah," I said. "For a while."

2
The Great Beer Commercial War

*Most of the pilgrims I met in Mexico were running from
something: financial woes, a pissed-off spouse, or a life that
hit a dead end. Regardless of the reason for the journey, the
Margarita Road will take you far from all those problems.
Still, there are no guarantees. A funny thing about the past—
it can catch up to you even on a remote tropical seashore.
Sometimes you bring it with you.*

It didn't take me long to settle into my new life as a beach
bar owner in paradise. Truthfully, it wasn't a demanding
career. Trust me when I say that serving rum drinks to girls
in tiny bikinis isn't that big of a chore. Eye strain was probably
the most common on-the-job injury. It also didn't take long
to realize I wasn't the only person in town who had taken the
Margarita Road to paradise.

A small community of American expats was beginning to
come together on that perfect little tropical beach. For some
time now, people like me had been drifting south, ending up

in Mexico with Jimmy Buffett songs playing in their heads. They left behind mortgages, failed marriages, and a lifetime of disappointments. Some of them came looking for a fresh start, and some were searching for a place to hide. A few were pulled by a dream they could never quite understand, until they walked down the beach to that crystal-clear water for the first time.

As I got to know my new neighbors, I found saints and sinners of every degree of good, bad, and strange. These aging adolescents thought of themselves as Peter Pan's lost children, and the beach was their Neverland. Having run away from home, they now were refusing to grow up.

They spent their days lying in the sun and their nights dancing on the sand. Every evening was an opportunity to break another Commandment, and every morning offered a new chance at redemption. My newfound friends were lazy, profane, adventuresome, often drunk, and free.

Few of my fellow travelers would have been acceptable to my old girlfriend in San Francisco. None of them was like the upwardly mobile go-getters I would have met in Manhattan had I gone north with Nicole. What we expats all shared, besides our love of the beach, was the enjoyment of slow-moving days without ambition or plans.

Giving up on the drive to succeed is a good part of what being an expat is all about. If you travel all the way to the Caribbean Sea, you probably have already decided to trade the dog-eat-dog competition of modern living for a hammock on the sand. At least that seemed to be the general plan for most of the wanderers I met. It was for both Tom and Eddie.

Eddie showed up in town first. Big Tom followed soon after. Each of them looked around the dusty streets that led down to that beautiful white sand and decided they had found the perfect place to drop anchor—which is how they ended up buying bars practically next door to one another.

The Mermaid Saloon sat in the middle of the block on a dirt road near the beach, stuck between a tattoo parlor and a small shack that sold great tacos al pastor. A local businessman built it when tourists started cruising down the coast looking for something besides the endless souvenir stands and overcrowded temple tours of Cancun. He bought the land for a few pesos, threw up some concrete block walls, and put a palm-thatched roof on top. Then he bribed some local officials for a liquor license. He never even opened for business but sold the place to the first person with cash who showed any interest. That was Eddie.

On the other side of the street, down a few doors near the corner, was the Lazy Lizard Cantina, a traditional Mexican brick-and-stucco building with a red tile roof. Originally it had been a bakery, until some guy from Germany bought it, gutted it, and turned it into a bar. When he ran into trouble over questions about his work visa, he decided to sell and head back to Frankfurt. About the same time Eddie was signing for the Mermaid Saloon, Big Tom was buying the Lizard for next to nothing.

It didn't take long for the two men to hear on the town's gossip grapevine that another American was opening a bar only a few yards away on the same street. It had all the makings of a nasty situation, since they would be competing for the same tourist dollars. The locals waited for fireworks. They waited and waited.

"Doesn't bother me," Eddie said, when anyone raised the issue.

"The more the merrier," was always Tom's reply.

Tom made the first contact, strolling over one day to take a seat at the bar in the Mermaid. He asked the bartender if the owner was around. "That would be me," said Eddie, drying his hands on a bar rag before offering one to Tom. It was a real Casablanca moment, as a great friendship began on a humid afternoon over cold Mexican beers.

Eddie was short and slender to the point of being gaunt, with a crop of wiry hair long ago gone gray. In his old life up north, he started each morning with a five-mile run, which for years was the only personal time he took. The rest of the day he spent as a lawyer in a big Chicago law firm. He had a blinding dedication to his job that eventually cost him his marriage. That overwhelming commitment continued until the day the head of the firm told him he was being replaced as lead trial counsel by the boss's son-in-law. When the shock of losing his job wore off, Eddie decided to never again keep track of his time. He packed his bags and headed south. He was finally going to enjoy life.

Tom was the physical opposite of Eddie. A big man, overweight to the point of looking like a bit of a slob even in a suit and tie, he wore a stubble beard because he thought it made him look thin and hip. He was wrong on both counts. When his partners in a Manhattan ad agency told him he was out of touch with the younger consumers, he laughed at them. After they exercised their option to buy out his share of the business, he responded by shouting, "Screw you!" on his way out the door.

Tom decided then and there that the rat race was over for him. He had never married and had no family. The way he figured, there was nothing to keep him from leaving his past behind and taking off for parts unknown. He decided he would live on a Mexican beach with blue water, "just like Tim Robbins at the end of that prison escape movie."

"Me, too!" Eddie said that first day as he listened to Tom's story. They soon recognized in the other someone who had also lived a life that demanded success at the cost of love or enjoyment. They both swore they would never do that again.

"Not ever happening," said Eddie.

"I left that life behind," said Tom.

They believed each other, and they believed themselves. They even clinked beer bottles and shook on it. Of course, that was long before Hollywood came to town.

It turned out having two bars close together was a good thing. People enjoyed wandering from one to the other and back again. On Friday nights, the little section of road between them became a street party. Mariachis and conga drummers would set up at opposite corners, and vendors would wheel churro carts into the crowd. I would often close down my own bar early to head for the Mermaid and the Lizard.

A free-spirited crowd would fill the narrow cobblestone street back then. Everybody danced, flirted outrageously, and had a good time. Spanish, English, Italian, and other languages and accents intermingled along with the bodies in motion. If on occasion someone drank too much or was pissed because his or her date ended up in another's arms, there were always good people around to chill things out. Sometimes I stepped in if one of the bars needed an extra bartender or bouncer, but mostly I hung out with old friends and met new ones.

In those early days, Paradise Beach had a cozy, small-town feel to it. However, as time went by, word of this hidden treasure reached the outside world. Tripadvisor and glossy travel magazines started taking note of the little place with the perfect beach. It wasn't long before the tourists began to flow in. Over the next couple of years, the town grew to accommodate the new business, and with growth came all the pluses and minuses that entails. Some folks liked it, while others hated it. One thing for sure: everyone had an opinion.

"A Starbucks!" said Eddie as he sat down, placing a couple more beers on the table. "Who the hell decided we needed a Starbucks in this town?" Tom voiced his agreement and reached for a beer. The three of us sat at a small table in the Mermaid overlooking the street. It had become a bit of a weekly thing to hang out there in the summer low season.

"Forget that," Tom said, working up some real aggravation. "The one that chaps my ass is that new fancy 'sports footwear outlet' down near the plaza. Are you kidding me?" He paused to gauge our outrage and, finding it sufficient, continued. "What idiot would wear three-hundred-dollar running shoes on the beach?" He lifted up his hefty leg to show us his rubber sand-encrusted flip flop—so old, worn, and sun faded it was impossible to guess the original color. It was patched in one place with black electrical tape. *"This* is what you wear in Mexico," he said, shaking his foot in the air. We all raised our beers in agreement.

Eddie put his bottle down and nodded toward the street. "Now there's something that hasn't changed around here." We turned to follow the direction of his gaze and saw a very pretty woman heading our way. Eddie was right. Paradise Beach still offered its fair share of eye candy. She was an in-the-flesh advertisement for southern California and all its temptations.

I watched her stride toward us on tanned legs that stretched out from tight linen shorts. The silver she wore on her ears and neck flashed in the sunlight beneath corn-silk hair. Her retro t-shirt advertised a tour for Led Zeppelin that probably took place before she was born. She saw me staring and smiled. I smiled back. I turned to Eddie and Tom and saw them both smiling at her, too. She walked into the shade of the Mermaid's awning and came right up to our table. "Hi, guys," she said brightly. "Do any of you know who owns this place?"

There was none of the slightly lost, worried look most tourists have when wandering about in a strange town in Mexico. She was obviously on a mission and would not be denied.

I nodded toward Eddie as Tom cocked his thumb at his friend and said, "Fast Eddie is the boss." Eddie smiled at her, agreed that it was his bar, and asked what he could do for her.

Opening the small bag that hung from her shoulder, she pulled out a business card and handed it to Eddie. "I'm Kelly Benson," she said.

Tom, Eddie, and I all looked at each other, trading grins. Another salesman. Or, in this case, a very attractive saleswoman. Eddie didn't even glance at the card before he said to her, "Sorry, Miss, but we aren't buying today."

She looked puzzled. "You're not buying what today?"

Tom answered for Eddie. "Whatever it is you're selling. We don't need popcorn machines, fancy sound systems, or napkins with funny sayings. We like things simple and laid-back down here. But we will buy you a drink if you care to join us," he said, giving her his biggest smile.

She had the good grace to laugh. She casually reached out and put a reassuring hand on Eddie's arm. "I'm not selling anything. I'm looking to rent a bar for a video and maybe make the owner famous." None of us had been expecting anything like that. Before we could recover, she added, "And I would love a beer."

While I pulled another chair up to the table—next to my own, of course—Eddie went for her drink. When he returned, he introduced us. "Tom here owns the Lazy Lizard Cantina down the street, and Poppa has a bar and grill on the beach."

She took a swallow from her beer while nodding a greeting to us. "Well, this makes my job easier. I was planning on getting around to all your bars eventually." She pulled some more cards from her purse for Tom and me. Across the top, they said *Airwaves Inc.* in a wavy script meant to simulate a wave, I guess. Under that was *Video and Audio Promotions* with an address in Los Angeles and her name followed by *Vice President.*

"V.P., huh?" I said. "Sounds like you're a big deal."

She laughed softly. "You wouldn't think that if you knew how many Vice Presidents we have."

Tom joined in her laughter. "You can have the title or the money but not both, eh? Yeah, we know how that works. Just one more reason we all left the real world to live here."

Kelly nodded in agreement. "Exactly. I'm not looking for the real world. I'm looking for paradise." She gazed around the table at our faces. "I was hoping you guys might help me find it."

She was good. She had us hooked, and we all knew it. "All right," I said, "let's hear your story." Hell, it was a warm afternoon in Mexico. There were worse ways to spend it than drinking cold beer and being hustled by a pretty lady. She gave me a grateful smile and began to tell her tale.

It turned out some big beer company was sponsoring a

popular country music star's tour back in the States. Kelly mentioned his name and then stopped suddenly. "You guys do know who he is, right?"

Eddie looked blank and shook his head. "The one in the cowboy hat," said Tom to Eddie. "He's kind of the new Jimmy Buffett. Sings about margaritas and beaches."

"Oh yeah," said Eddie, recognition dawning in his eyes. "Him." He turned to Kelly. "He's good. I like him."

Kelly smiled and continued with her explanation. In preparation for the upcoming tour, the beer company's PR department was looking for promotional ideas. They asked several production companies to come up with proposals for commercials to advertise the tour and their product. Kelly's firm had submitted an idea that the big shots liked well enough to give the go-ahead for some preliminary work.

She paused for us to ask questions, and so I did. "What's your concept?"

She spread her well-manicured hands on the table in front of her as if clearing space for the great idea she was about to share with us. "Living the dream," she said slowly in a dramatic voice.

Silence. She looked expectantly around the table at the three of us.

"What?" asked Tom. "Living the what?"

"Living the dream," she said again in a normal voice this time. "Escaping to paradise. It's what everybody back in the States working in some little cubicle or office thinks of doing. It's what Kenny and Buffett and all those guys sing about. That's why everyone buys all the CDs. That's why they go to the concerts." She began to get very enthusiastic. "Our video will start with someone in a suit and tie walking out of an office and ending up barefoot in a tropical bar. We want people to feel as if they could do it themselves." She gave a smile that encompassed all of us. "Like the three of you have done."

I laughed aloud. I couldn't help it. "So, they can live the dream if only they buy the right beer or listen to the right music." That earned me a little frown.

Before she could say more, Tom spoke up. "Yeah, we're living the dream down here," he said thoughtfully. "You could say that. It's not a bad description."

Eddie suddenly brightened and looked at me. "She's right, you know. Living the dream. It's a dream come true for me, that's for sure."

I stared at my friends in disbelief. Ten minutes ago, they had been deep into their complaints about how the town was going to hell, and now they were living the dream. The power of an attractive smile should never be underestimated.

Kelly started talking again. "We would like to film a scene inside a real Mexican bar. We don't want some franchise chain that sells margaritas out of a tap. We want the real thing." She looked around the Mermaid. "Like you have here."

I swear Eddie's chest expanded two inches, as he grinned broadly.

Kelly must have also seen Eddie's reaction, because she quickly added, "I'm looking at a lot of places, which is why I wanted to talk to all three of you." She explained she would head back to L.A. soon with a list of recommended locations and then return shortly to talk to the finalists. "If a bar is chosen to be part of the video, it could be seen by millions all over the world," she said. "The place we film could become famous."

"Well," said Tom grandly, "nobody around here wants to be famous, but if it would help you out, I'm sure all of us would be happy to show you around."

Eddie suddenly stood up. "Oh yeah. No problem at all. And as long as you're here, let me give you the grand tour of the Mermaid."

"That would be great," Kelly said, getting out of her chair to join him.

The grand tour of Eddie's place consisted of walking over to the bar, turning around and looking back at the three tables on the front deck area, then going up a spiral staircase to a second floor balcony that overhung the recently paved street. As they returned, I could hear Kelly saying, "It's adorable."

Before they could sit down again, Tom was on his feet. "Yeah, it's cute here for sure," he said. "Although you might consider a more traditional Mexican Colonial look for the video. My bar is just down the street, if you'd like to see that style of architecture." Even before she said yes, he had her arm and was leading her out the door.

Eddie turned to me with a *what the hell* look on his face. "Is he joking?" he asked. "A traditional Colonial style? It's a bar that used to be a bakery." He looked again at Tom leading Kelly down the street. "Somebody's beginning to think his shit don't stink. Style of architecture my ass."

And so the war began.

It escalated quickly. Within a few days, I walked by the Lazy Lizard and saw a truck being unloaded. I went over for a better look.

"Hey, Poppa," Tom called from the doorway.

"Hey, yourself," I answered. "What's going on?"

Tom stepped aside to make room for a guy carrying a

piece of metal furniture. "I bought some new stools for the bar. I decided to spruce the old place up a little." He motioned for me to follow him inside.

The Lizard was a big room with a large, circular bar in the center and tables and chairs scattered along the walls. The old wooden stools with padded seats were piled up in a corner, and in their place were wrought iron ones embossed with what might have been a lizard if you squinted a little. "Go ahead," said Tom. "Try one out."

I sat down. It was damned uncomfortable. "What was wrong with the old ones?" I asked.

"They didn't go with the ambience I'm trying to achieve here. I needed something more in keeping with the style of the room. You know, more Mexican." He grinned. "If this place is going to end up in a music video, I want it to look good." I wished him well with his redecorating and left without sharing my feelings about the comfort level of his new stools.

A few days later, I stopped by the Mermaid for a beer and found the place covered in drop cloths. Some guys were splashing bright green paint over the walls as Eddie closely supervised. He spotted me and came over. "Sorry, Poppa, we're closed for remodeling today."

"I can see that," I said. "Why? I thought the place looked good like it was. What's with this neon green paint?"

"It's called Tropical Rain Forest," Eddie said. "I'm just trying to create a more Caribbean vibe with some color."

"Christ, Eddie, why would you paint your walls baby puke green?" Tom had just walked up behind us, and the look on his face made it clear what he thought of Eddie's color scheme.

"It's Tropical Rain Forest," Eddie repeated fiercely. "It

opens up the room and evokes a natural feeling. That's something you should have considered instead of buying those scrap metal stools."

Tom gave him a dirty look. "Wrought iron. They're made of wrought iron and come all the way from Guadalajara."

"Whatever," said Eddie, as he turned to watch the painting. Tom gave a snort of dismissal and headed back to the street.

That Friday night, bartenders in both places were told for the first time in the history of Paradise Beach not to let people come in if they were carrying a drink from another bar. It seemed the Never-Ending Street Party was officially over.

The following week, Tom had two giant speakers placed on the roof of his bar. The next morning, the sounds of Kenny Chesney poured into the street at full blast, echoing through the surrounding buildings. When the music began to shake his walls, Eddie charged over to the Lazy Lizard. The bartender on duty told him Tom wasn't around and no, she couldn't turn the music off without the boss's permission. Eddie's face was a deep purple by the time he returned to his own bar.

After that, nobody saw Eddie for a few days. When he finally reappeared, it became the stuff of legend.

Those who were on the street saw Eddie and one of his bartenders pull a giant sign out in front of his bar. It was a wooden frame about six feet tall and just as wide. Stretched over the wood was a plastic tarp printed with a garish picture of the sun setting over the ocean. Across the painting, bright blue letters read *No Shoes, No Shirt, No Problem at the Mermaid Saloon*. On either side of the painting were poster board cutouts of busty, bare-breasted mermaids. The entire frame was wrapped in pulsating Christmas tree twinkle lights attached to an extension cord that ran back into Eddie's building. As a finishing touch, he glued cheap plastic margarita glasses on top and painted them green.

Eddie had just flipped the switch on the twinkle lights and stood back to admire his handiwork when Tom came barreling up. "What the hell is this?" he yelled as he approached. People on both sides of the street moved a little closer to watch.

"It's folk art," said Eddie. "Traditional Caribbean folk art." Tom almost blew a gasket. "Folk art? It's shit. I'm embarrassed to have it near my bar. It reflects badly on all of us who have businesses here." He waved his arms about as if speaking for all those standing around, although no one seemed to be agreeing with him. "I want it taken down. NOW!"

People began leaving their seats in the taqueria next door to come watch the show. Meanwhile, Eddie's anger at the insult to his artwork reached a point he had not experienced since his trial lawyer days. "You ignorant gringo," he screamed back at Tom. "This is the real thing. The genuine article." He gestured with both hands at the sign. "*This* is what living the dream is all about."

"This is living the dream?" Tom yelled back. "Flashing lights and hoochie girls? This garbage?" In a rage, he grabbed one side of Eddie's sign and raised it off the ground before slamming it back down again with all the force he could muster.

To both Eddie's and Tom's great surprise, the sign broke. The twinkle lights suddenly stopped blinking. One of the plastic margarita glasses fell off the top, and the wooden frame splintered, leaving a large piece of it broken off in Tom's hand.

Eddie went berserk, alternating between tearfully looking at his broken, now-lopsided sign and screaming at Tom. "You goddamned ape. You'll pay for this!"

Tom's anger seemed to be replaced for the moment by embarrassment. "I ... uh ... uh ..." He was finally at a loss for words. He stared at the section of wood in his hand before dropping it into the street and turning away to head back to his own bar.

Eddie's rage hit the red zone as he saw Tom discard the broken piece of the sign with what he thought was a supreme act of casual disrespect. With a roar, he scooped up the wood and, swinging as if he were trying to knock a baseball out of the park, struck Tom hard with it across the back.

"Mother FUCKER," Tom bellowed as he turned to see Eddie drawing back for another strike. Before Eddie could follow through, Tom unleashed a great swing of his own. His fist connected with Eddie's nose, sending the smaller man reeling backwards into his own beloved sign, which crumpled under his weight. Eddie, his nose bleeding profusely, came to rest on top of the collapsed pile of wood, plastic, and Christmas tree lights. He lay still as death.

Time seemed to stop. Tom stood as motionless as the man he had just knocked to the ground. No one in the crowd moved. It was as if the whole of the street had suddenly held its collective breath.

The spell was broken when Tom, with a great cry of anguish, fell to his knees. He scooped Eddie up in his arms and began to blubber. "I've killed him," he wailed. "I've killed my best friend." He crushed the smaller man to his chest, and Eddie gave a small moan. Tom shook him gently, cradling him in his arms like a colicky baby. "Eddie! Eddie, speak to me. Can you hear me, buddy? I am so sorry!" Huge tears rolled down Tom's plump cheeks.

When the cops showed up, it was possible they thought Tom, who still held Eddie in a bear hug, was trying to hurt him. They quickly surrounded the pair and began to pull them apart. Tom refused to abandon his fallen comrade and pushed the officers away in a scramble to stay by Eddie's side. The police responded by pummeling Tom with nightsticks, leaving him as bloody as his friend.

By this time, Eddie had begun to come around enough to get his bearings. When he started yelling at the cops to leave Tom alone, they gave him a few whacks, too. After a quick discussion, the boys in blue decided to arrest them both. They were handcuffed together and thrown in the back of the police van. Off they went to jail.

It was several hours before I heard the whole story and was able to negotiate a bribe for their release. After I paid the money in a discreet envelope, Tom and Eddie were escorted to the front of the station where I was waiting. Eddie held a towel over his broken nose, and Tom gingerly touched his bruised face and swollen eye. Despite their injuries, they looked less like street brawlers and more like two shame-faced schoolboys called to the principal's office for teasing girls or smoking in the bathroom.

Before we left, they were each given a citation. Tom had violated the municipality's sound level ordinance and would have to remove his rooftop speakers. Eddie was cited for obstructing traffic with his sign and prohibited from ever putting anything in the street again.

I offered to take them home or to the hospital, but they insisted on going back to the Lizard. It was dark and locked when we got there. The staff had left, not knowing if they would ever see their boss again. Tom opened the front door for us, and once inside I went behind the bar to get myself a beer. I figured I deserved it for putting up with their shenanigans.

Eddie hoisted himself up on one of the new iron stools, while Tom disappeared in the back. He returned in a moment with two small plastic bags of ice. He handed one to Eddie and held the other against his own eye. Eddie carefully placed the bag on his nose.

Tom took a seat next to his friend, and they stared at each other for a moment. "I'm an idiot," said Eddie finally.

"I'm just as big an idiot," Tom said. "Maybe we could start a club. I could be President. President of the Idiots Club, that's me."

Tom asked if I would grab a bottle of Don Julio from underneath the bar. I did and set it down between them with just two glasses. This was their party. Tom poured two shots, and Eddie picked one up. He had to move the ice bag from his face to drink. Tom took a swallow from his glass and winced when the tequila hit a cut on his lip.

Eddie starting talking slowly, as if each word were painful to say. "I guess I never admitted to myself how bad I felt about losing my job at the law firm. I always acted like it was no big deal and that they could kiss my ass. The truth was I was embarrassed and felt like a failure." He looked at Tom who was nodding his head in agreement.

"Yeah," said Tom. "I know. Me, too. And all of a sudden, here was a chance to show everybody back there I was doing great. That video of my bar was going to let those jerks who fired me see I was Mr. Cool down here in Mexico and they were the losers, not me." It was Eddie's turn to silently agree.

Tom gave a long sigh. "Well, we messed that up."

"You know, guys," I said, "from what I'm hearing, you

two weren't happy with your lives when you did nothing but work your asses off for other people." They shrugged. "You both say how you never had a real friend—a friend who had your back—until you came here. It's hard for me to think of you two as losers unless you let that friendship disappear."

They looked shyly at each other for a moment before Tom held out his hand. Eddie reached over and took it. In a moment, they were hugging. As I slipped out the door, they were pouring more tequila and laughing about the cops, already embellishing the story for future retellings. The war was over.

After that, things got back to normal. The Friday night street parties resumed, and on any given day, you could find Eddie over at the Lazy Lizard or Tom at the Mermaid Saloon. When Kelly Benson returned to town, the boys explained they were taking themselves out of the running for the video. They told her their friendship was more important than some musician's tour. Kelly said she was disappointed but understood. She never mentioned that another bar had already been chosen for the video.

A few months later, just after dawn on a Sunday morning, a parade of minivans stopped on the narrow street behind my bar on the edge of the beach. The drivers unloaded lights and cables, massive electronic boards of toggles and switches, and some good-sized video cameras. Fifty-some people crowded into my place and bustled about for hours, until the cameras were set to everyone's satisfaction. They put the main one facing directly past the hanging edge of the awning over the deck, looking out to the beach.

When everything was ready, someone yelled "Action." A guy in a suit walked through my bar. With the Caribbean Sea as background, he took off his coat and dropped it to the floor. He pulled his tie off and threw it out of camera range. Then he headed down the steps of the deck.

"Cut," the director said. Everyone huddled around a viewing screen and watched the replay several times. Then they all moved back and filmed the guy walking again. Then they did it again. And again. And again. They did it maybe forty times before someone liked what they saw. After that, all the stuff was packed back into the vans, and everyone drove away.

At least that's what Jorge tells me. I wasn't there. I had given him the keys and left him in charge. "Don't let them burn the place down or drink all the beer," were my only instructions.

Before the video company even showed up, I had pulled away in the jeep and driven over to the Royal Palms Hotel. Kelly Benson was waiting for me out front. As she climbed into the passenger seat, I asked, "Are you sure you want to go? Wouldn't you rather hang out and watch the video being made?"

"I'm the advance team," she said, settling back in the seat and letting the wind catch her hair as we pulled away. "I don't do anything at the actual shoot. My work here is over. In fact, I could be heading home right now if I wanted to." She gave me a sideways glance that had a cute little smile attached to it. "Only I don't want to."

"I'm glad," I said. We drove down the coast and took a bumpy dirt road through the jungle that ended at a small cove not many people know about. There were no margarita vendors, no loudspeakers playing music, no opening acts, no headliners, and no cameras. It was only us. We spread a blanket on the sand of the deserted beach and swam naked in the clear, open water of the Caribbean. We didn't see another person the whole day.

We were living the dream.

3
Lenny's Second Coming

Once you're on the Margarita Road, you can give in to all your daydreams. The wild party animal that was buried deep inside can finally break free. A life full of hot sex, high times, or whatever else you have fantasized about is now yours for the asking. Sure, there'll be a price to pay, but it will be worth it. At least you won't be the person you used to be.

I was heading to work, just as I had done every day for the last couple of years. For me, that meant strolling onto the deck of my little Mexican beach bar. Instead of fighting rush hour traffic jams, I started each day gazing out on glistening waves rolling across a stretch of pure white sand.

I sat down at a table and opened my laptop. Jorge brought over some coffee, a small glass of añejo rum, and an ashtray. In a little while, I'd have some chorizo and eggs fried up on the nearby grill. It had become my morning ritual to sit under the awning of woven palm leaves and read the New York Times online. It was a way of staying in touch with what was happening in the world, although I have to admit, I often wondered why I felt the need. Maybe I just enjoyed the contrast of reading about civilization's troubles while perched above a nearly deserted tropical beach.

Far in the distance lay poor Cuba, but all I could see was endless miles of clear blue water. Mexico's tropical coast has a vista that offers a combination of mind-numbing sameness and soul-stirring beauty. Even after a number of years living here, I still had to pinch myself sometimes to believe this was my home.

It wouldn't last. Eventually it would be time to move on. I knew in the not-too-distant future someone would think of this beach as a perfect place to build six floors of concrete and steel cookie-cutter condos. By then it would be flooded with Americans complaining about having to deal with all those Mexicans while vacationing in Mexico. Luckily, on this particular morning I still had the beach pretty much to myself. My view of the horizon wasn't yet spoiled by buildings or construction, although it wasn't without some distraction.

A few twenty-somethings in tiny bikinis were throwing a volleyball back and forth over the net I had strung up on the sand in front of the bar. To tell the truth, they didn't exactly ruin the view.

They weren't really playing any kind of game. Wiggling and giggling, they tossed the ball back and forth just trying to look good while not playing. They were succeeding. Each of them was damned adorable. They were at that special moment in life when they thought their bodies would never betray them by drooping, spreading, or growing old.

The arrival of college kids on spring break was something of a double-edged sword for those of us living in Paradise

Beach. It was a sure sign this heavenly coastline had been discovered. The real world was on its way with more people, more noise, and more of the problems expats try to leave behind. On the other hand, it also meant tourists were spending the money that beach bums like me needed for a life of leisure. Margaritas don't come cheap, you know.

While ruminating on the yin and yang of encroaching civilization, I saw one of the girls break off from the group. She yelled something to her friends and then made her way across the beach to the steps leading up to my deck. I watched her stop on the first step, all sun bleached hair and tanned limbs, prettily shaking the sand off each foot. She climbed up into the shade of the thatched roof and walked past me to where Jorge was standing at the bar. They exchanged a few words before he pointed in my direction.

She headed over to my table, stopped, cocked a hip, and smiled a smile that must have cost her folks a fortune. "Hi, I'm Stacy. Are you Poppa?" She half turned and pointed back at the wooden sign over the bar that said *Poppa's Bar and Grill*. "That Poppa?"

I considered a couple of possible answers. South of the border, you can't be too careful—even with a pretty girl. Especially with a pretty girl. I decided to risk it. "Yeah, I'm Poppa. What can I help you with?"

With the confidence that comes from never being told no, she sat down and pushed my laptop aside. "I'm Lou Ann's sister," she said brightly.

I had no clue who Lou Ann might be. If I had to guess, I would say she was probably one of the many tourists who had begun to drift through town over the last few years mistakenly thinking they were leaving an indelible mark on the locals' memories.

"How's Lou Ann doing?" I asked, because it seemed the thing to do.

"Oh, she's great. She graduated and got married, you know."

No, I didn't know. I really didn't care. I decided to keep that to myself. "Great. That's great," I said. "Tell her hello for me."

Stacy laughed a high-pitched Minnie Mouse laugh. "That's what Lou Ann said—to tell you hello. She says coming to Mexico was the best spring break she ever had. She loved hanging at your bar." Stacy leaned in, lowering her voice as if she had a secret to share. "I was hoping maybe you could help us find a guy called the Skipper." She paused to fix me with two of the bluest eyes I had ever seen. "You know, like the skipper of a boat?"

"The skipper of a boat," I repeated back to her. She smiled at my quick grasp of the situation.

"Exactly! Lou Ann said the Skipper could help us find some mad parties and, you know, make some connections." She waved an arm at the beach in the direction of her friends. "Lou Ann said your place was kind of in the center of what's happening down here, and so I thought you might know how to find him." She blasted me with another smile, opening her blue eyes a little wider as she waited for my response. A very effective interrogation technique, I must admit.

"You want to find Skipper," I said.

She nodded enthusiastically. "Do you know him?"

I finished the rum and started in on the coffee. In the distance, I could see a pelican dropping into the surf to snap up fish in the clear water near the edge of the beach.

❧

He hadn't always been called the Skipper. That didn't happen until he started wearing that stupid-looking sailor cap somebody gave him. When I met him the day he first wandered into my place, he was just Leonard E. Williams Jr., CPA and Financial Consultant. At least that's what it said on the business card that fell out of his wallet as he searched for money to buy a drink. I picked it up off the bar and read it. "Impressive," I said, handing the card to him. "Is that you?"

He shrugged, crumpling the card into a ball and tossing it back onto the bar. "Not anymore." After a moment, he said, "You can call me Lenny."

"Everybody calls me Poppa." We shook hands. "This is my place. What can I get you to drink?" I picked up the card and threw it in the trash.

He shrugged again. "I dunno. What should I have?"

Usually when customers are undecided, I tell them to think about it and I will come back later. However, from the looks of this guy, I didn't think that would change things. He needed some help. "How about a margarita?"

"Sure," he said without much enthusiasm.

I gave him the once-over while making his drink. Early 30s, thin, with a few days' growth of beard and a mop of dirty blond hair that needed a comb. He didn't look like the typical tourist who came into my place. For starters, he wasn't wearing Bermuda shorts or sandals over white socks. He wasn't wearing shorts at all, despite being on the beach. He had on a suit and tie, although he had at least yanked the tie loose from his collar.

The suit was expensive but wrinkled, as if he hadn't taken

it off in a while. There was a fancy-looking watch on his wrist, and his shoes, although dirty and scuffed, were Italian and pricey. When I noticed him getting out of a taxi earlier, he had a good-sized rolling suitcase with him. Now it sat on the floor next to his stool.

I set the margarita in front of him. I don't often pry into my customers' personal business. I'm usually not interested, and most times they end up voluntarily telling me their life story anyway. But this Lenny puzzled me. As he took a tentative swallow, I asked, "Vacation?"

He put the glass back down and sighed. "No. Not really. Well, maybe." He looked up and saw my puzzlement. "I mean, I don't know how long I'm going to stay. I may just live here for a while."

A runaway. We get plenty of them in Mexico. I know, because I was one myself. Only they usually weren't as uncertain about it as this guy seemed to be. "Then you should hang around," I said. "Later tonight, a lot of locals and expats will drop by. They can give you an idea of what life is like down here."

He thanked me and said that maybe he would. He went back to his drink, and I went back to filling the cooler. Later, I saw him sitting out on the beach, his shoes and socks next to him on the sand and his suit coat hung over the back of a lounger.

True to form, the expatriate crowd began to drift in around 8 p.m. Wet Willie plays guitar and sings most evenings, but he was on one of his binges, so Big Mike was sitting in. Nobody seemed to mind. They didn't come for the music. They came to get hammered, dance a little, and maybe hook up with somebody so they didn't have to stumble home alone.

As the night went on, Jorge and I stayed busy pouring drinks and making sure Dirty Jimmy didn't steal anyone's change off the bar or grab an unattended beer. I did notice that Lenny had wandered up from the beach and was talking with people as I had suggested.

At one point, I saw him sitting at a table in the corner next to Lucy, a middle-aged lady of some means who moved to Paradise Beach after three marriages and three very lucrative divorces. She had a few years on her, but what she lacked in youth she made up for in salesmanship.

A dedicated cougar, Lucy amused herself by chowing down on any fresh male meat that wandered into town. When I saw them leave together later, I thought *Welcome to Paradise Beach, Lenny.*

His night with Lucy must not have left too many scars, because Lenny stuck around. I started seeing him semi-regularly in my bar and at parties around town. At first he was quiet, keeping a low profile and hiding in his shell. Then, slowly, he poked his head out and began to look around. I guess he liked what he saw. It wasn't a bad spot where he landed. The town sat on the edge of the sea. It had good bars and a few decent places to eat if you ventured outside the growing tourist trap areas.

Oh sure, there was a gringo gulch where the sunbirds lived in the winter months. But if you avoided them, you might hook up with the small community of Margarita Road refugees: a group of wanderers from up north; a crazy Irish sailor; a few Italians; some young, fast-living kids from Mexico City; and one beautiful girl from Brazil. All in all, it was a nice place to stay—or hide, if that's what you needed.

Lenny found himself a small studio apartment a few

blocks from the beach and settled in. As his tan deepened, his confidence seemed to grow. By then, t-shirts and flip flops had replaced the suit. I never heard much about where he came from or why he ended up here on the edge of the jungle, but it eventually seemed like he had always been part of the local scene. Then he started to make his own scene.

I stopped by the Lazy Lizard Cantina late one night for a cold one. Kat was behind the bar and opened a beer for me before I settled on a stool. "What's up, Pops?" she asked, as she set the bottle down in front of me.

"Not much," I answered. "Just thought I'd have a quiet drink I didn't have to pour myself."

As if on cue, the place filled with raucous laughter. "Yeah," said Kat as she walked away, "good luck with that." I turned to look at who was making all the noise. Over in the far corner sat Lenny with a group of college-age kids behind a table full of empty shot glasses. When he noticed me looking, he stood up and walked over to the bar.

"Hey, Poppa! What's happening?" he said as he sat down beside me.

As we exchanged greetings, one of the girls from the group at the table stood up and came over to grab his arm. "Lenny, what about the party? We want to get going."

"Sandy, this is the famous Poppa," Eddie said, nodding at me.

Famous or not, the girl wasn't interested after a quick glance in my direction. I took a longer look at her. She was young—19 maybe, or even younger—and flying high. Too high for a tequila buzz. It appeared the stories I had been hearing about Lenny were true.

I gave him a harsh look. He took young Sandy by the

shoulders and gently turned her toward her friends. "You go on back and get everybody ready. We'll leave in a minute." Lenny spoke to her as if she were a small child, which didn't seem far from the truth.

She hesitated for a moment. "Go on," he insisted, "I need to talk to my buddy here." Lenny watched her stroll away and then turned to me with a grin. "Whatcha think, Poppa? Pretty fuckin' smooth, huh?"

I shook my head in disgust. "Are you making extra bucks babysitting now, Lenny?"

He looked seriously hurt. "Oh, come on. Don't be like that." He pointed with his thumb in the direction the girl had gone. "She's damned hot!" He glanced back at the group at the table. "And she's not even the best of the bunch." He smiled at his own good fortune.

"She's a baby, Lenny. And she's high. And I would guess you are, too."

He gave me a noncommittal stare. I wondered what the hell had happened to the timid guy who had wandered into my bar not so long ago. "Lenny, you're playing with fire. Even if you don't get in trouble for banging some wasted coed, you are way out of line if you are dealing drugs to these kids."

Lenny rolled his eyes. "Jesus, Poppa. I never would have guessed you for being one of those."

"One of what?"

"You know ... a killjoy."

I was so pissed I almost smacked him. While I fought my inclination to knock him upside the head, Lenny rambled on. "Poppa, there are people who live their life under a rock. I mean ... I'm not saying you are one of them ... but there are some types who never take a chance in life. They never get in trouble, they never have a thrill, and they never ever have any fun. I know because I used to be one of those people." He shook his head at his own memories. "Man, was I ever one of those. Now I'm out from under that rock. I'm so far out, I am on the edge! And it is a blast out here. So don't tell me to back off or quiet down, because that's never gonna happen again."

His mood seemed to swing from mellow to angry and back again, while he gave his little speech. I had no idea what he was going on about, but I decided to try to talk some sense into him anyway.

"Lenny," I said, "I'm trying to help you. I've lived down here a lot longer than you have. There are rules for us expats, and one of those rules is gringos don't deal drugs. The cops or the cartels or Jose down the street with his own little weed business are going to get pissed as hell if they find you selling. I mean pissed like Mexican prison pissed or a shallow grave in the jungle pissed. Would you listen to me, please?"

Lenny had been looking over at the kids waiting for him while I spoke. Now he turned to me and grinned as if he knew a secret.

"Poppa, you are just paranoid. Things are different these days. If I deal a little smoke, maybe some blow to the college kids, nobody takes notice. I buy my stuff from an Argentinean guy who brings it up from Belize. The Mexicans don't have a clue. If they did know, they wouldn't care. I'm small potatoes. The cops here don't give a shit about me and my dime bag sales."

The group at the table stood up and began to wander toward the door. Lenny got up from his stool and put a hand on my arm. "Don't worry. I know what I'm doing." Then he left with his fan club in tow. I remember thinking to myself as I watched them go that this situation would not end well.

It wasn't long after that night people began calling Lenny "Skipper," and he became the man of the hour. Every party in town was being fueled by his product, and tourists of all ages began to beat a path to his door. I couldn't stop him, but I made sure it didn't spill over into my business.

I really don't care what you use as a personal form of entertainment, but Lenny's little cottage industry was too blatant for my tastes. The last thing I needed was an overdose in my bathroom or undercover cops sitting at my bar. I told Lenny I would break his arms if he ever sold his shit there. He promised he never would.

Other places weren't as fussy. It got to be a daily routine for Lenny to put on his silly sailor hat and go cruising around town from happy hour to happy hour with a satchel full of goodies, making everybody a little bit happier.

Well, maybe not everybody.

About a year or so passed with little new or different. Things move slowly down here in mañana land. One day, I was lying out on the beach reading a battered old Travis McGee paperback when Jorge came down from the bar. He told me Lenny had just called and said he was in the immigration holding facility up at the Cancun airport. He wanted to know if I would please come see him.

Of course, I had to go. Whether I liked him or not wasn't an issue. In an expat community, your worst enemy still deserves your help against 'them.' And anyone with a badge is one of 'them.' I had Jorge take my shift at the bar and headed north up the highway.

At the airport, I offered the appropriate 'donation' to the guard at the immigration office. That bought me passage down a labyrinth of corridors and through a door to where Lenny was being held in a dormitory-style room with several bunks. It looked like he had the place to himself. He jumped up when he saw me and gave me a hug. We sat down on one of the beds.

"Thanks for coming." He looked tired and pale.

"No problem. So what's the story?"

He said he had been arrested for a violation of his visa status. "What's wrong with your visa?" I asked.

He laughed, but his face remained worried. "Nothing. This isn't about my visa."

I didn't like the sound of that. "Then what's it about?"

It was about drugs. He spilled it all out in an unbroken stream of words.

A cop had been tipped off by his wife's second cousin who was a bartender in one of the places on Lenny's delivery route. He passed the information along to his superiors. They passed it on to the Drug Enforcement squad where the news of Lenny's activities had not been well received. It seemed that Jose Rodriguez, Comandante of the state narco squad, did not take well to hearing that someone was selling drugs who was not a member of his police force or at least on his payroll. He felt something needed to be done.

From what Lenny had been able to learn, their first option was simply to get rid of him. However, the Comandante knew that making a popular member of the American expat community suddenly disappear might bring about some unwanted attention. Especially with the U.S. media obsession over Mexico's drug wars. So a less drastic solution was arranged. Immigration cops picked up Lenny for a technical error on his visa.

"How do you know all of this?" I asked Lenny.

"The Comandante sent someone to explain it to me. To give me my options."

"Options? What the hell are you talking about?"

Lenny took a deep breath and tried to steady himself. "The narcos will arrange to have me released with no immigration charges if I agree to work for them."

I had a cold feeling in my stomach. "Work for them how?"

"Doing what I'm already doing, only they will get a cut. Occasionally I'll point out some of the college kids I sell to so the local cops can arrest them and shake them down. You know, for money or sex."

"That's it?" I asked. "That's their deal? Take it or leave it?"

Lenny nodded. "Except for some cash I have to give them."

"What cash? How much?"

Lenny looked around the room as if there might be somebody else to help. There wasn't. "Ten thousand U.S. They said it was commission on the stuff I sold without their permission."

I threw my hands up. "Jesus, Lenny. Who are these freaks? They are making you their slave and having you pay for the privilege. Who has that kind of cash lying around anyway?"

"I do," he said softly. "I have it in my bank in Belize. I just need someone to get it for me and take it to the Comandante. They don't want to go themselves. It's too direct a link to them, I guess." He looked up at me, holding my gaze.

I suddenly realized what he was asking. "Oh no, Lenny." I stood up and walked away from him, shaking my head. "No. There is no way in hell I am helping you pay off those fuckers."

"Please Poppa …"

"No!" I went back and sat beside him. "Listen, if you have ten grand in cash, we can use it to bribe the guards here and put you on a plane back to the States before the narcos know you're gone. That's the best plan. I'll help you with *that* plan."

"No," said Lenny sadly, his head down. "I can't go back there. I'll be arrested if I go back."

"Come on, Lenny," I said. "Are you telling me you were dealing dope back in the States?"

He shook his head and gave a dispirited laugh. "No, I was just a loser. And an embezzler." Seeing my look of disbelief, Lenny began to fill me in on his life before Paradise Beach became his home.

He said he had been a basic social reject back in the States. Oh sure, he graduated from a top school and worked hard to establish himself as an accountant. He was good at it. It was his talent. So what? He smiled half-heartedly. "There is a reason people joke about how dull accountants are."

Life was all numbers and files for Lenny. His folks were gone, and with no family and few friends, he lived on his computer. Then he met Linda online in a chat room. It wasn't long before she suggested they meet in person. Lenny was scared witless, but he went on that first date. "She was gorgeous," he said. I could hear the puppy love in his voice. "I mean, she was way out of my league. A little older than me, but I didn't care."

He said he didn't quite understand why, but for some reason she fell for him. To his surprise, when he asked her to marry him, she said yes. "She told me she was going to change my life. She said there would be no more Mr. Dull Guy."

The changing of his life started with a honeymoon in Hawaii they couldn't afford. And if they couldn't afford that trip, they really couldn't afford to buy a timeshare on Maui. "But Linda wanted it so bad I couldn't say no."

Back at their new gated-community home, Linda showered him with gifts. Of course, she bought them with Lenny's money. Linda thought a wife shouldn't work but should stay home to take care of her man. Lenny reciprocated by buying *her* gifts. If he forgot, she bought them for herself. "The money disappeared faster than I could make it."

Even when he fudged his own taxes, there wasn't enough, he said. Then he started shaving a little from the clients' trust accounts. Money he was supposed to be investing for others was paying for Linda's out-of-control spending habits. It still wasn't enough.

After he told Linda there was no more money, she left him. Lenny knew the game was up when her divorce lawyer demanded an audit of his books.

"I panicked. I ran away," he said in a whisper of a voice. "I transferred my money to a bank in Belize under a phony company name. I filled up my pockets with as much cash as I could, and I came here." He looked at me with teary, pleading eyes. "Don't you see? I can't go back. They'll meet me at the airport, put me on trial, and send me to jail. Word will get out. They'll hear about it even down here. Everybody will have a great laugh over the crooked accountant too stupid to steal without getting caught."

I tried to reason with him. I truly did.

"Lenny, even if you have to go to jail, at least do it in America. It's white-collar shit. If you don't get a suspended sentence, you'll end up in some country club minimum-security facility. That's nothing compared to what they will do to you here. You can't trust these fuckers. You have to go back." I was pleading with him now.

He shook his head in frustration. "It's not just the jail. It's what people will think." I tried to interrupt to say he shouldn't give a damn about what people thought, but he kept going.

"Back there, I was nothing. A nobody. Down here, I have the life I used to dream about. People respect me. Guys want to be my friend. Girls who wouldn't speak to me back home will fuck me here." His face brightened at the thought of his success. "Down here, bartenders pour me free drinks when I walk in the door. I'm not Lenny the loser down here. Down here, I'm the Skipper. I won't give that up. Even if it kills me."

I told him it might. He still wouldn't budge. He said without paying the money, he would end up in some shitty Mexican jail where he would be forgotten or worse. "Please," he begged. "I'm not going back. If you get the cash and give it to them, at least I'll have a chance to stay alive. If you won't help me ..." His voice trailed off.

Lenny felt he had no other choice. I didn't have one, either. It was hard to tell which of us was more miserable about it. "Okay," I said. "Okay."

Before I left, he gave me his bank card and password. I went to a local branch, and they had the money transferred up from Belize the next day. They counted out $10,000 U.S. at the bank window, while I kept looking around to see who was watching. I stuffed it in a large paper bag and did a whole lot of kicking myself in the butt for agreeing to this insanity.

As I drove back to my little room above the bar, I kept checking the mirror. I practically ran up the stairs to my place and put the bag of money under the bed. Then I called the number Lenny gave me. When I said I was Lenny's friend, the voice at the other end told me when and where to go to hand off the cash.

The rendezvous point was a dirt crossroads in the jungle outside of town, a few miles inland from the main highway. The arranged hour was late that evening, and by the time I drove out there, it was pitch black. All I could see were the overhanging trees reflected in my headlights. Just before I got to the designated spot, I saw flashing lights in my rearview mirror. I pulled over, and a black Hummer stopped behind me.

I turned around and saw two armed policemen wearing the all-black combat uniform of the narcotics squad. They came up on either side of the car. One ordered me in Spanish to get out. I did as I was told and stood frozen while he frisked me. He leaned in the open door and grabbed the bag of money from the passenger seat, looked inside, and tossed it on top of the car. Then he waved back at the Hummer.

A tall, well-dressed Mexican got out and began to walk toward me, stopping just a few feet away. With his clothes and confidence, Comandante Rodriguez could have been a businessman in any big city. His business just happened to be selling drugs and running the state police's narcotics squad.

"Mister ... Poppa." He paused just long enough to let me know he found my nickname amusing. He reached over and took the bag from the top of the car. He didn't bother to open it or count the money. I guess he figured I wasn't stupid enough to shortchange him. He was right.

"Your friend should be out in a couple of days," he said in perfect English. He started to walk away and then suddenly turned back, as if he just remembered something he wanted to say to me.

"Your bar is very popular. Perhaps we could do business."

He watched me expectantly.

I felt sweat dripping down my back. "My people are lushes," I said. I could see he didn't understand, so I explained. "They're drunks. Their drug of choice is alcohol. I couldn't help you much at all."

He smiled, staring at me for a moment, and then without a word walked back to the Hummer, followed by his bodyguards. In a few minutes, they had vanished into the darkness. I was still standing in the middle of the road holding my breath.

Lenny came by a couple days later to thank me profusely before resuming his role as Skipper. He refused to listen to any suggestion that he should get out of town. He was his old self for a while, running little bags of dope to this bar and that hotel room and being at the center of any party that was happening.

Not long after, he began to drift away for periods of time. Nobody knew where he went or why. He didn't offer any explanations. Sometimes he would be gone a few days; sometimes it was a week or more. One day he just didn't come back. Nobody ever saw him again.

The rumor mill went crazy. It's that way in any small town and worse when it's a group of expats. So, I heard a lot of stories. Skipper was living the high life in Colombia or Cabo or Puerto Vallarta. Skipper was now a big-time negotiator for the cartels, flying in and out of the States under the radar to make million-dollar deals. No, Skipper was a Fed, a narc for the U.S. He was back stateside, preparing extradition papers for all his local customers. Everyone had a different story about where Lenny might have gone.

No one knew what really happened—not even me. I had

my own ideas, but I kept them to myself. I like to think maybe Lenny slipped across the border one night and is now living anonymously in some trailer park outside of Orlando. I don't believe it, not for a minute, but it's a nice thought.

As the stories of Lenny's exploits were retold again and again in bars and at beach parties, they reached epic proportions. In the end, the Skipper became a local legend.

Lenny would have liked that.

"Well? Do you know him?" Sweet little Stacy with the great smile was still waiting for my answer. I pushed the memories from my mind. "Yeah, I knew him," I said. "He doesn't live around here anymore."

She looked crestfallen. Her well-made plans for spring break debauchery were suddenly fading away. "Maybe you know someone else we could hook up with?" she pleaded. Those blue eyes brightened. "Maybe you could even come party with us."

I sighed inwardly. Yeah, I could help her out. After Lenny disappeared, and even before, there were lots of newly arrived hustlers who wanted a piece of the paradise party pie. Plenty of them had been willing to pick up where Lenny left off.

The invitation to join her was damned tempting. It had been a while since I had beach bunny for breakfast. But I kept thinking of this dream I have occasionally of Lenny lying in a hole in the jungle while bad people shoveled dirt over him. I don't like having that dream. So I told Stacy no, I couldn't help her.

She seemed surprised. I guess the image her sister had painted of me didn't square with someone too old and out of touch to be able to score a little coke. "Really?" she asked. "You don't know anybody?"

I shook my head. I picked up my glass and examined it closely. It was still empty. I looked back at Stacy. "Why don't you girls stick to tequila while you're on vacation? It's cheap and legal."

She sat back in her chair and gave me a look usually reserved for parents or other idiots of a generation not hers. "Yeah, okay," she said, trying not to roll her eyes but failing. She got up and headed for the beach without a goodbye. That hurt my feelings a little. Well, truthfully, maybe not so much.

After I watched her walk back across the sand to her friends, I signaled Jorge for another rum. Then I opened my laptop, wondering what Maureen Dowd was bitching about today.

4
Moto Marty Finds His Purpose In Life

Not everyone I met in Paradise Beach was running from something. Some pilgrims were philosophers looking for answers to big spiritual questions. Others kept their quest closer to home, searching for some meaning in their own lives. They almost never came up with any better answers down in Mexico than they found up north. However, every once in a while there was someone who surprised me.

"Poppa, you got a minute?" Marty came in one morning shortly after I opened the bar. He sat on one of the stools and waited to speak until I was finished loading a bag of ice into the cooler.

I wiped my hands on a bar towel and walked over. "Sure, Marty. What do you need?" It was early, but old rules like *no drinks until noon*—or five or whatever—don't count much when you are in sight of that Caribbean blue. People on the beach don't want to wait for their first adult beverage of the day, and besides, no personal judgments are allowed in my bar. If you want a shot of tequila or a rum punch to kick start the morning, I'll be glad to pour it for you.

As it turned out, Marty didn't want a drink. He fidgeted on the bar stool—looking out to sea, around the bar, and anywhere but at me. Whatever he had to say was apparently painful for him. He finally blurted it out.

"Poppa, I was wondering if … uh … if you knew anybody who needed … or wanted some kind of … you know … help around the beach."

It took me a moment to realize Marty was looking for a job. It was obvious this was a new experience for him. It also came as a bit of a surprise to me. I had never seen him do anything close to resembling work.

Marty was a good-hearted guy who loved babies and kittens. Everyone thought so. He wasn't mean or dishonest. However, he was a classic goof-off without any sign of ambition or plans for getting ahead. Although close to thirty, he acted like a kid. Living in ripped t-shirts and unwashed shorts, his attitude was that life should be lived on cruise control. "No worries" was his constant refrain, regardless of the situation or problem. All he wanted was a little weed, a little wine, some tunes, and no hassles. Nice work if you can get it, and up until now, Marty could.

Among the Paradise Beach expats, it was generally known that Marty was being supported by his family back in the States. That wasn't an unusual circumstance. He wasn't the only trust fund baby in town. More than a few local drifters were traveling on the dime of a family that wished them well but wanted them out of sight.

Marty never seemed ashamed of his status as what Mark Twain mockingly called a "remittance man." If you were willing to buy him a drink or three, he would gladly admit to his life of leisure and relate the story of the day his father had sent him packing on the Margarita Road. I heard it several times myself.

According to Marty, some years back his dad had called him in for what was billed as a serious talk about the future. From experience, they both knew ahead of time that 'serious' and Marty rarely crossed paths.

"He told me it was time for me to go. I asked where, and he said it didn't matter. The family decided to send me away to travel so I could find what I wanted to do with my life."

Marty didn't buy that 'it's what's best for you' stuff his dad was handing out. He might have been "a lazy good-for-nothing," as his late grandmother once called him, but he wasn't an idiot. This was about the family wanting him out of the way for a while. It wasn't as if they didn't love him. He knew they did, and he also knew they were bothered and confused as hell by the way he lived.

The way Marty saw it, his dad was a high-priced corporate lawyer who didn't understand why his son couldn't keep a job, let alone enter a respected profession or at least move out of the house. His mother, well known among charities and society salons across the south, didn't quite get why her son dressed like a bum and acted like a child. And he was certain his sister never forgave him for skipping her wedding because he got the dates mixed up. The truth was he never really fit in. He knew it, and his family knew it. "I always kind of felt like I was a stray they picked up," he would say with a sad grin.

Still, if they were willing to foot the bill for him to do a little traveling, he wasn't going to say no. Perhaps some time away was just what he needed. When his father asked where he would like to go, it was an easy choice. Marty had dreamed of Mexico ever since he saw Salma Hayek strolling across a Mexican street in the movie *Desperado*. So, Mexico it was. His father bought him a one-way ticket south and stuffed his son's pockets with enough cash to keep him going for a while. "I hope you find something you're good at," he said with a final goodbye hug. "Something that makes you happy."

Even if Marty didn't find Ms. Hayek waiting for him south of the border, he did find Paradise Beach, which was as far as he could go without breaking the line of communication—and flow of money—from his family.

He settled into his new life without a hitch. Like many newcomers to Mexico, he found his lack of responsibility reflected in the world around him rather than condemned as it had been back home. In return, he accepted the limitations of his new life. Even the occasional breakdowns of plumbing and electricity failed to rattle him. 'Don't sweat the small stuff' was not only Marty's attitude, it was the official motto of Paradise Beach, as well.

It took him no time at all to fall into a daily routine. He slept until noon, had beer for breakfast, and spent time on the beach ogling the topless Italian women tourists. Later, he would join the regular parade of other expats on the nightly bar crawl that would continue until dawn.

He bought himself a noisy, oil-burning, secondhand motor scooter and became a regular sight zooming around Paradise Beach's dirt roads, heading to bars, the beach, and back again. This earned him the nickname 'Moto Marty' among local Mexicans.

The expats' never-ending beach party often stopped by my place as they made their rounds, so over time I got to know Marty. I liked him. He might have been a screw-up, but he was pleasant and friendly. Most importantly, he never started brawls in the bar, never tried to sneak away without paying, and never hassled my other customers. Those virtues put him near the top of the Paradise Beach social register, as far as I was concerned.

Given what I knew of Marty's personal story, having him in my bar asking where he could find a job was more than a little puzzling for me. "Isn't your family still taking care of you?" I asked.

He shrugged, as if not quite sure of the answer. "Well, kind of. I have been living off my inheritance for a while. You know, my folks had been letting me take it early in installments. But things have changed over the last couple of years," he explained, his voice dropping. "My dad passed away some time back, and now my mom isn't doing so well." He looked genuinely sad.

"I'm sorry," I said. I meant it. Part of the bittersweet paradox of the expatriate experience is the distance from family. For many travelers on the Margarita Road, the people who drove you crazy up north were the reason you headed south in the first place. But you still missed them.

He gave me a lopsided smile. "Thanks. So anyway, my sister is sort of handling all the family money right now and, well, she's kind of behind in my monthly payments. I think she might be pissed at me." He rolled his eyes as if to show there was no accounting for his sister's attitude toward him. "So I need some way to support myself. You know, until my inheritance payments start up again."

"Hmm," I said. "That might be tough." Mexican law required a work visa for foreigners to hold a job. However, those work visas were almost impossible for an expat to obtain. As a result, the aging gringo children living the dream here in the sun scrambled for jobs as bartenders, servers, or tour guides where they could be paid cash under the table. Competition was high for those few slots. Marty's opportunities were going to be limited.

"What are you good at?" I asked. "What do you want to do?"

"That is the million dollar question, isn't it?" He grinned as if I had told an old familiar joke. "My dad always told me I should find what I do best. Figure out what my real purpose in life is. You know, other than getting high."

I didn't know why, but I suddenly felt a need to help the poor guy. Maybe it was the story about his parents that got to me. My own folks had passed away several years before I wandered down to Mexico, but I still thought of them. Or, maybe it was just that Marty seemed so vulnerable and lost.

Whatever the reason, I heard myself saying, "I may have something for you. I need a bar back to help out around the place—just somebody to clean up, get ice, and load the cooler. Stuff like that." Even as I said it, I knew I was making a mistake. But Marty didn't seem to think so.

"Aw, man, that would be great!" He grabbed my hand across the bar and shook it. "I won't let you down."

I told him what the job paid and said he should show up the next morning. He seemed so thrilled at the prospect of working; I suspected he had never done it before. He was still thanking me as I walked with him out to the street. He climbed onto his little scooter parked curbside.

"This is so great, Poppa. I can't wait to tell Lupe." The engine roared to life with a rattle and the small explosion of a backfire.

"Who's Lupe?" I asked, yelling over the noise.

Marty smiled wider than I had ever seen and got a dreamy look in his eyes. "She's the love of my life." Off he zoomed.

"Oh no. Not Lupe." My buddy Chaz put his head in his hands and started laughing. He was a short, lean Irishman with sharp sailors' eyes, a prominent nose, and a deep-water tan. Chaz had left Ireland long ago to work and travel his way around the world several times before dropping anchor semi-permanently here in Mexico. He was one of the few real friends I had in Paradise Beach. He had stopped by the bar for a beer, and I was recounting my conversation with Marty for him.

"What's wrong with Lupe?"

Chaz looked up, still chuckling. "Lupe is an 18-year-old hooker who dances in a piece-of-shit topless club in the barrio. She has Marty wrapped around her little finger." He wrapped an imaginary string around his pinky. "This is a disaster waiting to happen."

"Come on, Chaz," I said. "It can't be that bad. Lots of guys get hung up on some good-looking girl with a heart of stone who takes them to the cleaners. I may have done it myself once or twice. It's part of life. The worst thing that usually happens is you lose a little money and end up with a tattoo you regret." I unconsciously rubbed the ink on my shoulder.

Chaz saw it differently. "This isn't a guy hung up on a local dancer. Marty is in love with a capital 'L'. He has fallen for this girl. Completely." Chaz sighed at the hopelessness of Marty's situation. "I keep telling him, 'Marty, give her your heart or your wallet, but never, never both of them!'"

I knew Chaz liked Marty and looked on him like a kid brother, but I figured he was worrying too much. After all, the guy was a grown man. How bad could it get?

I was about to find out.

At first, Marty was a good employee. He wasn't exactly a self-starter or management material, but more often than not he would do what I told him as long as I told him two or three times. Sure, he would come in late most days, but that really wasn't unusual in the land of 'maybe later.'

After a while, I began to see Chaz's point. Lupe was the center of Marty's life. He covered her rent, enrolled her in an English-language school, and took her on weekly shopping sprees. Marty also reported that Lupe felt much better now that she had an air conditioner in her apartment. He was forever asking for an advance on his pay to buy something for her. It seemed Marty gave her all he had, and everything he gave her made him adore her more. Anything else, including his job, was second to Lupe.

When I expressed some concern over this situation, Marty tried hard to convince me all was well. "Honestly, Poppa, Lupe is the best thing that ever happened to me. She makes me happier than I have ever been before." It's hard to argue with happiness, so I let it go, figuring eventually Marty would come to his senses. Maybe he would have, but before that happened, Lupe disappeared.

"She's gone, guys," Marty said sadly. He sat dejectedly beside Chaz at my bar while I leaned over to join the conversation. Marty was actually supposed to be working, but I was too anxious to hear the latest about his love life to tell him to get busy.

"She said she was going to her pueblo—some little village

south of Mexico City—just to see her family," he said. "That was weeks ago, and the cell phone I bought her is disconnected." I thought he was going to cry.

"How did she get a ticket to go?" Chaz asked.

"I gave her the money," Marty said sheepishly.

"You idiot." Chaz gave a half laugh, half angry snort.

"She was really sweet, guys. I'm going to miss her."

Chaz almost exploded in exasperation. "Marty, she stole all your money!" he yelled.

"No," said Marty firmly. "She didn't steal anything from me. I gave it to her."

I could see his point. It wasn't as if she had cleaned out his bank account at gunpoint. He had pulled the money out of his pockets voluntarily. I had faint memories of doing much the same thing once upon a time.

Marty continued his sad tale. "I just want to know if she's all right. I went over to the club where she danced, but they wouldn't tell me anything." He looked from me to Chaz and back again. "Maybe if someone else went and asked about her … ?"

Chaz answered first. "No way! Let it go and count yourself lucky she's gone."

Marty turned his tear-filled puppy dog eyes to me. "Poppa?"

Oh hell.

"You're a bigger idiot than he is," Chaz said to me. I didn't disagree. That night I headed out to find some answers for Marty.

If you drive away from the beach, past the ever-expanding line of hotels, bars, and restaurants of the tourist zone, you end up in the neighborhoods. This is where Mexican people who wait your tables and serve your drinks actually live. There are no margaritas or beach chairs here. Tourists rarely see this part of Mexico. They don't want to.

I drove past neat little cinderblock houses lining well-maintained but unpaved roads. I kept driving until the street got bumpy and there were fewer homes. I started seeing small shacks with dirt floors and plastic tarps for roofs and people gathered around open fires cooking their dinners. Mongrel dogs came barking at the car as I drove by.

I drove still further until the road stopped. That's where I found La Selva, the place Lupe had worked. This so-called 'gentlemen's club' was a squat cement building without any windows. The front was painted in bright, garish colors with a mural of jungle foliage and a cartoonish girl with impossibly large breasts in the embrace of an equally cartoonish jaguar. I parked my jeep out front and gave the door man some pesos to make sure the tires stayed on the car before stepping through the bead curtain that marked the entrance way.

It took a minute for my eyes to adjust to the low lighting, and by the time they did, a waiter already had a hand on my elbow and was leading me to a table. He acted with all the submissive servility usually reserved for big spenders being welcomed to a Vegas casino. Only this was no casino. The floor was covered in various colored tiles laid down in no particular pattern, as if someone had used whatever they found on sale or had fallen off the back of a passing truck. The tables and chairs were made of cracked plastic and imprinted with the faded logo of the local beer company.

In the middle of the room was a small, elevated platform a foot or two higher than the floor and about six feet square. In its center was a tall pole around which a very young and very bored topless woman danced.

My new best friend directed me to take a seat next to the stage and asked in rapid Spanish what I would like to drink, as he placed a menu in my hands. He had to shout to be heard above the electronic music blaring from speakers over the stage.

A quick glance showed that in addition to various tequilas and mezcals at ridiculously high prices, the menu offered condoms, lubricants, and other paraphernalia guaranteed to spice up the evening. I pointed at the listings for beer. The waiter looked disappointed and left.

Behind me was a badly-made wooden bar with a linoleum top. Along its front was a row of stools upon which sat a number of the ladies who worked for the club. There were four or five other patrons in the place, but as I was the only non-Mexican, they focused on me. Gringos always meant money. I was careful not to make eye contact in the hopes of avoiding attention from any of them. I wasn't there for that kind of fun. I was on a mission.

The waiter returned with my beer and made a show of pouring it into a glass that appeared to have a lipstick smear on the rim. Then he loudly asked if I would like company.

My Spanish can be a little rough, but it's good enough to make it through most days. However, this situation was tricky. I tried my best to explain I wanted to talk to someone about a girl named Lupe who used to dance there. When the waiter looked lost, I scaled back my request. Could I speak with anyone who had been a friend of Lupe's? "Amiga de Lupe?"

He seemed to think about this and then raised a finger to indicate he would be a moment, before heading off. I looked at my beer and decided not to risk it. By the time I had reached this conclusion, the waiter returned with a girl in tow.

She looked to be in her early twenties, maybe younger, with a heavily made-up face and a thick body barely concealed in a sheer wraparound dress. Her hair was cut shoulder length and styled to try and hide a scar running from her temple to the corner of her eye. "Lupe," the waiter announced, before depositing her in my lap and walking away.

The girl snuggled in close and wrapped her arms around me, burying her face in my neck. I pushed her back a little by the shoulders. "Lupe?" I was practically shouting to make myself heard above the music.

"Si," she said before returning to my neck.

Again, I pulled her up so I could talk. "La conoces Lupe?" That seemed to get her attention. Without answering, the girl suddenly stood up and pulled me by the hand as she headed for a hallway in the back of the club's main room. I was glad to get away from the blaring noise and prying eyes.

As we entered the narrow hallway, we passed a large guy with his hair pulled back into a ponytail and wearing a Steelers t-shirt. He stood against the wall with his thick arms folded on his massive chest and gave me a cursory glance as we passed. The bouncer, I figured.

The hallway was lined with doorways over which curtains hung. The girl suddenly stopped in front of one and pulled the curtain aside. It revealed a small closet-like space with a light fixture and a single bed with a worn blanket on top. She stepped inside and motioned me to follow her. "No, señorita," I said, shaking my head to emphasize this was not what I wanted. "I want to talk about Lupe."

The girl grinned and said, "Si, Lupe. Mi nombre es Lupe." Then she suddenly grabbed me by the belt and yanked me toward her with surprising strength. Caught off guard, I stumbled into the cubicle. With one hand still on my waist, she used the other to pull the curtain closed behind me.

As I tried to figure out how to loosen her grasp and walk away without actually hurting her, she managed to undo her wrap dress with her free hand so that it fell to the floor, leaving her nude but for preposterously tall high-heeled shoes. She didn't stay standing for long, however. She quickly knelt in front of me.

Obviously, her idea of a conversation was different from mine. I started backing away, but she followed, scooting on her knees while keeping one hand on the waistband of my pants and reaching for my zipper with the other. I tried to stop her full frontal attack, all the time repeating, "I only want to talk."

We must have made a bit of a commotion, because the giant I had noticed earlier suddenly filled the doorway. The girl and I both froze, my back against the wall and her hand in a death grip on my crotch. "Is there a problem?" he asked me in a clear American accent.

I gave a sigh of relief. "You speak English."

He nodded. "Sure. What do you need?"

I gave him a thumbnail sketch of the situation. He looked confused at first and then irritated that I was not actually there to pay for companionship. "You don't want this girl?"

"No," I said firmly. "It's Lupe I'm looking for."

He glanced down at my 'date' still kneeling in front of me and told her in rapid Spanish to return to the bar. She finally released her hold and stood up. Picking up her dress, she threw it over her shoulder and held out a hand expectantly.

I looked at the bouncer for help. After all, I hadn't touched her. His face was impassive, and I got the message. I reached in my pocket, took out two hundred pesos, and placed them in her hand. She waited with her hand still out. I added another hundred. She rolled her eyes, gave a smile to the bouncer, and walked away.

"Lupe doesn't work here anymore," the giant said when the girl was gone.

"Yeah, I got that impression. Do you know where she is?"

He looked at me suspiciously, as we walked back out to the main room. "Why do you want to know?"

"It's for a friend. He's worried about her."

The bouncer suddenly grinned. "El gringo rubio?"

I told him yes, the blond American who had been coming around was my friend. "He is in love," I said.

The big man seemed unimpressed with that news. "Lupe's gone," he said flatly. "She went with some guy who told her he could get her a job working in a fancy club in Veracruz. There's big money for dancers over there. That town is booming. Oil business, you know. I'm thinking of heading there myself."

I had to make certain for Marty's sake. "So she didn't go to visit family somewhere?" The bouncer gave me a stare of surprise and then exploded with laughter. "Family? Hombre, come on! These girls don't have families."

The next day at work, I let Marty know what I had found out. I figured I should tell him the truth, although I expected him to freak out a little. To my surprise, he seemed to take it very well.

"I'm just glad to know nothing bad has happened."

I couldn't help myself. "Marty, after taking you for all that money, she goes off with some guy who says he can get her a better job in a higher-class whorehouse. You aren't upset by that?"

Marty gave a sympathetic look as if he felt sorry for me being unable to understand the situation. "That's Lupe's life. It's what she does best. If she can do it where they treat her better and she makes more money, then how can I not be happy for her? I sure wouldn't want to hold her back."

When I later relayed all this to Chaz, his response was simply, "I told you he was crazy."

Crazy or not, no matter how much Marty wished Lupe well in her new life, I could tell he still missed her. For a few weeks, he moped around at work looking sad and sighing heavily every once in awhile. He just wasn't his old 'no worries' self.

Then suddenly one day his period of mourning ended. The Marty I knew was back, with a spring in his step and a ready excuse why he never did anything I told him.

He had met Sofía. Once more, Marty was in love.

I saw Sofía a few times when she came to the bar to pick Marty up after work. Cute with long, wavy black hair, she had bright eyes and a quick, friendly smile. She spoke semi-good English and actually seemed to care about him. Hopefully, she would have more staying power than Lupe had. However, she did have one thing in common with her predecessor: she was also a stripper and a prostitute.

"Entertainer, Poppa. She is an entertainer," Marty kept telling me. He was probably right, although I didn't think I would see her on America's Most Talented in the near future.

Once again, Marty's paycheck went to improving his girlfriend's life. He paid for Sofía's new clothes, makeup, hair styling, and whatever else her heart desired. He squired her around town to the best places he could afford (usually a high-end taco stand) and made regular appearances at the club where she danced. He couldn't have been happier—at least for the moment.

One day not long after Marty met Sofía, he showed up very late for work. Coming in the door, he saw me behind the bar doing his job of putting beer in the cooler. He made a beeline over, but instead of apologizing for being late with a lame excuse like he usually did, he simply sat down on a bar stool. "Poppa," he said, "I need some time off."

I had to laugh at how ballsy he was. I was tempted just to say no and tell him to get to work, but my curiosity got the better of me. Marty always needed money, or rather Sofía needed money. And the little work he actually did when he bothered to show up wouldn't tire anybody out enough to need a vacation. So why would he want time off? I couldn't help myself. I asked.

"My sister is in town, and I need to spend some time with her."

That was not what I expected, but it was a better story than any I had anticipated. In fact, for Marty, that was a legitimate reason.

"Well, okay then. Take a couple of days off. I'm glad to see you are staying connected to your family. Does this mean things are patched up between you two?"

"I don't know." Marty didn't look thrilled at the prospect of a family reunion. "We'll see."

His sister Adrianne had checked into the Caribe Azul International Hotel, Spa and Marina, a mega resort near Cancun. She spent her days getting massages and sipping margaritas, only breaking off from this wearing schedule to lecture Marty.

The reunion apparently was not a particularly happy one. When Marty returned to work a few days later, I found him sitting on a case of beer in my storeroom. Rather than sweeping it out and stacking the boxes against the wall as I had told him to do, he was morosely smoking a cigarette and staring into space. I asked if there was a problem. When he explained what had transpired with his sister, I was stunned.

"She wants me to go back with her, Poppa. Back to the U.S."

I sat down next to him on the stack of cases. "You mean for a visit?"

"No. She wants me to come back forever."

That was big news. The family wanting you back is either an expat's dream come true or the nightmare they were dreading. Or a little of both.

"Adrianne says it is time for me to grow up. She says I need a real home with family, and if I go back with her, she will see I get all the money Dad put aside for me. I just have to move to the States and live a normal life. You know, like with a career and stuff."

I tried to imagine Marty in any kind of job in the real world. After seeing his work at my place, where he managed to screw up or ignore the simplest chores, I was fairly sure his level of competence was near the bottom of the scale. I was surprised his sister couldn't see that, as well.

"What kind of career does she have in mind?"

"I don't really know. She mentioned something about working for her husband in his office. Some kind of desk job, I guess."

"What kind of business does your brother-in-law have?"

Marty blinked as if he had never really considered that question before. "I don't know."

He and I talked for quite a while. I played devil's advocate and pointed out that he had been mourning the loss of his family's fortune for some time. This was a chance to return to their good graces and get his money flowing again.

"Family is important," I suggested. I didn't know if I really believed that, but it seemed the thing to say.

"Yeah, I know. But what about Sofía?"

"What about her?"

Marty's voice filled with real concern. "Who will take care of her? How will she survive? What will she do?"

I wanted to say that she would probably continue to take her clothes off and have sex for money. Instead, I tried to offer some help. "Marty, all I can suggest is that you think about yourself for a change. Set your sister and Sofía and everyone else aside for the moment and focus on what will make you happy."

It was a corny cliché, I know, but it was the best I could come up with, and I meant it.

Marty thanked me for my advice, and I went back to work wondering if Paradise Beach was about to see the last of Moto Marty. I knew he loved his south-of-the-border lifestyle, but I also knew he really wanted the money his parents had left him. Perhaps the pull of that bank account would be too great to withstand.

A day or two later, a well-dressed woman walked into my place. Actually, overdressed was more like it. Maybe she would have fit in on a high-end cruise ship—but not so much in my funky little bar and grill.

She wore an expensive, gauzy pantsuit that I'm sure was

advertised as tropical loungewear in some pricey department store. She was draped in a gold chain necklace and earrings that matched her multiple rings. Her makeup had taken some time to apply. She was definitely slumming by coming to Poppa's.

She did a quick glance around and then strolled up to the bar. I was about to give her my standard welcome speech but didn't have a chance. "Where's Marty?" she asked firmly. "He said he works here." She slapped the bar top with her hand. "Where is he?"

Before I could answer, Marty came in the back door near the end of the bar with a case of beer. He did a full stop before saying, "Hi, Sis. What are you doing here?"

"What do you think I'm doing here? You were supposed to come see me two days ago. We have a lot to do to arrange for your trip home. Now put that box down and let's go."

Instead of putting it down, Marty came behind the bar with me. He set the beer in front of the cooler and then turned to his sister. I watched him steel himself for what he was about to say. "Adrianne, I've made a decision. I'm not going with you." Marty looked a little scared as he uttered these last words, but there was also a hint of defiance in his eyes.

Adrianne stared at her brother for a moment, as if trying to decide if she had actually heard what she thought she had heard. When she figured it out, she did not take it well. "Are you out of your fucking mind?" she yelled across the bar at him. "What's to decide? You're coming home and being part of this family. That's all there is to it."

This was followed by several reminders of all the precious time and money Adrianne had spent to come down to rescue him from his godforsaken, do-nothing life. Marty's observation that he had not asked to be rescued didn't help the situation.

At this point, I tried to intervene, suggesting that perhaps they could have this conversation somewhere more private and not in the middle of my bar. The only sign either had heard me was Adrianne's raised palm held in my direction, clearly instructing me to butt out.

Marty did his best to make his sister listen. He tried to explain he had never felt as accepted anywhere as he did in Mexico. She was right, he said, he needed a real home with real family. He had found that home and family among the people of Paradise Beach. He really was happier here than he had ever been before. And wasn't that the real question: what would make him happy?

Adrianne ignored that last query, probably because she wasn't prepared to answer truthfully. "That's it then, Marty," she yelled, loud enough to cause people out on the deck to turn and look. "If you decide to stay here with your worthless life, there won't be a second chance."

"I know," said Marty.

"I mean it," Adrianne bellowed.

"I understand."

"This is it, Marty. If I leave without you, you will never again get a penny except for the trust payments."

"Okay. If that is how it is going to … What? What did you say?"

Adrianne threw her hands up in exasperation. "Marty, haven't you been listening to me this past week?"

Actually no, he hadn't been listening. All the time his sister had been talking about banks, trusts, and interest payments, he had been worrying about leaving Sofia and giving up his life in Mexico. However, he was listening now.

Adrianne leaned in toward Marty and thankfully lowered her voice. "I explained all this to you before," she said, her exasperation giving way to anger.

"Yeah, well, tell me again, okay?"

Between clenched teeth, Adrianne tried once more to make things clear. "Our parents set up a trust for us. It pays us a certain amount each month for the rest of our lives." She cast a sideways glance at me that obviously meant I should go away. I ignored it. There was no way I was missing the rest of this exchange. It *was* my bar, after all.

"Money for the rest of my life?" I could see Marty thought this wasn't a bad deal. Adrianne disagreed.

"That's chicken feed, Marty. The good news is we don't have to wait for the money to dribble out. My lawyer says with Dad gone and Mom with dementia, we can ask the court to end the trust and give us the money now. But it takes both of us to do it. We have to both agree to break the trust."

I could see the wheels turning in Marty's head. He knew himself pretty well. He could make a big stash of money disappear overnight. Maybe it was better if he got it a little at a time like his father planned. Maybe his Dad had understood him after all. He said as much to his sister.

"But Marty," Adrianne practically wailed, "if we had the principal, you could give your share to me and then Hank could invest all that money for both of us. That's our plan. He says he can probably double it, guaranteed." Hank was Adrianne's husband, and Marty had never liked him much, that being the real reason he skipped their wedding.

"What happens if things stay as they are?" Marty wanted to know.

"Then the lawyers tell me I will have to go back to sending you your pathetic little pile of money each month until it is all used up, which would be one of the dumbest things you have ever done in a life full of dumb moves."

Marty smiled. "Maybe," he said, "but that's what I want." After a few more attempts to convince her brother to leave with her, Adrianne stormed out of the bar in a barely contained fit of rage. Marty just gave me a sheepish grin as if to say, *See what I have to put up with?* Then he started loading the beer into the cooler.

A few months after Adrianne left Mexico, Marty came in one morning with a sad look on his face. He said he had decided to quit working for me. "Poppa, I feel just terrible to leave you like this."

I did my best not to smile. He had not been an exemplary employee. Between his no-show days and his tendency to take naps in my storeroom, I figured his leaving wouldn't affect my business much. "It's all right," I told him. "I understand. With your inheritance payments back on track, there's no need for you to have to work here anymore."

"That's true, but really it's mostly because I'll be taking care of Sofía for a while after the operation."

"Operation? What operation?"

It turned out Sofía had noticed that the middle-aged American tourists starting to show up at the club tended to focus more on girls with large chests than their less voluptuous counterparts. For Sofía, it was an easy calculation. Bigger boobs meant bigger tips. She told Marty she really needed the extra cash to help support her infant son who lived with her mother in central Mexico. Sadly, though, she could not afford the new boobs on her present salary.

Of course, Marty agreed to foot the bill for breast implants. He told me that since Sofía would be laid up for a while, the best thing would be for her to move into his place while he provided around-the-clock nursing care. "So I can't work here anymore," he explained. "Sofía will need me with her."

I took a breath and decided to put it all out there.

"Marty, please don't get upset, but I just have to say … "

"I know what you're going to say. Chaz has already yelled at me about this."

"Well, maybe you should listen to him."

"But I love Sofía, Poppa!" he pleaded.

"You loved Lupe, too. And look what happened. She took all your money and then split. Do you really think Sofía is going to stick around any longer than Lupe did? She is taking those new tits on the road first chance she gets."

Marty hung his head while I read him the riot act. "Yeah, you're probably right," he said, still staring at the floor. "You, Chaz, my sister. You are all right, I know it. But Sofía needs me, just like Lupe needed me. She did, you know. Lupe really needed me."

I felt bad, but it was time to bring the curtain down on Marty's foolish infatuation with strippers. "Marty, you know Lupe didn't love you. And you know Sofía doesn't love you."

Marty's eyes grew big, and he started to speak, but I cut him off. "These girls trade what they call love for money. It's a business to them, and you are their best customer. You're a cash cow they milk for all it's worth. When Sofía sees a bigger sucker with more money, she will drop you just like Lupe did."

When I finished my speech, Marty sat silently with his head down. I felt like a heel. Maybe it was the right thing to say, but I still felt bad about being the one to say it.

He lifted his head and looked me in the eyes with as sincere an expression as I had ever seen on his face. "I know you think I'm stupid—that I just give away my money and get nothing back. But it's not just about the money for me or for them. I know you think that's it, but it's not. Girls like Lupe and Sofia don't have anything. They don't have anybody. Nobody loves them. Nobody ever helps them." Marty's voice suddenly became fierce. "That's not right. Everyone deserves a helping hand now and then. Everyone should have someone love them at some time in their life, even if just for a little while. Even if they don't know how to give any love back. That's what I do. I love them for a while and don't ask them for anything in return. And it makes me feel like I'm doing something important—something worthwhile that nobody else can do. Yeah, they get the money, but I get to feel like I made a difference."

He reached out across the bar and placed his hand on my arm. "Tell me something, Poppa. Who's going to love those girls if I don't?"

He had me there. You don't often hear words of wisdom in my bar, but once in a while, it happens. I wished Marty the best and told him to stay in touch. We had a beer together and shook hands. Then he went back to Sofia.

As predicted, it wasn't long after her breasts healed that Sofia took off for richer pastures just as we all knew she would. Just as Marty knew she would.

"It's okay," was all he said. "She'll be fine."

I worried about how Marty was going to handle this latest rejection, but I needn't have.

A short time later, I heard from Chaz there was a new

lady in Marty's life—a dancer, of course. Some girl from a crummy club out on the highway. Marty had moved her into his little apartment and was buying her new clothes. He was in love once again. For all anyone knew, maybe she was in love with him, too. Maybe this time it would last forever.

It didn't really matter, though. Marty had finally found something he was good at.

5
The Fairer Sex

There aren't a lot of rules or regulations on the Margarita Road. You won't find much in the way of adult supervision, either. What you do and who you do it with is generally no one's concern but your own. Still, there are exceptions. Even in paradise, not everyone thinks freedom is a good thing. There are always some people who want to make sure the fun times don't get out of hand—especially if they're not having any of the fun.

"Poppa! Another pitcher of margaritas, please."

The request was shouted from the group of five women seated around the big round table under the umbrella on my deck. It was accompanied by joking cries about how someone had already had enough and how it was too early in the afternoon to get drunk. While the laughing exchanges went back and forth, I looked over to the table just to confirm the order.

Molly caught my eye and nodded, holding up one finger. Whenever there was a question about the order or the bill, or as far as I could tell any aspect of these women's lives, Molly would render the final judgment.

I mixed up another pitcher and carried it over, circling the table and filling glasses. The conversation had quieted down a little and seemed to have taken on a more serious tone. Several of the women were speaking at once.

"Nobody can blame her. He's the one screwing around."

"That's right. It's not her fault she's married to a bastard."

"She might not even know what's going on."

"It's that whore's fault."

Molly's voice rose above the rest. "And that's why I invited Katie to come by today. It will give us a chance to let her know what her husband is up to with Jennifer. Better she hears it from her friends rather than from some stranger."

Molly must have seen me unconsciously grin at that last bit because she quickly gave me a dismissive, "Thanks, Poppa. We can pour the rest."

"Sure thing," I said.

I didn't mind. I could still hear them from the bar. I set the pitcher on the table and headed back inside, leaving them to plan their next crucifixion.

These women were regulars in my place. They would gather on sunny afternoons to drink and gossip in view of the Caribbean Sea, deciding who in town was worthy of their attention or judgment. I called them the "Ladies Who Lunch," and Molly was their founder and unanimously-agreed-upon, unofficially-appointed-for-life chairperson.

Molly had come to Paradise Beach several years back. From what I heard, her life had stalled right after finishing college. Available jobs in rural Arkansas where she grew up were limited to the local burger joint or being a teller at an out-of-the-way bank branch. Molly wanted more than that. She planned on going places. As she saw it, the only problem was that most of the places she wanted to go put too much emphasis on who was prettiest or had the best grades or knew the right people.

To make matters worse, the boyfriend who had shown so much promise (the only one since high school) took off for California. He had halfheartedly invited Molly to join him, but she made it clear the west coast held no attraction for her. "Why would I go to L.A.?" she said after landing in Paradise Beach. "You have to be a blonde bimbo, all tits and no brains, to get anywhere out there. I have bigger plans."

While trying to figure out how to leave Arkansas for someplace other than California, Molly came across a blog by an expat living in Paradise Beach. It described gringos getting in on the ground floor of a future tourist empire, which sounded good enough for her to buy a one-way ticket. Mexico had the added attraction of being as far from her mother and the trailer park as she could afford to go.

She became part of the second wave of expats heading into town. Following the drifters and adventurers who first landed on the beach, this new group shared a sense of manifest destiny with more of an interest in payoffs than paradise. They came to put down roots where there were fewer rules and less competition. As these self-styled entrepreneurs set about staking their claims, the idea that it was someone else's country never became an issue.

Molly would sit in my bar telling me of the boring, stupid world she had barely escaped and laying out the blueprint for her new life. "This town is mine for the taking," she would say over several margaritas. "There are so many opportunities; I can't even decide which one to start with."

Unfortunately, none of those plans for success ever quite

happened for her. Life on the Margarita Road doesn't always cooperate, especially with ambition.

The job managing rental properties for condo owners back in the States only lasted one season. Her monthly pamphlet for tourists offering *Recommendations for Fun in the Sun* was nicely written, but no one wanted to advertise in it. Even the receptionist gig disappeared when she stopped sleeping with the hotel manager.

She didn't starve. There was always some job she could hold onto for a while and another after that. She could usually find enough money to pay rent on a room far from the beach and almost cover her bar tabs. But having success on a scale to write home about? Not so much.

Molly's hopes for a love life turned out to be equally elusive. Let's face it, trying to find romance while wandering through the happy hours of Mexican beachfront dive bars is a crapshoot, at best. Semi-sober guys with all their teeth, no mommy hang-ups, and a desire to settle down and start a family are scarce among the potential dates drinking their way through the tropics.

I don't know why, but Molly just couldn't find her niche. Maybe it was because she thought she should be boss in any job or relationship that came her way. That didn't mesh with a beach lifestyle that put a high degree of value on no one being in charge. Or perhaps she just got lost on her planned way to the top. A steady diet of booze and bitterness can do that.

Whatever the reason, while she never gave up on her dreams, as the years passed she did develop a thick hide and sharp teeth. She wasn't alone. She eventually found other women who shared her anger at a world that hadn't yet recognized their talents. I guess that's how the Ladies Who Lunch was born.

I heard Bridgette chime in from the table. "Well, I think we are doing that poor girl a favor. She needs to know what a piece of shit that husband of hers really is." If Molly was the leader of the Ladies, Bridgette was their moral backbone. "Most of all, she needs to know Jennifer Langston is not someone to be trusted."

A little older and wider than most of the women around the table, Bridgette had come to Paradise Beach from Milwaukee. Her husband took an early retirement and insisted they move here, despite her qualms. He had gladly traded in his job doing heating and air with the local school system in exchange for the complete Jimmy Buffett Parrothead experience of flip flops and tequila shots. Bridgette, on the other hand, was a little less enamored of the tropical lifestyle.

She didn't care for the beach, hated the sun, couldn't swim, and refused to learn any Spanish. "All my friends are Americans, so why bother?" she often said. Bridgette considered her friendship with the Ladies Who Lunch to be the sole saving grace of her life in Mexico.

Eventually, her husband must have tired of the constant public bitching about the weather, the Mexicans, and him. One day he took off with a cute, redheaded creative-writing teacher passing through on sabbatical from a community college in Cleveland. The last anyone heard, they were heading for a Jerry Jeff Walker concert in Belize.

That's when Bridgette's strong sense of moral outrage kicked into high gear. She became more and more vocal about condemning the "tramps and sluts" in town. In Bridgette's eyes, most of the women in Paradise Beach were strong candidates for that status.

Molly and Bridgette were the core of the Ladies Who Lunch. There were other members, of course. Ashley was a trust fund baby who ran a puppy rescue operation out of her house. Her furnishings and mortgage were paid for by donations people gave to help abandoned street dogs. Linda wrote a blog about the trials of being a single mother in Mexico, although her son spent most of the year with his father in Colorado. Natalie was able to live quite well in paradise thanks to the skills of a great divorce lawyer. Others came and went, depending on the season and the judgment of Molly and Bridgette.

The ladies had a semi-regular agenda. Besides alcohol consumption, they were the self-appointed protectors of the morality of the gringos in Paradise Beach. That moral code required no one be freer or happier than they were. Any transgression of that code was met with gossip and social shunning. Today, as far as I could tell, Jennifer Langston had become their latest target.

I had known Jennifer for years. She was a tall, leggy strawberry blonde with a wide grin and big brown eyes that required an entire afternoon to fully explore. Like me, Jen had been an early arrival on the beach.

She had floated into town on the arm of a captain sailing his boat to the British Virgin Islands. They stopped for a few nights to wait out some weather problems, and when he sailed away, she remained behind. "I do love these Mexican boys with all their macho posing," was the only explanation for her decision to stay.

Jen always claimed she had come by her wanderlust early in life as the child of a child of the Sixties. "I'm lucky I wasn't named Moonglow or something," she would say.

Her mother had been a bead-wearing, flowers-in-the-hair hippie chick who nested in the corners of L.A.'s Laurel Canyon back in the Age of Aquarius. Jen was the result of a few blissful days spent in a vine-covered cabin with a bass player from a second-tier band that never went beyond playing bars on the Sunset Strip. A signed album cover was her paternal inheritance.

Jen's mom had a gypsy soul, and as the two of them traveled about, there were crash pads near Malibu, marijuana farms north of San Francisco, and a spell with an artist commune in Arizona. She would be the first to agree it was a weird and sometimes less-than-perfect childhood. "How many 14-year-olds get joints instead of candles on their birthday cake?" Regardless, she never seemed the worse for it. Somehow, she managed to reach adulthood with a sense of independence and self-confidence not seen in her sisters with a more traditional upbringing.

In typical beach-bum fashion, Jennifer survived by giving massages on the beach, babysitting tourists' kids, and taking the occasional gig as a receptionist or bartender at whatever hotel was shorthanded.

Since she spoke Spanish like a local, she also helped out at a nearby grade school. "I'm just a glorified recess monitor," she would say, but I could tell she had a great time with the kids. Maybe she was reliving her own early years on a more normal basis through them. Or maybe she was just a big kid herself.

No matter where she worked or what she did, her real career was being free, and she had found Paradise Beach the perfect place to practice her occupation.

There seemed to be no particular guy in her life, although

she did enjoy men and made no secret of that. And if a married man passed through her bed now and then, she figured that was between him and his wife and didn't concern her. Jen was a wild child who answered to no one but herself, and the Ladies Who Lunch considered that a direct insult.

From what I could gather listening to the conversation out on the deck, Jen's latest affront to the Ladies was their belief she was having an affair with a married British expat named Peter Billingsly. It seemed Peter's motorcycle had been seen parked outside the little duplex where Jen lives. "It wasn't just parked for an hour or so. I saw it there early in the morning. It had obviously been there the whole night!" The others audibly gasped. "And that wasn't the only time I saw it parked there." Molly sat back, her final argument for conviction completed.

There they had it: solid, unquestionable proof that Jennifer was a slut and that Kate Billingsly's husband was the type of scum drawn to such women. It was now their duty to expose these two immoral players to the world—or at least to their dear friend Katie. "We owe it to that poor girl to tell her the truth about what's going on behind her back," Bridgette said with a righteousness that would have been the envy of a judge from the Spanish Inquisition. "We have to do this for her."

Peter Billingsly was a journalist. He was tall and thin with a wild mop of hair and beard that made him look a bit like a giant dandelion. His wife Katie was compact and athletic with short brown hair and an English overbite. She resembled a cute chipmunk. They had left England, as Peter explained it, "because it was too bloody cold to live there a minute longer." They bought a boat in Jamaica and had been sailing around the Caribbean with extended stays on various beaches, as

Peter wrote a book about the adventure. Currently, they were anchored in Paradise Beach. They must have liked it, as they had been here several months.

Katie was not exactly membership material for the Ladies. For starters, she had a wicked sense of humor and used it mercilessly when dismissing fools from her life. She also had a habit of skinny-dipping in front of my bar when she'd had a few too many tequilas. "I couldn't do this in England," she would yell on the way to the water.

Some found her behavior shocking. Personally, I considered it quite charming.

However, even if Katie was not up for a permanent seat with the Ladies, they obviously felt a degree of sisterhood with her that demanded they wreck her marriage by exposing her husband as a cheating cad. If at the same time they could paint a big red 'A' on Jennifer Langston's bra-less chest, so much the better. I was more than a little curious to see how this would play out. I didn't have long to wait.

Katie walked into the bar while the Ladies were on their third round. She was accompanied by a big sand-covered golden retriever I knew as Sam. She glanced at the group out on the deck and then stopped at the bar to lean over and give me a quick peck on the cheek. "Hello, Poppa. Is it all right if Sam comes in with me?" I said it was no problem and filled a bowl with cold water for him. The dog was one of my best-behaved patrons.

As I handed Katie the water, I said, "I'm a little worried about you."

"For goodness sakes, why?" she asked as she bent to give Sam his water. "The girls invited me for a drink. What could go wrong?" There was a mischievous glint in her eye.

I nodded toward the group at the table. "They can be a little rough."

"No worries, my dear," she said with a grin. "It will be a pisser, you'll see."

I hope so, I thought, as she headed out to the deck. Sam wandered over to settle down on a shady spot under the awning where he could keep an eye on things.

The Ladies all greeted Katie solemnly, as if they were attending a funeral. As she took a seat, I walked around from behind the bar and went over to the table. I set a clean glass in front of her. "Katie," I asked, "are you good with a margarita?" I nodded at the pitcher on the table. "Or would you like something different?"

She looked up and gave me a big smile. "Oh, give me a minute to think Poppa. Hmmm." She placed a finger to her lips. Out of the corner of my eye, I could see Molly frowning in irritation at my delay of her planned lynching.

"By the way," Katie said to me suddenly, "how are you enjoying the bike?"

"I love it," I said. "It's so much easier to drive that thing in town than my old jeep. I can zip in and out of traffic and park it anywhere. It fits in any little space I want to leave it. Please make sure to tell Pete how much I like it."

"Oh, I will," Katie said.

There was a sudden stillness at the table. Then Molly snapped to life, practically jumping out of her chair. "What are you talking about?" she said half to Katie and half to me, her eyes going back and forth between us. "What bike do you mean?"

Katie looked a little shocked at the forcefulness of Molly's question. "Well, uh, we were talking about the motorcycle

Poppa bought from my husband Pete."

I chimed in at this point. "You know that old banged up blue motorcycle Pete drove all over, don't you Molly?" Molly could barely nod her head yes. "I bought it from him about a month ago." Now it was my turn to act puzzled. "Why? Is there a problem?"

Molly's eyes burned into mine. "No," she said finally. "Of course not. I've seen the bike parked around town and wondered who was driving it these days."

"That would be me," I said and smiled.

"Where have you been parking that scooter?" Bridgette practically spit out at me.

"Anywhere I want to." I smiled my biggest smile at her.

"At Jennifer Langston's house?" Bridgette was turning red in the face.

"Why yeah, it's possible it was parked over there on occasion. I think Jen's a pretty special person, don't you?"

I turned back to Katie. "So about that drink … "

"Oh, a margarita is fine, Poppa. Thanks."

I took a slight step back to get a view of the whole table. The Ladies silently looked up at me with frozen faces. "If you need anything more, let me know," I said.

As I headed back to the bar, I heard Katie say, "So what should we talk about, girls?"

6
Part Time Paradise

Travel agents and Tripadvisor eventually discovered Paradise Beach. Fewer drifters arrived via the Margarita Road, while more and more tourists were coming in a never-ending stream of cheap flights from the States. Each new season found the beach covered with winter-pale bodies from places like Buffalo and Omaha. After a week or two, the visitors from up north couldn't imagine being anywhere else. That's the danger of a vacation in paradise: you want it to go on forever.

The first time I ever saw Bernie, he was encouraging his wife to climb onto my bar and pull her underwear off.

"Go on, honey. Get up there."

It had been a tradition since I opened the place. Any lady brave or drunk enough to remove her undergarments while dancing on the bar was rewarded. The rewards ranged from a free shot of tequila to a night of drinks on the house, depending on my mood and my own alcohol intake. However, the real enticement was that the garment would be hung from the ceiling in permanent tribute to its owner. There were close to a hundred thongs and panties hanging from the rafters already.

Some folks say my attitude is misogynistic. Others say it's tasteless. I just think it's fun, and I figure everybody could always use a little more fun. It didn't hurt anyone, and it gave soccer moms who would never do such a thing back home a chance to be a little naughty on vacation. Besides, as I always say, "My bar, my rules."

Feel free to drink somewhere else if it bothers you. One of those places with a giant plastic amphibian out front just opened down the beach. They serve prepackaged fun and sugary drinks with cutesy names. Go there if you want. Lots of people do. Places like that seem to be the wave of the future for Paradise Beach.

Regardless, I still had my share of tourists, and it was in the middle of a good-sized Saturday night party crowd when I saw them. He was holding one of his wife's hands while putting his other hand on her rear end. He gave her a little boost as she climbed up on a stool and started to put a knee onto the bar.

"Hold it right there," I said.

They both froze as I walked down to where they stood. This gave me a chance to look them over. She was cute, in her late thirties with wavy light brown hair, and wearing the same sundress every other woman tourist was wearing that season. He was about the same age, a bit pudgy with a face flushed from too much drink and sun.

She started to sit back down on her stool. "I'm sorry," she said, looking a little embarrassed.

The guy had a different reaction. He put his hands on the bar, and his voice took on an edge when he spoke to me. "We were told if she danced on the ... "

I raised a hand to quiet him down. "Take it easy, cowboy."

He was wearing a straw Stetson with a Cuervo hatband and sporting a Parrothead concert shirt. "This pretty lady can dance on my bar anytime." The woman blushed and smiled. "But those shoes have to come off." I pointed at her sandals. "Barefoot only on this bar."

I gave them a big smile to let them know we were all friends. The guy relaxed and grinned. "Okay, then." He turned to his wife. "Let's do this, honey."

She slipped off her sandals and carefully stepped onto the bar as I cranked up the stereo. Once she started to sway to a Bob Marley song, the crowd began to shout, "Take them off!" Her husband was yelling the loudest.

She gave him a questioning look. "Should I?" she mouthed. When he gave her an enthusiastic nod yes, she reached up under her dress with one hand while holding the hem below her crotch with the other. In a moment, a tiny bit of silk slid down her legs to her ankles. As the crowd roared its approval, she bent over and picked up the thong. She held it out to me, and with a slight bow, I placed it inside my shirt with a showy flourish.

She laughed and climbed down to sit on a stool. Bright red with embarrassment, she smiled from ear to ear as her husband began to gush about how hot it had been. As I wandered away, Jorge was already making her one of his specialty margaritas as a reward.

Throughout the rest of the evening, I noticed the same couple dancing and introducing themselves around. *Friendly folks,* I thought. He might have been a little pushy, but what the hell, everybody gets to cut loose on vacation. Besides, Jorge smiled a lot when serving him, so I guessed he was tipping well. That gesture will cover a multitude of sins in a bar. It was a busy night, and I never really noticed when they left.

The next morning, the same guy in the same cowboy hat showed up at the bar without his wife, looking a lot worse for wear. He stumbled in, his face a light shade of green. He climbed onto a stool and put his hands on either side of his head, holding it as if it might fall off.

"How's it going?" I asked, as I cleaned the bar in front of him. "Come for a little hair of the dog?"

He closed his eyes and moved his hands to cover his face. "I think I may die right here," he groaned.

I took pity on him. After all, I did have his wife's panties hanging above my bar now. "Let's start easy, then," I said. I filled a tall glass with ice. Pouring lime juice to the halfway point, I added a good dash of sweet syrup and then filled it to the top with sparkling water. I set the drink in front of him.

He opened one eye and peeked between his fingers to look at it. "What's this?"

"It's called a Suero," I said. "It's the Spanish word for IV—you know, like an intravenous drip. It's a local hangover cure. The water helps hydrate you, the lime settles the stomach, and the syrup give you a little sugar boost. Drink it down. It will help."

He did as he was told. When he was done, I made him another, and he drank about half of it. He sat up and began to look around. It appeared as if he might live. "Hey!" he said. "That's not half bad. Maybe now I'm ready for something stronger. A margarita maybe?"

I nodded and started to build his drink.

"I'm Bernie, by the way. Bernie Huffman." We shook hands.

"I'm Poppa," I said. "This is my place."

"It's a great bar," he said. I thanked him. "Say, Poppa, I noticed that your bartender was taking some photos last night when my wife Kathy was on the bar."

I knew what was coming. "Yes, Jorge usually does that when a good-looking woman is up here." I patted the bar top. "Sometimes he posts them on our website, but if you want, I'll ask him to e-mail them to you. Just give me your address."

My suggestion had the opposite effect than I had expected. Bernie looked like the floor had given way beneath him. "Oh, God no, don't let him do that." He looked scared. "Not either one. If anyone back at my school ever sees those photos, I ... well ... oh shit, that would be bad."

Personally, I never saw a little bar dancing in Mexico as anything to worry much about. "What's the big deal?"

"It could just about ruin my career," he said.

It turned out Bernie was a lawyer, although he had long ago decided his career was in the classroom, not the courtroom. As he put it very proudly, he was a Professor and Senior Lecturer of Business Law at a small university in Iowa. Bernie said he preferred the ideals of the classroom to the sometimes dirty real world of business and lawsuits. "And, it's a nice steady paycheck."

As I listened, I got the impression he wished some days he could actually run things himself instead of just lecturing to a bunch of bored college kids. Of course, it didn't matter to me what he did or didn't do. It was his life, and if he was happy, then all was good.

What was important at the moment, however, was Bernie's fear that his colleagues or academic superiors at the college might see how he and his wife were spending their vacation. "It's an old school with lots of heritage and dignity.

The senior staff is very conservative. I could lose my job if they saw those photos."

Still, Bernie wanted to make sure I knew he didn't share his employers' sense of provincial propriety. "I am the most liberal member of the university's faculty," he explained. "In fact," he said with a failed attempt at a humble look, "they call me the Wild Man back there."

"That so?" I said, placing a light-on-the-tequila margarita in front of him. I figured he needed to start slow. "This one's on the house, by the way."

"Thanks," he said, raising the glass to his lips for a taste. He nodded appreciatively before putting the drink down and continuing his story. "I mean, I usually don't care what people think. Kathy and I can get crazy on vacation, if you know what I mean." He gave me a sly grin to show we were both sophisticated guys who understood exactly what he was talking about. "Those old fogeys where I teach might have a heart attack if they knew some of the things we do." He laughed softly at his own mental image of his aged and non-wild colleagues. "So if you could tell your bartender … "

"Jorge," I interrupted.

"Yeah, Jorge. If you could tell Jorge to make sure those photos from last night don't get posted anywhere on the internet, I would really appreciate it."

I told him I would see to it.

"That's great," he said, picking up his margarita. He raised the glass to me. "You know what they say. What happens in Mexico stays in Mexico."

Yeah. That's what they say.

I saw Bernie quite a few more times over the next week. He and his wife became regulars during their vacation. By the end of his time in Paradise Beach, he knew many of the expats by name. On their last night in town, he threw an impromptu going-away party for himself. He bought several rounds of drinks, which is always encouraged and appreciated by any bar owner.

Near the end of the evening, he got a little teary-eyed as he told various people from around town he would miss them and how much they meant to him, although he had met them only a day or so before. He even got on stage to sing some Toby Keith songs with Wet Willie.

Willie is a middle-aged Brit who showed up on Paradise Beach several years ago with a love of American rockabilly music, a decent enough voice, and a six-string guitar. He had been a regular singer—and drinker—in my bar ever since. With his battered cowboy hat over a long gray ponytail and fancy Mexican caballero boots beneath faded cargo shorts, he makes quite a sight. The expats in town adore him, and the tourists see him as part of the local color.

At the end of the night, Jorge yelled, "Last call!" Bernie suddenly jumped back on the little stage next to a startled Willie. Grabbing the microphone, he screamed above the feedback he caused, "I love you guys. I'll be back next year!"

It's nice to be loved, even by an inebriated law professor in a XXL Tommy Bahamas shirt stained with sweat and enchilada sauce. However, no one there took Bernie's promise to return as a General MacArthur-like commitment. Most tourists say that on their last night, and some actually make it back. For others, next year never comes. Their intentions are good, but mortgages and payments on the kids' braces seem to get in the way. I figured Bernie for one of these folks. Boy, was I wrong.

"Poppa! We're home!" Bernie shouted as he and Kathy rolled in the door of my place about six months later. While slurping margaritas, Bernie explained they were down during the university's spring break. I said I was glad to see them, and that was the truth. I am always a bit pleased when folks figure my town and my bar are worth another trip.

I saw quite a bit of them over the next few days. They seemed to like my place and hung out there often. Bernie was a gregarious guy who would chat up my other customers whether he knew them or not. It was like having my own Walmart greeter while he was in town.

That was just the beginning for Bernie. It wasn't even another six months before he and his wife were back again, this time for two weeks of their summer vacation. "I love Paradise Beach, Poppa," he said. "It's like I have always lived here." This time around, they rented one of the hideous new condos that were beginning to take over the beach not far from my bar. Once they settled in, Bernie began to ask some of the expats over for dinner and drinks.

I was invited one evening but bowed out with some made-up reason. The truth is, I spend too much of my life listening to drunks telling the same gossip over and over. When I have time off, I like to spend it alone or with somebody special.

I did hear that my friend Chaz went once, so I asked him about it. "It was weird, Poppa," he said.

His story was interrupted by the arrival of Handsome Harry. Chaz and I were sitting beachside at Harry's restaurant, and he stopped by the table to say hello. It was always fun to see Harry. He stood out as a character even on Paradise Beach, where everyone had a story.

Handsome Harry wasn't particularly handsome, though he did have a striking appearance with bright blue eyes and long white hair he wore braided down his back. He told everybody the sun bleached it, but in truth it had turned snow white when he hit his late fifties.

Harry looked a little like Keith Richards, with lines of laughter and pain that had long ago settled into a creased map of the life he had lived. He also had a voice that sounded like a cement mixer turning. He always claimed his distinctive sound was the result of a complex and somewhat acrobatic multi-partner sex act he had learned while traveling in the Far East during his younger days. According to the tale he told, it had all gone wrong when one of the ladies involved lost her balance during a moment of passion. In the subsequent fall, she had landed in such a manner as to elicit a scream of pain from Harry long and loud enough to damage his vocal chords.

That was the way Harry told it, at least. Personally, I figured his gravelly voice came from too much booze and too many cigarettes.

Whether fact or fiction, his supposed adventure added to the air of mystery he cultivated. He would recite the story to a crowd of fascinated tourists sitting in my bar, a glass of fine tequila in hand. Or he might tell it before launching into his a cappella version of *House of the Rising Sun* in an attempt to impress a woman half his age from Oklahoma or other points north. Harry was my idea of a true citizen of paradise— carefree, irresponsible, and fun to be around.

Chaz had suggested lunch on the beach, as he heard Harry had hired a new woman bartender with a voluptuous stature and minimalist wardrobe. Unfortunately, we had seen no sign of her. We mentioned this to Harry who promised us the lady in question was running late but that we wouldn't be disappointed. He bought us a round of beers to help ease the pain of waiting.

When Harry moved on to another table, Chaz resumed his story about dinner with Bernie.

"Like I say, it was weird."

"Weird in what way?" I asked. I was really curious now. As a sailor drifting from one Caribbean resort town to the next, Chaz had seen plenty of things strange and wondrous. He wasn't the type to be surprised by the seemingly limitless antics of people on vacation.

Chaz gave it some thought. "It's hard to describe. I remember when Bernie first came down to Paradise Beach; he treated me like some sort of celebrity because I live here."

I couldn't help but laugh. "You're a star, Chaz. We all know that."

He laughed, too. "No, I don't mean just me. He treated everybody who lives here like that. Now he acts like we've been best mates forever. He did a whole lot of talking about how "we" should handle the tourists and how Paradise Beach has changed since the old days. If I hadn't known better, I would've thought he'd been living here for years."

"That is weird," I agreed. Just as I was about to ask for more details, the new bartender arrived and distracted me. Harry had been correct. She didn't disappoint.

A few days later, Bernie stopped by my bar with his new prized possession. He strolled into the place as if he were the owner and called out, "Hola!" to Jorge. He made a beeline for my table. I was enjoying a moment's peace in the afternoon lull before the rush of the party crowd that evening. Sitting down, he put a small flip phone in the center of the table. "It's my Mexican cell phone," he said proudly.

"Yeah?" I said, not quite understanding the importance.

"It's a Mexican cell phone," Bernie repeated. "It's a cell phone with a local Mexican number. We can call each other now whenever I am in town." I couldn't imagine why we would do that, but I kept my mouth shut.

Bernie opened his new phone and pushed some keys. "Give me your phone number, and I'll put it in here." I didn't know how to say no, so I reluctantly gave it to him. "Excellent," he said. "This way we locals can all stay in touch with each other."

Over the next couple of years, Bernie and Kathy came to Paradise Beach every chance they got. It became their obsession—or at least Bernie's. Kathy seemed content to lie on the beach with a good book and sip her drinks. Bernie, on the other hand, had begun to think of himself as an expert on the place, offering lectures and instructions about life in the tropics to anyone at the drop of a hat. Maybe it was the professor in him, but it got to be a little irritating.

Bernie was in my bar one day as I was chatting with a young couple from New Jersey who had stopped by for mojitos and advice. They had asked me if I thought a drive down the coast to see the Mayan ruins in the pueblo of Tulum was worth the trip. Before I could answer, Bernie suddenly appeared at their side. He had overheard their question and began his spiel before I could say anything.

"You're going down the coast to Tulum? I can help you out."

I couldn't get a word in edgewise as he told them how to get there, what to see, and even where to go for lunch afterwards. "It's a little place the tourists don't know about," he said, "Tell them Bernie sent you, and they will treat you like a local."

When he was back in the States after his many vacations, Bernie continued to offer his expertise on numerous internet forums that focused on Paradise Beach. He posted under the name 'Tequila Bern' on such important topics as who had the best pork tacos and whether it was preferable to visit the beach in February or March. Those who dared argue with him were regularly dismissed as mere tourists. "I practically live there," he would write.

He might have come on a little strong with his opinions, but he wasn't the only one who did that. Plenty of visitors to paradise can't seem to let go of their vacation attitudes, even when their time on the beach is done. Who can blame them? Just about everybody coming here lies back on a lounge chair, umbrella drink in hand, and while gazing out at a cloudless sky over a calm sea exclaims, "I should live here!"

Sadly, it's not that easy. It takes a lot of work to be free. As Kris Kristofferson sings, "Freedom's just another word for nothing left to lose." Being free means cutting loose the ties to your old life and throwing most of your baggage overboard. It means jumping off a cliff without quite knowing what's waiting below. That's too scary for most folks. So, the daydreamers end up just pretending to be expats for a while. That's fine by me. We all need a little bit of fantasy in our lives. However, Bernie eventually took it to a whole other level I hadn't seen before.

"Poppa," he said, his face practically glowing, "I just bought a bar here."

He had called ahead on his precious cell phone to tell me he was in town for a few days and was coming over with some big news. Of all the possibilities I considered while waiting for him, I hadn't expected this.

"That's great, Bernie," I said, and I meant it. Maybe his dream was coming true. Good for him. "So I guess this means you and Kathy will be moving down here."

Bernie acted shocked at the idea. "Oh no, we couldn't do that. Well, someday maybe. But right now? It's not possible. You know, we have the kids, and they'll eventually head to college, and you know how expensive that is these days. I've got responsibilities. Plus I have tenure now so … " His voice trailed off.

I was confused. "How are you going to run a bar down here and keep living up north?"

Bernie gave me a condescending look. "Poppa, come on. I have a law degree, for goodness sakes. I think I can handle managing a little bar, even long distance. I'll have the phone and internet. And I'm in town all the time. It's not like running a bar is a complicated thing. It's not brain surgery."

"Or law," I added.

"Exactly," he said, missing my sarcasm. "This way when I am here I will always have a place to party."

I resisted telling him that in my experience partying in your own bar could be disastrous on many levels. Instead, I asked, "So where is this place?"

He really got excited then. "It's right here on the beach. Can you believe it? We're going to be neighbors. It's the old Blue Lagoon bar. You must know it."

I did know it. I knew it was at the farthest end of the beach—a concrete shell near where the dive boats tied up. I knew the boat motors churned up the seaweed into a dead brown stinking mess that washed up on shore every night. I knew it was owned by an Italian guy famous for his money laundering, drug smuggling, and the ability to make people disappear who got in his way. I knew it had five different tenants in two years.

"You bought that place?" I asked.

Bernie came down a notch in his excitement level for a moment. "Well, no. But I have a great long-term lease at a terrific rate, and I bought all the bar equipment." He explained he was taking some time off between spring and summer semesters to come down and supervise the renovation and grand opening of his bar. "It really just needs some paint. The best part," he enthused, "is that I already have an experienced manager who can handle everything. My new landlord recommended him."

I asked if he was worried that his bosses at school might be upset about him owning a bar in Mexico.

"No reason for them to know," he said smugly. "I told them I will be spending some time south of the border because I am doing research on international business laws in Central America." He laughed at his own cleverness. "Like I always say, what happens in Mexico … "

Yeah, I had heard it before.

I tried to talk a little sense into him that day. I told him that opening a bar in a tourist town is tough in the best of times. It's hard to get the word out that you even exist. You need to bribe taxi drivers and hotel receptionists. You need people to talk about you on Tripadvisor forums and have tour companies hand out your cards. You need a reputation, a following, and a lot of luck.

Plus, opening in the low season of the summer months can make it a thousand times more difficult. Most of all, you have to be there every day to count the bottles and the money or they will both disappear faster than a cold beer on a hot beach.

He didn't hear a word I said. His mind was made up. I could only wish him the luck I knew he would need.

True to his word, Bernie was back at the end of May. He came by himself. When someone asked about Kathy, he said she would be down later in the year, but for now, he was 'flying solo.' This was accompanied by an exaggerated wink. I wondered if Kathy was as enthusiastic about Bernie's new project as he was.

A couple of weeks later, I went to the grand opening of Cowboy Bernie's Beer Barrel Bar. It was quite a party. As planned, Bernie had painted the place and not much more. However, it was packed that night with the curious, the thirsty, and the regular local crowd. These people didn't care where they drank, so long as it was cheap.

The bartender was a guy I once fired for pouring rotgut tequila into an empty Herradura bottle. I ordered a beer.

I hung around for a while watching the action. A small band played on a corner stage. Bernie spent much of the evening singing with them. When he wasn't indulging his inner rock star, he walked through the crowd taking photos of every pretty girl he passed. Eventually he spotted me and came over.

He grabbed me in a bear hug. "Thanks for coming. Isn't this great?" I agreed it was. "Say, Poppa," he continued after releasing me from his grip. "I've been meaning to talk to you about something." He paused for a moment to wave at some people coming in.

"What is it, Bernie?"

"It's Cowboy Bernie in here," he said pointing at his straw

cowboy hat. "Well, I was thinking that I might hire Wet Willie to play here on Friday nights."

"You know Willie plays at my place every Saturday, right?" I asked.

"Oh yeah. Of course. Is that a problem? I mean he's free on Fridays, isn't he?"

I waited while Cowboy Bernie took another photo. When I had his attention again, I said, "The problem is that there are only so many tourists at any given time. If they see Willie at a place on the beach one night, they may decide to do something different the next." I almost said this wasn't brain surgery, but I didn't. "Why not get somebody different?"

Bernie looked thoughtful, or as thoughtful as he could with a head full of tequila. "It's just that we all love Willie. Jeez, Poppa, I'm not trying to steal customers from you." He looked hurt that I would even suggest such a thing, "I just think it would be more fun for us locals if we kept the party on the beach going all weekend."

"Bernie, I'm not here to party with the locals or with anybody. My bar is my livelihood. It's how I pay the bills. Do you understand? Bernie?"

He hadn't heard me. He was cheering on a middle-aged woman who had climbed onto his bar and pulled her shirt off. She was bouncing her bare breasts in the direction of the Cuban guy who had spent the last week on the beach telling anyone who would listen that he was a spy. Meanwhile, her husband was staring daggers at both of them.

I figured it was time to go. "Good night, Bernie," I said. I don't think he heard me. He was busy taking pictures of his half-naked customer and exclaiming loudly that they were going up on his website that night.

Bernie went home to the States not long after that, and I didn't hear from him for a while. However, I did hear about his bar. The whole town did. Unfortunately, Bernie was the last to know what was happening. In fact, he didn't find out until he returned to Paradise Beach months later. When he did get the news, he came storming in the front door of my place shouting at the top of his lungs.

"What the hell happened to my bar?"

"Hi, Bernie," I said.

"What the hell happened to my bar?" he repeated. A few of my customers turned to see who was shouting. I came around the bar and motioned for him to join me on the deck.

"Calm down, and I will tell you what I know." We sat on some chairs outside under an umbrella. "Do you want something to drink?" I asked. I could see he was near tears.

"No, I don't want anything to drink. I got all these great reports from the manager about how well the bar was doing, and now I come down here and find it's closed! I want to know what's going on!"

I explained that what was going on was a familiar story. As soon as the gringo boss headed north, the manager who could 'handle everything' started selling the liquor inventory to a friend with a cantina in the barrio. Most of the money that came across the bar went into his pockets instead of the till. Bills went unpaid. Taxes weren't filed. No one went to city hall for the licenses. Inspectors from the Palacio Municipal eventually came by, and as there was no one around with the money or authority to pay the requisite bribes, they posted giant *Clausurado* signs. Bernie's bar was officially closed.

As soon as that happened, the landlord said the lease had been broken. He quickly rented the property to someone else.

Bernie was out, and there was not a thing he could do about it.

"It's not fair," he wailed.

"It's Mexico," I replied. But I suspected he neither understood nor accepted that answer.

Then Bernie got angry. At me. "Why didn't you do something about this?" he demanded.

In fact, I had tried. I sent a message to the owner of the property that perhaps he could wait to find a new tenant until Bernie returned. Word came back that if I didn't keep my nose out of other people's business, it might be sliced off with a machete. As I had gotten used to having my nose right where it was, I decided to follow that advice.

"Sorry, Bernie. There wasn't a lot I could do. Those guys you were in business with are not very nice people."

Bernie wasn't having any of my explanation. "You were supposed to be my friend. I thought we locals looked out for each other."

"Bernie," I said sadly, "you have to face some hard facts. We're not really friends." He gave me a shocked look. "I like you, but we see each other, what, a week or two every year when you come down on vacation? You buy drinks in my bar. We barely know each other. You're a customer."

He tried to interrupt to proclaim the true nature of our deep friendship, but I just kept going. "Yeah, sometimes my customers take the time to get to really know me and we do become friends, but that's a rare thing. You never took that time. You were too busy making sure the party never ended, which is fine. But it doesn't make us friends. For the record, neither one of us is a local. The only locals around here are the Mexicans. It's their country. The gringos who live here are expats, and most of them are just passing through.

And Bernie, you aren't an expat or a local. You're just another tourist."

He acted as if I had just punched him. Or shot his dog. He leaned across the table with a look of pure disgust. "I don't have to take this shit from you. You're nothing but a fucking bartender." He said *bartender* like it was leaving a bad taste in his mouth. I wanted to point out that I was a bartender who still owned a bar, but I figured that wouldn't help the situation.

Bernie continued to rant. "I came down here because I thought this place was special. I thought this was where people really cared about each other. I thought everyone was family. Then when I started my own business, you all got jealous."

I tried to tell him that nobody was jealous of him. The drunks and drifters that populate any beach town are always happy to see a new bar or business. It keeps the scenery from getting too stale. Even those like me with already established places tend to welcome newcomers. The more the merrier is part of the expat attitude.

But you have to jump off that cliff I was talking about if you want to be welcomed into this particular club. You don't get to sit in the cheap seats and pretend you are on the team. However, Bernie was not listening. He interrupted me to vent some more.

"You all want to keep the beach just for yourselves, so you set me up and stood by while this worthless corrupt country stole my money. Fuck this shit. I can see now the only way to get ahead down here is to be as dishonest and shitty as the Mexicans are. You people deserve each other." While I was trying to figure out who 'you people' were, he stood up and walked out of my bar. I never saw him again.

As much of a pain in the ass as Bernie had been, I actually

felt a little bad for him. It's not fun to have your tropical escape fantasies dashed on the rocks by reality. Not fun at all. Still, you can't fake being on the Margarita Road. Either you are or you aren't. There is no in between.

As far as I know, Bernie never came back to Paradise Beach. I heard he made a fuss for a while on some internet travel forums, complaining about his betrayal by all the people who lived here. After that, I guess he went back to his old life. Maybe he vacations in Orlando now.

Down here, things went on much as they had before Bernie ever showed up. Other than me, I doubt anyone remembered him after he disappeared. Truthfully, I only thought of him when I noticed his wife's panties hanging in my bar, waving in the breeze along with all the others left by tourists over the years.

7
One of Our Own

Most of the Americans wandering down the Margarita Road to Paradise Beach hadn't come south of the border for a cultural exchange. They cared little about Mexico's history, politics, or traditions. Hell, few of them bothered even to learn the language. All they wanted was cold beer and to be left alone to stake out a spot on the beach. That was fine with the locals—until some of the gringos decided they wanted more. Some of them wanted everything.

"I've never had to pay a woman to touch me."

I was carrying beer to the cooler when I passed Chaz and Geoffrey sitting at my bar in deep conversation. I was intrigued enough to stop and listen further. Besides, it was a slow day. The beach in front of my place was empty as it usually is during late fall. The crowds wouldn't be back until Thanksgiving when things got chilly north of the border.

"Jeezus, Geoffrey," Chaz said after he swallowed a mouthful of beer, "we're not talking about getting laid here. We're talking about real massage. Legit stuff for what ails you. You really can't have a problem with that."

I liked Chaz. He had a wicked sense of humor and an eye for the ladies. Unlike many, he was good for his word. When Chaz said he would do something for you, he actually did it. That made him a rarity among the expats.

"What's going on?" I asked, setting the beer case on top of the bar.

Chaz pushed his Dive Naked ball cap back on his head and nodded in the direction of the guy on the stool next to him. "Old Geoffrey here was just equating massage with prostitution."

Geoffrey defended himself. "No, that's not what I said."

"What did you say?"

Geoffrey sighed in disgust at having to explain himself to mere mortals. He was tall and a bit overweight, with a mass of curly brown hair and a sparse mustache. On his face was a look of contempt, a common expression for Geoffrey. He took his glasses off, polished them on his t-shirt, and put them back on. He blinked once or twice before reacquiring the smirk that seemed to have a permanent place on his face.

"What I said was that some guys needed to pay for a woman to touch them. Massage, blowjob, fuck—it doesn't matter. I just made the point that there are other guys who never have to pay for it."

"Like you, Geoff?" I called him Geoff because I knew he didn't like it.

"Never had to, never will," he said smugly and took another swallow of beer. "I have something the ladies can't resist. They never say no to me." That was Geoffrey—one of the least likeable and most successful people in town.

Over the years, I had learned expats are a varied lot. There are plenty of reasons one might suddenly head south on the jet stream. For example, the explorer types want a life full of new experiences. To them, the sense of adventure is what it's all about. Still others just want out of the craziness of the modern world. They think peace or nirvana or whatever is waiting for them on a beach somewhere.

And then there are those with a sense of entitlement. They want to be king or queen of whatever shore they land on. They figure the only reason they haven't achieved the success they deserve is all those pesky rules society puts in their way. So they head south to Mexico or the islands figuring that's where a little extra cash can set those impediments aside.

To these greedy fast-buck artists and hustlers, any native-born people they encounter are simply rungs on a ladder to be used as a boost up on the way to the top. Lowlifes of this ilk have been landing on tropical beaches ready to rip off the locals ever since Columbus sailed to the New World. Geoffrey was part of this breed.

After inheriting a boatload of money from the early death of the father he never cared much about, Geoffrey quit his unsuccessful career as a salesman at a computer chain store. He then spent a year or two bumming around the Caribbean with his wife. They took the Margarita Road through Jamaica, the American Virgin Islands, and Belize, all the time looking for an advantage or hustle that would work for them.

When they drifted into Paradise Beach, they finally saw dollar signs where most people just saw a beautiful bay. Geoffrey started buying property and flashed what was left of his dad's cash at a few local Mexican families who had never seen more than a couple hundred dollars at a time. To a simple fisherman whose family of seven lived in a two-room house with a plastic tarp for a roof, Geoffrey's greenbacks were a gift from the gods.

You have to give him credit for planning ahead. He soon had titles and leases to half a dozen lots around town. He and Karen then opened a low-end youth hostel with a small café near the beach. Next, they bought a ramshackle set of rooms a few blocks in from the water and called it a 'resort hotel.' As a result, when the local tourist business really took off a few years later, Geoffrey and his wife were already on the ground floor, renting rooms, arranging tours, and offering their services as the resident experts of Paradise Beach.

It always seemed to me like Karen did the real work. Geoffrey spent most of his time in bars or on the computer writing about his life south of the border. He had a popular blog and sold articles to online travel magazines. His writing must not have been half-bad, because he eventually built up quite a following that he then turned into a cottage industry.

Geoffrey hustled payoffs from local businesses to recommend them to his readers and badmouthed those who wouldn't pay. He sold tour vouchers, discount meal coupons, and maps to supposedly hidden beaches that any local kid on the street could direct you to for free.

Through internet chatter and the recommendation of travel agents who received a kickback, he began to build a favorable reputation among the folks coming to Paradise Beach for vacation. The snowbirds from up north started to seek him out, and on most evenings in the season you could see him holding court with a crowd of adoring tourists at a table in the Mermaid Saloon. He fancied himself the unofficial mayor of Paradise Beach's resort zone.

When he was alone with other expats, Geoffrey would crack up about how he had everyone fooled. As he told it, all he had to do was put a note out on his blog that he needed someone to haul something down from the States for him—car parts, Heinz catsup, a new cell phone, whatever—and sure enough someone would bring it. "And guess what?" he would ask, before answering his own question. "They won't let me pay them for it. Whatever I ask for, they bring it to me as a gift!"

He laughed in big breathy chuckles at their foolishness. "They think knowing me puts them in some locals inner circle. They love me! They buy me drinks and eat up whatever shit I feed them. Half the time, I can get my dick sucked, too. One guy even asked me to do his wife! What a bunch of losers!"

Yeah, he was a treasure all right. The Ugly American was George Clooney next to Geoffrey. It didn't matter to me all that much, though. Jerks like Geoffrey are generally not my problem. But if they work at it, they can be. Not long after our chat about massage techniques, Geoffrey started working at it.

I walked into my place late one afternoon and found a shoebox-sized package wrapped in brown paper and shipping tape sitting behind the bar. I picked it up and went out to where Jorge was grilling burgers on the deck.

"What's this?" I asked.

"I don't know, Jefe. Some guy came in for a drink and asked for you. When I said you weren't here, he left it." He flipped one of the burgers.

"Okay," I said. "Do you know what's inside?" I held the package up.

Jorge gave the *I don't know* shrug so popular in Mexico.

"Well, did the guy say anything?"

He brightened up as he suddenly remembered. "Oh yeah,

he said Geoffrey Ryan would come by to pick it up."

"Did he say what it was?"

Jorge shook his head as he went in with the spatula to attack another burger. "Nope."

I went back inside and climbed the stairs to my little room above the bar. It's not much, but the window opens up on the best beach in all of Mexico. I swear that on a clear day I can see Cuba from my house. I wonder if that means maybe I can run for Vice President some day.

I sat on the bed, thought for a moment, and then pulled out the little Fred Perrin pocket blade I always carried. The package had been left in my bar, so I figured I had a right to see what was in it. Besides, I'm a naturally suspicious guy. Mexico does that to you.

With the first cut, I knew what I was holding. The aroma of really good and very pungent weed filled the air. I took some rolling papers from my bureau drawer and rolled a small joint for myself before taking the rest of the brick down to the beach.

I smoked the joint as I walked along the shore, tossing handfuls of grass into the ocean. It didn't take long before the whole of Geoffrey's shipment was sinking in salt water and mixing with the seaweed.

Now, I have nothing against a nice little buzz to mellow the mood every once in a while, but Poppa's was my business. We expats can get possessive about whatever corner of paradise we have carved out for ourselves. Perhaps I overreacted, but I knew for sure I didn't need the local cops coming to hassle me about my bar being used as a drug drop. That's what I told Geoffrey when he came by for his stash.

"Dude! I can't believe you're upset over this." Geoffrey

said dude a lot. He thought it made him cool.

"Geoff, I don't let anyone sell shit in my bar, and I never will."

Geoffrey seemed insulted. "Selling?! Selling? Who's selling anything? It's my personal stuff, that's all. Nobody is selling anything. God, Poppa you are scared of your own shadow."

"That may be. Still, it's my shadow and my bar, and I don't want anyone using it as a post office for their dope. Why didn't you have your connection drop it off at your hostel?"

He threw up his hands in exasperation. "Karen would give me shit about it. She thinks I spend too much time getting high with some of the local girls." He smirked. "And she's right, of course."

"That's not my problem, Geoffrey."

He finally gave up. "Fine. Just fine. You won't see me or my dope around here anymore. Just give me my stuff and I'll leave."

When I told him I had trashed it in the sea, he went crazy. Screaming and shaking his fist at me, he demanded I pay him for the weed. I told him to screw himself. Finally, he stormed out.

Geoffrey and I didn't speak much after that. He wrote on his blog that I had ripped him off and that people should avoid my place. My regulars didn't seem to pay much attention, and my business went on about the same as before.

After that, I wanted nothing more to do with Geoffrey and did my best to avoid him. He obviously felt the same. So I was more than a little shocked when his wife came into the bar several months later as I was having a cup of coffee out on the deck. She made her way over and took a chair opposite me without saying a word.

I had been having a nice, sunny Sunday morning watching seabirds skimming the surf on the beach in front of me and listening to a distant church bell. I wasn't in the mood to break off from that important activity to be bogged down in some local expat drama. Still, I couldn't really concentrate with her staring at me from across the table. "Karen," I said. "I'm surprised to see you in here. Is there something I can help you with?"

She was a little older than Geoffrey but still younger than I was. Her blonde hair was pulled back in a severe bun, and she wore a shapeless, sack-like sundress. Her thin face was plain and without makeup. The early morning sun made her look more uptight than usual.

"It wasn't my idea. It was Geoffrey's. He said you wouldn't refuse." I could see she was upset and struggling to keep herself under control.

"Refuse what?" I asked.

"Geoffrey was arrested last night. I need money to get him out."

That threw me for a moment. "What did he do?"

Karen looked out to sea. "Nothing."

"Karen?"

She shook her head. "Really. Nothing. He got in an argument with some local guy. The cops stepped in. You know how it happens here."

She was right. I did know. The local cops were never averse to hustling a gringo off to jail in order to force the paying of a bribe. Still, I couldn't figure out why she came to me. "Hell, Karen, you and Geoff pull in way more money than I do. Why can't you use your own cash to get him out?"

She sighed. "We keep our money in a bank in Belize, and

they can't wire it for 48 hours because tomorrow is a holiday here."

I began to see the picture. Many of the Americans living locally kept their money back in the States or in some other country. It was just safer not to have large sums of cash around in Mexico. Somebody might always ask you—not very politely—to give it to them, or they might try to take it from you. Expats usually wired money to a local bank on an as-needed basis. That made things dicey when you had an emergency on a day when Mexican banks were closed.

I could hear the worry creeping into her voice. "Poppa, if he is in there for too many days, they will hurt him very badly."

I had to agree with her. My first thought was to let him rot, but some sliver of nationalistic camaraderie won out. No American was going to spend time in our local jail without some permanent reminders of the stay. I decided I couldn't let that happen, even to someone as disagreeable as Geoffrey.

"How much do you need?"

She told me. It was a lot, but I had that much on hand from the bar's receipts. I went to the safe in my room and brought it back to her. She thanked me—if not profusely, at least with real gratitude. "We will repay you when the banks open." Then she left, and I went back to the important business of counting waves.

Just as Karen had promised, Geoffrey waltzed though the door late in the afternoon a few days later like we were the best of friends. I was sitting at the bar sipping some pineapple juice and Cuban rum.

The place had been empty most of the day, so Jorge and I were entertaining ourselves by discussing the respective vocal ranges of Shakira and Beyonce, among their other attributes. As Geoffrey took the seat beside me, Jorge moved down the bar without acknowledging him. I thought that was a bit strange.

"There it is, dude." Geoffrey slammed an envelope on the bar with a flourish. "Every penny. And I gotta say thanks. You were a lifesaver. Those boys in there were gonna have me for lunch." He looked down at Jorge, waiting to catch his eye and order a drink. Jorge kept his head down, busying himself with some glasses that were apparently very dirty.

I picked up the envelope. "Glad to help, Geoff. A word of advice? Knock off the drug shit. They will kill you someday."

He started laughing. "Dude, I keep telling you I don't deal. I get high, but I don't share my stash with anybody."

That I could believe. "So, what was it?" I asked. "What was the trouble?"

"Oh, you know. The same old shake-the-rich-gringo-down-for-some-bucks shit." He yelled to Jorge, who seemed intent on ignoring him, "Hey, can I get a drink here?"

I called Geoffrey's attention back to me. "I don't understand. What did you get arrested for?"

"I told you, Poppa. The old Mexican shakedown. Some little chica was coming on to me and ... well, you know." He winked at me. "I showed her a good time. We did some partying, and then she started complaining. I knew she just wanted money." Geoffrey swelled up his own chest and pointed to it with his finger. "That ain't happening. Not with this boy."

I still wasn't getting it. "She called the cops because you didn't pay her?"

"Yeah. Well, no. Not exactly."

"What exactly?"

"What the hell, dude. What is this, twenty questions? I got it on with this babe, and then after, she was all like 'oh no, I didn't want that.'" Geoffrey fluttered his eyes and shook his hands up by his face in imitation of the girl. "The next thing I know, her daddy is down at the police station telling them I did something to his daughter. Of course, that was bullshit. She was the one coming on to me. I figure the cops and her family were working some con to snag the gringos. It was my bad luck to get caught in it."

Geoffrey looked at me and must have seen the expression on my face that mirrored the coldness in my stomach. "What?" he asked.

I spoke slowly. "Geoffrey, what exactly did you do?"

"I didn't *dooo* anything," he said.

"I know," said Jorge suddenly from the end of the bar. "I know what he did."

Walking toward us, Jorge picked up a bottle of Don Julio tequila. He stopped in front of Geoffrey and filled a shot glass to the brim. Geoffrey looked uncertain.

"Is that for me?" he asked.

"Yes," said Jorge, "it's for you." He picked up the glass and threw the tequila in his face.

Geoffrey jumped up from his stool, knocking it over. "What the fuck are you … " Jorge stood rock still behind the bar.

I was a little shocked myself and waited for Jorge to say something. He turned to me while Geoffrey continued to sputter and spit tequila. "He raped a 15-year-old girl that cleans the rooms over at the hostel he runs. The money was to pay off the cops when her family wanted justice."

I could hear Geoffrey sucking in air beside me. "How do

you know?" I asked.

"She is my wife's cousin's youngest daughter." Jorge took a breath. "And she wasn't the first one this piece of shit has ruined."

I turned toward Geoffrey, seeing red. He backed away quickly.

"That is *not* what happened," he yelled. He pointed at Jorge. "Are you really going to believe him? Poppa, come on, he's a Mexican. They're all Mexicans." He said it like that explained everything.

I told him to get out. I used some choice words and a couple of threats. I was giving serious thought to punching him into the floorboards. Jorge hurried around the bar and stood in front of me, putting his hands on my shoulders. "No, Jefe," he said. "It will cause you too much trouble."

"That's right," yelled Geoffrey. "I have friends. Important friends. You touch me and you are going to jail!" As he moved toward the door, he kept telling me how he would ruin me if I said a word about this to anyone. Nobody would ever come to my bar again; he would see to that. Then he was gone.

Jorge took the bottle of Don Julio off the bar and walked outside to sit on the edge of the deck. I went out and joined him. We silently passed the bottle back and forth for a while, as the sky over the Caribbean Sea began to darken from pink to purple.

"How many?" I finally asked.

"I don't know," he answered, "Some girls probably don't say anything. I've heard of three other times he paid off the cops."

"Do you know this for sure?" I asked.

Jorge shrugged. "I hear things," he said. "You know David

who brings the water truck?"

I nodded. I knew him—a small, very fat man in a perpetually oil-stained t-shirt who pumped water into my cistern once a month while humming mariachi songs to himself.

"His daughter killed herself in the sea two months ago. David thinks it was because of Geoffrey Ryan."

"How … ?"

Jorge seemed to read my mind. "He picks on the young ones—the ones working as maids or dishwashers. The ones who live out in the barrio and only come into town to work for white people. The ones who think the resort zone is some sort of heaven, like where Jesus would go on vacation. He tells them they are pretty. How important he is. Then he makes his move. Sometimes they say yes; sometimes they get scared and say no. Geoffrey only hears yes, no matter what they say. Then he sends them home to their families."

"How come nobody has cut his throat?" It was a serious question.

Jorge shrugged and took a hit from the tequila bottle then handed it to me. "In Mexico, poor people have learned to be quiet. People like that are afraid to speak up."

"Who are they afraid of?" I took a drink and passed the tequila back to him.

"Of everybody. Mostly the police. The money Geoffrey pays the cops keeps him out of jail when a family complains, but it also makes the police his partners in the lie. They would be very tough on anyone who exposed that. And … " His voice trailed off.

"And what?"

Jorge said nothing.

"And what?" I insisted.

"They are afraid of the gringos. Everyone knows what would happen if a gringo was killed by a Mexican." He paused while thinking. "What is it that you say when everything is very bad and there will be much trouble?"

"Shit storm," I said.

Jorge smiled but with no happiness. "Si, that's it. Shit storm. If a Mexican killed a Norte Americano because the gringo fucked a Mexican girl, there would be a shit storm."

I started to speak, but Jorge held up his hand. "The gringos have a lot of influence here. All the money we make comes from the tourists. No one wants to see that end."

I interrupted him. "That's not right, Jorge. There is no reason to fear the expats over this. Do you really think the Americans would take the side of a man who does this just because he is American, too? Is that what you think of all gringos?"

Jorge stalled by taking a swig from the bottle, and, realizing it was empty, lowered it into his lap. Then he said, "Maybe not all." He gave me a sideways glance. "Do you really think that none of Geoffrey Ryan's gringo friends know about this? Do you think he never talks about all the Mexican girls he has fucked?"

He waited as if expecting me to say he was mistaken. I couldn't.

"Does no one see what he is? The ones who buy him drinks and bring him presents—do you think they would believe a Mexican if Geoffrey said he did nothing wrong?" He lifted the empty bottle and ran his fingers lightly over the wrapper that proudly proclaimed *Hecho en Mexico*. Then he pulled back his arm and sent the bottle flying out onto the beach where it landed with a thud. By morning, the tide would carry it away.

"He doesn't belong here, but the Americans don't care," Jorge said. "He's one of theirs."

Somewhere I heard a night bird cry out over the water. It was the only sound for a long time.

Then I asked Jorge, "So who?"

"Who what?"

"Who is stronger than the local police? Who are the local cops afraid of? Who can get to Geoffrey without anyone else being hurt?"

Jorge shrugged his shoulders, "I don't know."

I thought about that for a while.

"Jorge?"

"Yes, boss?"

"I need to talk with Jose Rodriquez up in Cancun. Can you get a message to him?"

Jorge's eyes grew wide. He considered it for a few moments. Finally, he said, "Yes. I know someone who can talk to him for you."

"Good," I said. But I didn't feel good. Then I told Jorge what I had in mind.

He asked if I was sure.

I told him yes. Somebody had to do something. Like it or not, Geoffrey Ryan was an American. He was one of ours.

A few weeks later, we were well into one of the slowest low seasons I had seen. There was nobody in town and no one on the beach. More importantly, there was no one in my bar, even on a Saturday night. I figured what the hell and decided to close early. I sent Jorge home, dimmed the lights, and started stacking chairs. To be truthful, I really didn't mind that things were so slow. I like having the place to myself occasionally.

By the time Jorge left, it was too dark to see the water, but I could hear the waves crash on the sand and then make that hissing sound as they pulled back into the sea. I stopped for a moment to light a smoke and enjoy being alone. Except I wasn't.

As I took a drag on the cigarette, I caught movement on the sand. My first thought was that a couple from the hotel down the beach was skinny dipping and having a little recapture-the-romance moment. It was becoming a regular event, as more and more tourists were drawn to Paradise Beach. Then I saw the guns shine in the moonlight.

As they moved into the dim light of the bar, I could see they were dressed in the all-black, SWAT-style uniform of the narco squad. They even had their faces covered with black bandanas from the eyes down. There were three of them. One stopped at the steps just outside and stayed there. The other two came inside. I froze with my hands in the open while they moved past me as if I weren't there.

One went into the space behind the bar then came out and walked over to the bathrooms. He entered each one in turn, and when he was satisfied I was alone, he took up a position against the far wall and stayed there.

The third guy stood in the center of the room and waited for the all clear from his buddy. Then he motioned me to take a seat and walked over to claim his own spot against the wall.

Yeah, I was scared, but I knew what was happening. I had been expecting this visit; I just hadn't known when. I finished my smoke and waited for my final visitor. A moment later, he stepped out of the darkness.

Comandante Rodriguez was immaculately tailored, as

always. Italian silk suit cut to his lean form, shoes that cost more than I made in a month, and with just enough gold on his wrists and fingers to impress without being gaudy. For a crooked cop, he was styling—I had to give him that. He looked around with interest as he entered, acting more like a real estate appraiser than the head of all narcotics law enforcement along Mexico's eastern coast. Of course, as the chief narcotics cop, he was also the head of all drug trafficking in the area. He pulled out a chair and sat down across the table from me.

"Good evening, Poppa," he said in accented English.

"Buenas noches, Comandante," I replied.

He smiled at my Spanish, whether in appreciation or amusement was hard to tell. I figured I had better switch to English before I said something by mistake that could cost me later.

"I see you got my message," I said.

He nodded. "Yes, but I have to admit I was very surprised." He sat back and crossed his legs, the picture of the relaxed businessman at the end of a day. "At first I thought it was a joke. Then I wondered if something had been lost in the translation. As you can tell, foreign languages can be difficult for me at times."

I couldn't help myself. I laughed aloud. "You speak better English than my whole family back in Boston. I bet you even went to Yale."

He stared at me and then joined my laughter. He smiled a real smile. It made him look younger. "UCLA." For a moment, he seemed lost in a memory. Then his attention came back to me. "What about you, Señor Poppa? Where did you go to school?"

"I don't know if I did. It was too long ago to remember." Suddenly the fear turned to exhaustion. I was tired of the chitchat, tired of his Mexican game of let's-be-nice-before-we-pull-out-the-knives. And I was tired of myself and what I had done. I wanted this evening to be finished. "So let's get to it. How is this going to work?"

He raised his eyebrows in mock surprise. "How is what going to work?"

I put my hands on the table, maybe a little too forcibly. It brought his guards to attention. I leaned forward. "How do you want me to sell drugs for you?"

He grinned like the Cheshire Cat. "Ah, yes. The deal you proposed. If I killed Geoffrey Ryan, you would sell my products though your bar. That was the deal, wasn't it?"

In a panic, I tried to remember what I had said in the message passed through Jorge up to Rodriquez's office in Cancun. "What? No! That wasn't my deal. I said that I would sell your drugs if you got Geoffrey to leave the local girls alone. I just wanted him scared off somehow. I never asked you to kill anybody." My sudden outburst caused one of the bodyguards to take a step toward me, but Rodriquez waved him back.

"Then you are a fool," he said. "What did you think I would do? Arrest him? Arrest a Norte Americano businessman on the word of a mixta child?" He laughed at the thought. "I would be in trouble with my country and yours if I did that. No, Poppa, you did not give me many choices. Regardless, whatever your idea might have been, we both know he deserves to die."

Before I could protest further, Rodriquez lifted his hands as if in surrender to me. "It doesn't matter now. As you must know, your friend Geoffrey left Mexico a few days ago to take up residence with his in-laws in the United States."

Yes, I had heard. Everyone was talking about it. Geoffrey and Karen left town—abandoning their home, their furniture, their businesses, everything. They had boarded a late-night flight back to Minnesota out of Cancun. Before they left, Karen told some neighbors that her mother was ill and needed full-time care. She didn't know when, or even if, they would return. Geoffrey would be blogging from the tropical shores of Lake Superior from now on. I figured Rodriquez was the cause of their sudden departure.

"What did you do to him?" I asked.

The Comandante gave me a look of indifference. "I did nothing. Señor Ryan and I had a short conversation, that is all. Perhaps that had something to do with it."

"You threatened him."

Rodriquez shook his head dismissively. "No, I explained the facts to him." He leaned back, put his fingertips together, and spoke softly as if giving a lecture to a child. "I made it clear that his activities had brought him to the attention of those beyond the local police—specifically, to my attention and the attention of my special forces officers. Of course I did not tell him how this matter came to me." He smiled at me as if we shared a secret. Which we did.

He gestured toward one of the nearby black-uniformed statues. "I told him my men would respond differently than the local police if he continued to rape young Mexican women. I pointed out that while the local officers were content to demand monetary bribes, my special forces would cut off his balls and shove them down his throat, after which he would be beaten to death." He looked at me to see the effect of his words. I didn't move a muscle.

"Then," he continued, "I suggested that he might avoid such an unpleasant circumstance by immediately leaving the jurisdiction under my authority. Or even better that he should leave Mexico. He was most appreciative for this information."

When he paused, I took a deep breath. The ball was in my court now.

"Okay," I said. "As long as he is gone and is no longer raping girls here. That's something at least. Maybe he will be scared enough to stop." Of course, I knew that wasn't likely.

"At least he will be raping white girls now," the Comandante said with sudden fierceness.

I stared back at him. "I don't care about the color of his victims."

"I do," he said coldly. Then he relaxed. He brushed at some sand that had stuck to his pant cuff. "Regardless, it is finito. I appreciate you having brought this matter to my attention, but I see no reason we need to engage in further business together."

It took a moment to sink in. "You don't want to operate out of here? You don't want my bar?" I could feel my heart pounding.

He looked around once more, nodding as if liking what he saw. "Well, perhaps I might stop by for a margarita from time to time. I hear your bartender makes the best ones in town. As for anything else—no, I do not plan on doing business here." Then he leaned over the table between us and looked directly into my eyes without smiling. "You did me a favor. I am returning it."

Without saying more, he stood up and started toward the stairs, his bodyguards following behind. I should have let him go, but I couldn't help myself. "Why didn't you kill him? If you thought he deserved it, why didn't you kill him?"

The Comandante stopped for a moment at the edge of the deck, staring out at the blackness of the sea. He spoke, still looking into the night. "Because, my friend, I have no doubt that if I killed him, you would have gone gringo on me. You would have tortured yourself about whether he should have had a trial and a lawyer and be given a chance to reform. After all, Geoffrey Ryan is one of your people."

He turned to look at me, and in that exchange of glances, we both knew he was right. "You would have unraveled, maybe even tried to tell someone about our arrangement. Then it would have become necessary to kill you to keep you quiet."

He sighed heavily as if very weary. "I just didn't need all that trouble." Then he grinned at me. "Besides, I like you, Poppa. I don't like many gringos, but I do like you."

He walked down the steps to the beach, disappearing into the blackness of the night.

8
The Sexiest Man
In Mexico

Not every wandering pilgrim on the Margarita Road is looking for a permanent break from reality. For some, the journey is a temporary escape from a daily routine that isn't working so well anymore. They want an experience to shake things up that will be more than a vacation but less than a lifetime. After hanging out on the beach for a while, they can return with a new attitude to the old life they left behind. It's a very good plan, as long as your feet don't get stuck in the sand.

The sexiest man in Mexico was a short, pudgy American. He was not particularly good looking. In fact, he had never thought of himself as being very attractive. Yet there was no denying it: my friend Lucas had something going on with the ladies of Paradise Beach.

We met when he came into my bar one night with an attractive señorita. They took a spot on the deck where the breezes off the beach kept the candles on the tables flickering.

She ordered a margarita, and he had a Coke. I didn't pay them much attention, but when she went to the ladies room, he made a beeline toward me. When he reached the bar, he leaned over and spoke in a soft voice. "Can I ask you a small favor?"

I gave him a noncommittal nod of the head. You learn in the bar business not to agree to anything until you know the whole story.

"I'm kind of new in town, and I was hoping to take this girl someplace nice for dinner. Any suggestions on a good restaurant? Something a little high end." That type of favor I could handle, but I had to think for a moment. High was not my normal end.

"The Happy Lobster might work. White linen tablecloths, guacamole made at the table. Pick your own lobster from the tank. A little touristy, but still good. She'll be suitably impressed."

Lucas gave a relieved smile, said thanks, and offered a hand as he introduced himself. I took it and told him to call me Poppa. "How long are you around town for?" I asked.

"I don't really know yet. I'm teaching English over at the language academy. I have a three-month contract, but if I like it, I may stay longer." He grinned. "At this point, I still get lost about twice a day."

He seemed like a good guy, so I told him he could stop by whenever he needed some help. "I'm here most days."

A frown suddenly crossed his face. "I'm a friend of Bill's," he said a little defensively.

"And I'm not, so we have that in common." He hesitated only a second before laughing. "Seriously," I added, "come whenever you want. I make a great cup of coffee."

"I will," he promised.

His companion arrived back at the bar, slipped her arm around his waist, and kissed him gently on the neck as she pressed against him. I remember thinking to myself that maybe he didn't need to impress her much after all. She was already there.

I began to see Lucas more and more after that. Poppa's Bar and Grill became a regular spot for him to start the evening with his dates. And there were many dates, always with attractive young women. I couldn't figure it out. Maybe I was a touch envious. Regardless, Lucas and I eventually became good enough friends for him to tell me about how his journey had started.

It seemed that up north he hadn't been the popular ladies man he was south of the border. That wasn't surprising. He was shorter than average, maybe a little too round in the middle, and had premature pattern baldness he inherited from his grandfather. He knew he was no Brad Pitt, and he accepted that. He decided being a nice guy was enough for him.

Sadly, though, even nice guys can stumble and fall. That's what happened to Lucas. He began drifting while in college and started heading down a bad path of too much booze and too many drugs. Before he knew it, he had an addiction: first to crack cocaine and then to booze. Or maybe it was the other way around. Maybe the drinking came first and the drugs later. Regardless, he ended up a drunk, a stoner, and alone.

His family tried to help, but Lucas wasn't listening. He had surrounded himself with a wall of dependency that only he could break through. Jail or the morgue seemed more and more to be his likely end. Instead, fate—or something—intervened.

As Lucas would recall, he woke up one morning with his head resting in a pool of his own vomit and a policeman pounding on the door. During the night—or, actually, early in the morning—he had passed out with his radio playing alternative rock full blast. The neighbors weren't happy with the screaming, tuneless vocals and repetitive bass playing loud enough to be heard on the next block. Someone called the local station house to complain.

He groggily answered the door and went into shock. When you are full of booze and drugs, the last thing you want to see is a uniformed police officer.

Still half-stoned and half-asleep, Lucas did something very stupid. He invited the cop in, while he went to lower the volume of the music. When he turned back from his stereo, the officer was standing over the table where Lucas's head had rested a minute ago. He was taking it all in—the crack pipe, the coke residue, the empty scotch bottles, and the vomit. He looked into Lucas's eyes, and the two of them stood there silently for a moment.

"What's this?" his visitor asked finally.

Lucas stammered as he tried to think of something to say that might save his ass. "Uh … it belongs to some friends. I was out and some friends came here to party. It's not my … "

The policeman waved a dismissive hand. "Not this shit," indicating the crack and the pipe. "This," he said, stabbing his finger at something else that lay on the table. "What's this about?" Lucas stepped closer and looked. He realized he had thrown up all over an open phone book. This was back before people carried the internet in their pockets. "Looks like you were planning to call for some help last night," the cop said.

Lucas peered at the open book. Beneath the smeared

vomit, he could just make out listings for Alcoholics Anonymous. "I guess I was," he said, although he had no memory of any such thing.

The policeman stared at him for a moment. Then, nodding to himself as if in agreement with some inner voice, he said, "Okay, you get one chance. I should haul you in. But if you really want to pull yourself out of this shithole, I'll step back. Is that what you want to do?"

Lucas couldn't believe it. Seriously? The cop was going to let him walk because he had vomited on a particular page in the phone book? This was too good to be true. He thought he must be the luckiest guy in the world. "Yeah, absolutely!"

The officer gave him another hard look and said, "Go to the meetings. You don't want to fuck this up. Trust me, I know." He walked out, closing the door behind him.

Lucas let out his breath. Then fear shook him. He suddenly wondered if the cop was just fooling around and would come charging back in to arrest him while laughing at his gullibility. He waited. Nothing happened. After a moment, he opened the door and stepped outside to look down the long hallway. There was no sign of the cop. *That's weird,* he thought.

Years later, when telling of this day, he would mention the passage in the Bible that speaks of people entertaining strangers while unaware they are actually angels. But that was a long way off. At this particular moment, he just thought he had gotten away clean. Regardless of what the cop said, he wasn't going to go all rehab just because he threw up on the phone book.

Lucas took a shower, all the time thinking what a tool the guy had been to just let him go. He was home free. Yet he couldn't quite shake the moment from his mind—not after going out to grab some breakfast and a new bottle of vodka at the package store and not later when he rolled his first joint of the day. Even stranger, while laughing to himself about how lucky he was, he started wondering what it would be like not to be high all the time.

Whether by divine guidance or some instinct of personal survival, it finally dawned on Lucas that he didn't ever want to wake up in his own puke again. He suddenly found himself dialing the phone. He couldn't honestly tell you today why he did it, other than it seemed to be time. Maybe there was no other place to go—no direction left to turn but this one. For whatever reason, he called a number on the page, starting the never-ending road to being clean and sober.

It wasn't easy. Hell, no. The way he told the story, it sounded hard and scary. He said he thought of the pipe and the bottle about a thousand times a day at first. Still, he didn't go back to getting high. He drank the bad coffee in the church halls and went to the meetings every damned day and sometimes a couple times a day. He read the book, called the sponsor, recited the prayer, and earned a chip after a year. Then, in another year, another chip. Eventually, he would have a drawer full of chips.

Still, that didn't make life perfect. It was certainly better, but not perfect. Rehab can be very lonely. While Lucas showed amazing courage and made personal strides that undoubtedly saved his life, being in a twelve-step program wasn't any more conducive to starting relationships than being a drunk had been. Ex-boozer and ex-junkie were not high on the list of sought-after qualities on most computer dating services.

So in his early thirties, Lucas found himself clean, sober,

and pretty much on his own. Oh, he still had family and friends, but nobody special. Not to mention that a little intimacy wouldn't have hurt.

He kept wondering how he could meet people, specifically women, who would give him the time of day. Dating another friend of Bill's wasn't a great idea. He had more than enough work just to maintain his own sobriety without taking on someone else's path at the same time. Cruising the bar scene was obviously out of the question. Now that he was finally sober, Lucas had no idea where he could get a date, let alone a steady girlfriend.

At some point, his family began to worry. They wondered whether his life was bogging down so much that he might veer back into the same rut that took him down the first time. The thought crossed Lucas's mind, too, and it scared him.

One day, a friend from AA showed him a magazine. "Lucas, take a look at this," he said, pointing to the folded-back page. *Teach English as a Second Language in a Tropical Wonderland. No Experience Necessary,* it read. The ad offered employment in various language schools along Mexico's Caribbean coast.

The whole idea captured Lucas's attention right away. He figured that since he spoke English, he met most of the qualifications, and he could resurrect his high school Spanish with a bit of work. Most importantly, a change of scenery was just what the doctor ordered.

Many recovering addicts tend to be tempted when continually confronted with the same old faces in the same old places where their troubles began. A fresh start is often helpful in staying sober. *What the hell. Why not?* Lucas thought to himself. Plus, the ad showed a girl on the beach in a bikini. Even better. He sent in an application and had almost forgotten about it when he received a response. To his utter amazement, they hired him. He was going to teach English as a second language to Mexican adults.

After a quick two-week Spanish immersion course and a few hours of taped lectures on how to teach a class in a foreign country, he was handed a three-month contract, a lesson plan, and a plane ticket south. He kissed his family goodbye, promised his friends he would be back soon, and took off for Mexico.

Lucas was assigned to teach at a school in Paradise Beach. It didn't take long for him to fall in love with the place. Like most people who come here—whether for a week or a lifetime—he couldn't take his eyes off the turquoise sea. He was constantly walking barefoot in the powder-soft sand. And he loved hearing the night birds sing as the sunset turned the sky above the palm trees a coral pink. He actually might have seen more of Paradise Beach's beauty than most gringos did. By not drinking, he avoided the long hours slamming tequila shots in local bars and the even longer hours recovering from hangovers in the 90-degree heat.

He was happy. He knew someday he would head back north to his real home and his family. However, for the moment, he was content—especially with his love life.

"So what's your secret?" I asked Lucas one day. It was a lazy summer Sunday, and we were floating on the Caribbean in a fishing boat we had chartered. The captain was apologetic that we weren't catching anything and kept moving around trying to find some fish. The truth was, Lucas and I were content to sit back and enjoy being on the water.

"Secret to what?"

"Your secret that makes all those women chase you," I

replied.

He laughed. "Oh. That secret. You know, I have wondered about that myself." He sat silently looking out at the sea with a grin.

"Knock it off," I said. "Let's have it."

Lucas chuckled as he opened the thermos for some more iced coffee. "It really isn't any secret. I kind of have a ready-made dating service at the school."

"It's got to be more than that," I said.

He shrugged. "Maybe. I guess I'm just different to most of those women. I have something they aren't used to, and it fascinates them."

I gave him a skeptical look. "Now I really am intrigued. What is it you have that's ... different?"

"Well, not *that* for sure." We both cracked up.

"Seriously, I think it's just that I don't look like the tourists they see in Margaritaville t-shirts and sandals with socks. I don't even look like the locals or expats who don't really spruce up too much." I glanced down at my own regular ensemble of cargo shorts and sleeveless t-shirt with a faded image of a comic book hero. I had topped it off with a sun-bleached ball cap that said Randall Knives. Well, yeah, I guess I could understand his point.

He continued. "The girls see me come to school in a clean shirt with pressed pants and my hair combed. Plus, here I am a figure of some authority—a teacher—helping them learn English so they can better themselves. I'm kind of a special savior for some of them. It impresses them enough they end up asking me out." He grinned. "I don't even have to make the first move."

He shook his head in amazement at his unbelievable luck.

"Trust me," he said, "this has never happened to me before." He looked somewhat embarrassed. "And some of them probably think they can make me fall in love and take them back to the U.S."

"Is that a possibility?" I asked.

Lucas looked horrified. "Oh, hell no. The last thing I need is to drag a wife back home with me. I can barely take care of my own problems. Who needs that kind of complication?" He shuddered at the thought. "Maybe someday, after I've gone back to the States, I'll think about getting married, but not now."

We sat watching the horizon for a while. Not far away, a pod of dolphins broke the surface of the sea.

"Do you miss America much?" I asked him.

"Of course," he said.

"What do you miss most?"

He thought about it for a moment. "Well, my folks, some of the people I knew back there, old friends."

"What about living in the north? What about that do you miss?"

Lucas's eyes watched the rolling blue sea. He was silent for a few moments. "Hmmm, that's a good question," was all he said. I didn't push, figuring it best to leave him to his thoughts. Every expat has to decide for himself when to hold onto those old memories of a past life and when to let go.

As the months passed, Lucas stayed true to his plan and kept on dating one new woman after the next. When the school offered a longer-term contract, he grabbed it. Oh, sure, he still would talk about going home from time to time, but more and more his focus was on his new life.

He completely immersed himself in Mexico, moving

into a small apartment in a neighborhood far from the tourist area. He found he slept better in a hammock and became a regular at a nearby open-air restaurant where every morning he feasted on rice, beans, and eggs covered in hot salsa. Days off were spent diving or going to dinner with other teachers. And of course, he did dearly love the ladies.

It wasn't hard to understand. Mexican women are something special. They learn early on that men are subservient to them. They are trained by their mothers in the use of this power over these lowly creatures.

Baby girls get their ears pierced within the first year. As young women, they learn that high heels are the appropriate footwear for all activities other than swimming. Even female executives wear miniskirts and low-cut blouses. Life in Mexico can be a bachelor's dream come true. As it turned out, Lucas had his pick of the whole social spectrum at his school.

His students included a fair number of professional women working in banks and law offices that dealt with English-speaking people. They saw learning English as a path to advancement. Perhaps more importantly, it was a way to distance themselves from their poorer sisters of Indian blood who cleaned rooms and still made homemade tortillas on stone grills.

There were also the daughters of local families who wanted more out of life than the traditional roles of wife and mother usually available to women in Mexico. They hoped knowledge of English would get them a job as a bartender or receptionist in one of the big resorts that were beginning to fill up the coastline around Paradise Beach.

There were even a few girls from the local strip clubs who needed to speak English to do business with the growing gringo clientele. Lucas said he had to bite his tongue to keep from exploding in laughter when one young lady earnestly explained she only needed to be able to tell her American customers, "It will cost you more to put it in my butt." He never imagined his teaching could make such a difference in someone's life.

Regardless of employment or social status, the women of Paradise Beach needed to learn English, and they wanted to learn it from Lucas. He was the key to their futures. They swarmed around him and showered him with the kind of attention usually reserved for rock stars. He was one happy man. He had gone through hell and emerged out the other side clean, sober, and much in demand by the female population of a tropical paradise. It seemed there was nothing he couldn't have if he wanted it.

Then he met Anjelica.

"What am I going to do, Poppa? This girl has me going in circles." Lucas had stopped by and was sitting at my bar. In between waiting on customers, I was hearing about this new woman.

According to Lucas, she sat in the front row the first morning of the first day of the new session of classes. She sat there as if having beautiful long wavy black hair, gorgeous dark eyes, and a smile that blinded before it seduced was the most natural thing in the world. She sat there and stole Lucas's heart.

When class ended and she walked out, she gave him a little glance and smile. His new dress shirt was soaked with perspiration. It was a scene repeated on a daily basis as the semester moved forward.

"Have you taken her out yet?" I asked him one day.

Lucas looked shocked. "Oh, hell no! I can't even call on her in class without forgetting what I was talking about." I stopped washing the glass I had in my hands and gave him my best tough love look.

"Who is this I am talking to? It's sure not my friend Lucas … the pride of Charleston, the playboy of the western world, and the sexiest man in Mexico."

Lucas morosely shook his head. "I wish I were those things."

It was time for a pep talk. "You are!" I insisted. "I have watched you for over a year now bringing one beautiful lady after another into my bar. Women adore you, and men envy you—including me. So pull up your socks and ask her out. Remember how lucky she is to have you interested in her."

Lucas suddenly looked like his old self. "Damned right," he said. "I'm going to ask her out tomorrow."

I saw him again a few days later. He sat on a stool in the bar, his head in his hands, the Coke in front of him untouched. "So, how did it go with Helen of Troy?" I asked.

"Strange," he said glumly. "Very strange." He explained in detail how he had taken my advice to heart and decided to show a little courage.

As he told the story, what followed left him more confused than ever.

He had started out casually, calling to her as class ended and students were walking out.

"Anjelica," he said, "may I see you for a moment?"

She walked up to his desk at the front of the room. "Yes, Señor Lucas?" she asked, standing in front of him in her crisp white blouse and almost-too-short navy blue skirt. By this time, her English was just about perfect. Much better than

Lucas's Spanish.

"Anjelica … " he started to stall while looking into her eyes but forced himself back on track. "Anjelica, I was wondering if we might get together outside of class for some coffee or lunch or something." His voice began to trail off as he lost a little of his nerve.

She frowned. "Have I done something wrong, Señor Lucas?"

He rushed to reassure her. "Oh no, not at all. I just thought maybe we could get to know each other better."

"Better? I don't understand. Better than what?"

Lucas was drowning and saw no choice but to try to swim to shore. "I just mean perhaps we could be friends. And, you know, maybe go out for lunch." His voice began to falter under her gaze. "Or … something."

She stared at him disapprovingly for a moment. "Señor, I don't know you. I cannot go out with a stranger."

Lucas was stunned. "Of course you know me. I'm your teacher." He was really confused now. And embarrassed. He had completely misread this girl. She was not the least bit interested in him.

Anjelica nodded wisely. "Yes, you are my teacher, and that is how I know you—in the classroom. That is not a social situation, yes? More importantly, my family does not know you. You understand that, yes?"

Lucas could do no more than nod his head in bewildered agreement. Yes, he didn't understand.

Anjelica continued, "Before I can go out with you socially, you must be properly introduced to my family, and you must ask them if it is all right for you to invite me out. I promised my parents when I left home that I would not see any young man without my family's approval."

The last of Lucas's confidence slipped away. "It's only lunch. I … uh, I don't … uh … What? Uh … where do your parents live?"

"Merida," she replied calmly.

"But Merida is almost 300 kilometers from here. I can't drive to Merida to ask if I can take you on a date." Lucas wondered if he had missed something. "Can I?"

"No, that will not do, will it?" Anjelica placed a manicured fingernail on her adorable lower lip and thought for a moment before speaking. "I know! Mi Tia Diana," she said suddenly, her face beaming with happiness, as if the idea had just then occurred to her and not been planned for some time. "That will be sufficient. You may present yourself to my Aunt Diana. Yes. Tia Diana will consider your request that I have coffee with you. Come," she said and turned for the classroom door.

He followed her down the hallway and out the front of the school. He said later that he felt like a small puppy chasing after its owner. Anjelica's heels clicked on the cobblestones as she moved with determination down the street.

"Uh, Anjelica, where are we going?"

She didn't break stride or even turn to look at Lucas. "To meet my family, of course."

They stopped just inside a little open-air restaurant about a block from the school. A short woman with a broad, smiling face stood behind the counter that separated the tables from the kitchen. When she spied Anjelica, she quickly came around to hug and kiss her.

"Did you come for lunch, mi angelita?" she asked.

"No, Tia. I came because I want you to meet someone.

This is Señor Lucas from the language academy." Tia Diana did not seem surprised at this news.

"Buenos dias, Señora," Lucas said, glancing sideways at Anjelica to make sure this met with her approval.

Tia Diana gave him a look of disdain usually used for unruly customers or her ex-husband. "My English is okay," she said. "You can speak English." There followed an awkward silence. Lucas glanced at Anjelica who gave him a go-ahead look. When he failed to understand what he was supposed to do next, she sighed and spoke to her aunt, who was waiting patiently.

"Tia Diana, Señor Lucas has something to ask you."

Tia Diana turned to focus all her attention on the now completely flustered Lucas. "Yes, Señor?"

"I ... uh ... I was wondering, Señora, if I might ... uh ... be allowed the ... uh ... privilege of taking Anjelica out for lunch someday." He stared at the old woman. He was holding his breath without realizing it.

Tia Diana drew back and gave Lucas a hard once-over glance, as if this situation had never been discussed at length with her niece before today. Finally, she nodded. "All right, Señor."

Lucas began to relax, but only for a moment. The old woman continued. "This is my younger sister's youngest daughter, and she is very special to me." She wagged a finger in Lucas's face. "She is a good girl. Do you understand?" Lucas was sure her question included the unspoken phrase *you ignorant gringo*.

"Yes, Señora. I understand perfectly." He nodded, practically bowing to her. "I will treat Anjelica with the greatest respect."

Tia Diana smiled a smile that now included both Lucas and her niece. "Then I give my consent." With that, she suddenly turned and walked back to her smoking grill.

It took Lucas a moment to regain a sense of where he was. When he remembered the lovely girl beside him, he pulled himself together and spoke to her in a quiet voice. "Anjelica?"

She looked at him with questioning eyes. "Yes, Señor Lucas?"

"Anjelica, now would you like to have lunch with me?"

She gave him a sweet smile. "Thank you, Señor Lucas. It is so nice of you to ask. But I am afraid I have other plans today. Perhaps another time."

With that, he said, she walked out of the restaurant as Tia Diana softly laughed to herself from behind the grill.

As Lucas finished his story, I laughed, too. "That girl is great!" I exclaimed with real enthusiasm for the woman I had never met. "She has set her hook, and now she will just sit back and reel you in."

"No way," he said. "I am not playing her game any longer. There are too many other women just waiting for me to notice them. I'm not even sure I'll ask her out again." He nodded to himself. "She had her chance."

A good fisherman will haul in 20 fish and still be obsessed with the one that swam by his hook without biting. That was Lucas. Although I'm sure his intention was good, his resolve and pride quickly disappeared. He asked her out again the next day. She said yes this time.

However, things turned out differently than Lucas expected. For starters, Anjelica didn't come on to him. She flirted a little, to be sure. While she was obviously interested in him, there was none of the 'come hither' promises he got from most of his other dates.

When the evening ended and he drove her home, she gave him a quick kiss on the cheek and a "thank you for a lovely evening," before she confidently got out and walked into her apartment building alone.

"Well, that's that," Lucas said to me when he stopped by afterwards. "I am not wasting my time on her."

He asked her out again the next night. And every night for the next week. Sometimes she said yes, and sometimes she said no. When she said no, Lucas would sit with his coffee at my bar and stare at the ceiling fan.

"You got it bad, son," I said one night as he sat silently. I freshened his coffee. "So what's this girl doing that has you so worked up?"

"Nothing. She doesn't lead me on. She doesn't hint that she wants to go to America. She loves Mexico and acts like she wants me to love Mexico, too. I just don't get it."

"Hmmm." I got it. She obviously did, too. I wondered how long it would take Lucas to get it.

"She's really perfect, you know," he said, suddenly putting his cup down on the bar as if he just had an epiphany. "She is gorgeous, smart, funny, and level-headed. Perfect, right?" He looked at me for confirmation, even though I had never met her.

"Lucas, old buddy, it sounds to me like you may have found The One." I said *The One* in a deep voice, like pronouncing judgment on him.

Lucas looked shocked. Or maybe scared. Or both. "Oh no. No. No sir. Not for this boy. I am having way too much fun to limit myself to one lady. No way. I'll string her along and then it's 'hasta la vista, baby.' On to the next one."

We'll see about that, I thought to myself.

Lucas continued to date Anjelica. She took him to little restaurants far from where tourists ever roamed. They would eat marinated pork tacos and chili peppers so hot he cried while she laughed behind a hand held to her face. She took him to beaches where they picnicked with local Mexican families on tortillas filled with chorizo sausage and Oaxacan cheese. Lucas played soccer on the sand with the children. ("Fooootball," the kids kept correcting him.)

She even took him to church for the festival of the Virgin of Guadalupe, the patron saint of Mexico. I had to laugh when I heard that one. Lucas in church.

They grew closer and closer, and those goodnight kisses in the car at the end of the evening got longer and steamier. Still, their passionate embraces were far short of those Lucas had enjoyed with his other dates. One night, he decided it was time to change that. After all, he was the sexiest man in Mexico. Just ask all his other girls.

However, when Lucas recounted the evening to me, it became apparent that Anjelica was nothing like all his other girls.

"Lucas, what are you doing?" Anjelica shrieked.

He pulled his hands back as if he had grabbed hot coals.

"I … uh … I just thought … " he stammered.

"I know what you thought," Anjelica said sternly from the passenger seat as she adjusted her clothes.

Lucas regrouped for a new tactic. "Anjelica, we have been seeing each other for six months! I adore you, but a man has needs." He figured falling back on his machismo status was a surefire winner with a Mexican girl.

Her face softened. "Oh, mi amor. I adore you, too. I love

you, and I am sure you love me, too. Don't you?"

The answer was yes. He had come to realize that he truly did love this extraordinary woman. It was something that had never happened to him before. It frightened him a little, and he wasn't sure what to do about it.

Anjelica saw the answer to her question in his face and smiled. "Then, my love, I want to give you everything."

Everything rang like a giant bell reverberating through his heart and mind—and other places. He was on his way to home plate. He reached for her again. She quickly raised a hand to his chest and stopped him mid-embrace. "Everything will be yours when you stop seeing other women, when you meet my parents, when you take instructions to become Catholic, and when you marry me."

She smiled a smile that lit up Lucas's world. "Oh my darling, I am so happy." She kissed him quickly and got out of the car.

As soon as he drove away from Anjelica, Lucas stopped by my small room above the bar to give his full report, sitting on the floor and holding his head in his hands. The more I heard about the evening's events, the more I liked this girl.

"She is the best," I said, putting the coffee pot on to brew. "I swear, if you don't marry her, I will."

Lucas's hands muffled his voice. "Poppa, I can't get married. Not now. I'm still fighting for my sobriety. I can't ask her to sign on for that."

"Did you tell her? What did she say?"

Lucas lifted his head out of his hands. "She says that her love will help keep me sober."

I had to ask. "Lucas, truthfully, are you worried about being a drunk or about giving up all those girls who hit on you?"

He smiled sadly. "Maybe a little of both," he admitted. "I can get lucky with so many women. I used to be a drunk and a junkie. Now, I am the sexiest man in Mexico." He said the words in a self-mocking, exaggerated way, but I knew there was a note of seriousness there, too. "Do I really want to give that all up? Is this girl worth giving up America for? She says she won't go to the States. She wants her babies born and raised in her country. I can't stay here for the rest of my life. At some point, I have to go home."

I poured two cups of Chiapas-grown coffee and walked over to hand him one. "I can't help you with that, my friend. I'm not sure where I call home or if it's even important to me." I sat down at my little carved wooden table facing Lucas. "How does anybody figure that kind of thing out on a permanent basis? Is home where you were born? Where your parents live? Where you have a job?" I shrugged my shoulders. "Who knows?"

Lucas got a little irritated at that point. "Oh come on, Poppa. Look at your own life. You're as carefree as a bird. You sure haven't tied yourself down to one woman. I never hear you complaining."

"No, I'm not complaining," I agreed with him. "But I also know that if I had someone back in my old life who believed in me like Anjelica does in you, I might not have gone wandering around the world in the first place. At least I wouldn't have gone alone."

Lucas sipped his coffee silently, looking miserable. "You are going to have to decide, my friend," I said. "This girl won't wait forever."

"Yeah," he said. Then he gave a small, soft laugh. "Wow.

Mexico."

All of that was a long time ago. A year or so after that evening, the company that hired him as a teacher made Lucas permanent director of the school in Paradise Beach. Over the next couple of years, they put him in charge of three more schools along the coast. That kept him busy.

As time passed, Lucas and I didn't see each other as much as we once did, but we stayed good friends. And every now and then, I would get the occasional invite to Sunday dinner. I remember thinking how happy he seemed the last time I was there.

Lucas and I sat at the dining room table. I drank a cold beer, while he sipped an orange soda. Anjelica came in, setting down plates in front of us. She served us one at a time, using her free hand as she carried the baby in her other arm.

"Let me help," Lucas said, starting to rise from his chair.

She placed a hand on his shoulder and gently pushed him back down. "No, my husband," she said. "You sit and talk with our friend Poppa." She bent and kissed him thoroughly before heading back to the kitchen.

"Looks like you are still the sexiest guy in Mexico," I said.

Lucas grinned ear to ear, watching his wife walk away. "No," he said. "Just the luckiest."

"Ever think about going home anymore?" I asked.

He looked at me quizzically. "I *am* home."

9
Mrs. Timmons
Gets a Tan

The Margarita Road isn't just about flip flops and late night beach parties. Running away can be hard work. Deciding to cut loose from all the old obligations and connections to go wandering on the Gulf Stream is only the first hurdle. The aftermath of being uprooted from your job or family can leave even the most freedom-loving of spirits a bit dazed and confused. If you mix in questions of love, the situation can get damn near impossible to handle.

"Hey, buddy, I'll have another one of these." He raised his empty beer bottle and waved it at me.

I reached into the cooler and grabbed a Sol, wiped it dry, popped the cap, and set it in front of him. I didn't offer any more limes. He hadn't touched the ones I set out with the first bottle.

He took a swig. "How much are these again? Two bucks?" He sounded slightly outraged.

"No. Twenty pesos. About one seventy-five in U.S.

money."

"Man!" He did a mock shudder to show his surprise at the price. "I can get a six pack at the supermarket out on the highway for not much more."

My customer was wearing a Rolex, $300 prescription sunglasses, and a silk camp shirt stretched across a belly grown fat from many years behind a desk. He was smoking a Cuban cigar he paid way too much for, even if it had been real, but he wanted to bitch about what I charged for a beer.

It didn't bother me. I had heard it before from guys just like him. More and more tourists were showing up in Paradise Beach wanting the best money could buy. The only problem was they resented paying the price, especially in Mexico.

"That's true," I said. "But you'll have to drink it sitting in the parking lot. The grocery store doesn't offer any beachfront accommodations." I pointed at the Caribbean Sea just steps away. My bar backed up against a frontage road and overlooked a white-sand beach and blue-water vista that took your breath away.

He turned in his seat to look where I was pointing, but I'm not sure he even saw the ocean. Two girls strolling the beach in bikinis caught his attention. They stopped to spread their towels in front of my place. He whistled softly under his breath.

"Boy, oh boy. I gotta give it to you. You sure are living the dream here."

Yeah. I had heard that one before, too. I reached over to the satellite radio behind the bar and clicked on the Margaritaville station. Then I turned up the speakers so he, Jimmy Buffett, and I could all live the dream together.

He started getting chatty after that, telling me it was his

first time to Mexico. "We usually take a cruise around the islands, but the wife insisted on someplace new. So here we are." He seemed insulted when I asked if they were staying in town. "No way. We're at the Golden Mayan Sunrise Palace Golf Spa and Resort."

I knew the name. It's one of those giant all-inclusive mega encampments cropping up on the highway outside of town. The place is so huge you have to take a bus across the property to find the beach. All the employees speak English, and all the travel blogs say the Italian restaurant is to die for. It's a fortress for travelers with plenty of money but no spirit of adventure.

"We're safe there and don't have to worry about what we eat or drink," he said. I wondered if he thought those of us living in town were in constant fear and took a bus to the resorts when we got hungry or thirsty, just to be safe. Truthfully, I never quite understood the whole thing about visiting another country and then staying in a place that made you feel like you were back in the States. Why not just go to Vegas? Or Orlando? Oh well, to each his own.

Out of curiosity, I asked him why he had decided to brave the dangers of coming into town. "My wife wanted to see it. She says she feels cooped up in the resort. So we took a cab down here. She's off wandering around that shopping area spending my money. You know the one?"

I said I did. It was little stretch of cobblestone street not far from the beach, where local artists and vendors hustled the tourists. Visitors from up north filled the market, buying t-shirts and 'genuine Mexican silver' for twice the price they would pay in the mall back home.

"Yeah, well, I hung in there for a while and then decided I needed a drink. Some guy in a store said you had great margaritas, so I told her I'd be here." I didn't point out that he hadn't yet had a margarita.

He kept ordering beers and making what he thought were humorous jokes about how Mexicans sleep all day, all the while telling me how great my life was without a 'real job.' After an hour or so of this, I was ready to pour the next drink over his head. Then his wife showed up.

She was better looking than I expected. Or, rather, better looking than I thought he deserved. Maybe late thirties, with a still-slim body. She had long, strawberry-blonde hair framing a face with a lot of laugh lines that gave her character. She also had the pale look of somebody who didn't spend enough time in the sun.

While her husband bitched about how long it had taken her to get there, she put her bags of recently purchased treasures on the floor and sat down. She seemed experienced at ignoring him. I walked over and put a paper napkin on the bar in front of her.

"Something to drink?" I asked.

She turned and gave me a smile. It was a good smile. She looked a little tired, but maybe it was just irritation at her husband who wouldn't shut up. "I hear you have good margaritas," she said. I returned her smile.

"The best in town," I said and pulled a glass from underneath the bar.

Her husband suddenly held up a hand, palm out like he was a traffic cop. "Hold on a minute," he interrupted. "The concierge at the resort said we should stick to beer in town, remember? I heard even the ice cubes can make you sick."

She gave me a questioning look. I grinned to let her know hubby was full of crap. "The resorts always say that so you don't spend money in town. They like to keep you and your cash on the property. My water and my ice are both purified. It's probably safer than the water you drink wherever you live back home."

"Chicago," he said automatically.

"Well then," I said, still looking at her, "I can guarantee I use better water than you get out of the tap in Chicago." I might have said *Chicago* as if I were saying *dung heap*.

She laughed. "A margarita it is, then."

I pulled out the stops. No blender, just the shaker with some ice, fresh lime juice, a generous pour of Herradura Añejo, a little Centenario Silver, a dash of Grand Marnier, and a quick pour of syrup. I threw in the least little bit of orange juice and shook it all up. I salted a glass, filled it with ice, and slid a lime slice onto the edge. I placed it in front of her and poured through the shaker's strainer. "Here you are. A Poppa's Special."

"Don't say I didn't warn you," hubby said, raising his hands as if he were finished trying to talk sense to her.

She lifted the glass and took a tentative sip, rolling it around in her mouth like she was sampling an expensive wine. Then she took a bigger sip. She set the glass down and looked at me with a sparkle in her eyes. "That is a very good margarita."

I gave a little bow. "Thank you, Ma'am. At Poppa's Bar and Grill, we try our best." I held out my hand. "I'm Poppa."

"I'm Lynn," she said placing her hand in mine. "Lynn Timmons."

"I'm Ralph," he said.

I kept holding her hand as I gave him a nod and then turned back to her. "Nice to meet you both."

I was going to move to the other end of the bar to give

them some space, but she quickly drew me into their conversation. Actually, it was just her conversation, as Ralph appeared bored and was amusing himself by watching the action on the beach. She wanted to know the usual stuff: how long had I been here, did I love it, and was it really paradise? What did the Japanese writing on my tattoo say? Eventually, she had to ask. "Do you have another name besides Poppa?"

"Not anymore," I said.

"Wow! Look at that." Ralph had decided to rejoin the conversation, but his gaze was still on the beach. "Is that legal?"

I glanced up to see what he was talking about. At first, I couldn't tell why he was so concerned and then realized he was staring at the girls who had settled in on the beach in front of my bar. They had removed their bikini tops and were now out splashing in the surf.

"Oh my," Lynn said, as she twisted around to look for herself. She turned back to me. "Is it?"

"Legal?" I chuckled. "I don't think anyone around here ever took a vote or passed a law about boobs on the beach, so yeah, I guess it's legal. It's fairly common," I added. "We get a lot of European tourists. They don't seem as hung up as the Americans do."

Lynn again shifted on her stool to take a better look at the girls on the beach. "I bet that feels pretty freeing," she said wistfully. Realizing she had spoken aloud, she added with a laugh, "You must get a great tan doing it."

Her husband frowned at her. "Maybe if you're twenty-something. Not for a woman your age. Nobody wants to see some middle aged broad get naked." He picked up his beer and swallowed the last of it. "We should get going." Then to me he added, "What do I owe you?"

I didn't slap him upside his head, but it was a fleeting thought. "Let me see … five beers is a hundred pesos."

As he pulled his money from his pocket, I saw it dawn on him. "What about her margarita?"

I looked at Lynn, speaking to the embarrassment I saw in her eyes. "In this bar, a beautiful woman always gets her first drink free."

That brought a little smile. "Thank you," she said.

Ralph rolled his eyes and put the money on the bar. Exact change, no tip. "Let's go," he said impatiently.

I picked up the cash. "Come again anytime."

She took her packages from the floor. "Maybe we will."

Ralph was already at the door to the street. "Come on, Lynn. We still have to find a taxi to take us back to the resort."

I ignored him. "You should. Come tomorrow night. We'll have some live music—a local guy and some friends of his."

As she mulled that over, Ralph said, "We have some pretty good entertainment at the resort, you know."

"Yeah, I hear the Michael Jackson tribute show is a must-see," I replied.

Ralph missed my sarcasm, but Lynn laughed. As she walked out the door behind her husband, she threw me a backward glance. "We'll try and make it."

I put Ralph's beer bottle in the empties case and her margarita glass in the sink. I figured I would never see them again but hoped I would. Well, at least her.

There was a good crowd the next night. There always is when Wet Willie is playing. Willie was into his second set and his fifth shot of tequila when Ralph and Lynn walked in the door.

I left Jorge in charge behind the bar and went over to greet them. "Welcome again," I said. Ralph looked like he would rather be anywhere but here. She looked excited.

"Is there a place to sit?" she asked, yelling to be heard above the noise of the crowd and Willie's version of *Folsom Prison Blues*. "It's okay if there isn't. We can stand." Ralph's look made it clear that was not exactly true.

"Follow me," I said, as I led them through the crowd and out onto the deck outside.

There was a plastic table in the corner. I looked around and saw a couple of empty chairs and pulled them over. "Here you go, guys. Sea breezes and you can still see the stage."

"This is perfect," Lynn gushed as they sat down. Ralph was silent. It was obvious who decided they should come back to my bar. I told them I would send Jorge over to take their drink order and went back to work.

As the evening progressed, I kept my eye on them and occasionally went over to the table. Lynn seemed to be having a good time sipping her margaritas and chatting with people around her. Occasionally she came to the bar to talk with Jorge, and later I saw her dancing with Crazy Sammy. I kept my eye on them to make sure he behaved. Every time I glanced over, which I admit was often, she was laughing and smiling.

Ralph on the other hand didn't seem to be having as good a time. He started with a few beers over the first hour or so but soon added tequila shots. As his wife walked around, danced, and made friends with everybody she talked to, he sat sullenly in the dark corner of the deck. It became rapidly apparent he was getting very drunk very fast. At one point, I saw her take his arm and try to pull him up to dance, but he refused to budge. That is, until later—when he saw the Hernandez twins.

Marti and Luisa Hernandez are perfectly matched 19-year-old bookends with beautiful mocha-colored skin and long black hair. They are sweet, fun, and well known around town for teasing the boys with duets on the dance floor. This time they were kicking it as Willie did his Elvis imitation with a not-half-bad version of *Burning Love.*

Like most everyone else, I was watching the girls and applauding as they spun around the small space we use as a dance floor. Suddenly, I caught some movement out of the corner of my eye. Ralph was off his chair and doing a drunk stumble toward the girls. He pushed through the crowd and came to a halt in the middle of the room, weaving precariously from side to side.

Marti saw him first. I could see the look in her eyes as she decided she did not want to pull him into the dance with her sister. That was an honor reserved for young, buff guys or old, harmless ones. Ralph was neither.

She grabbed her sister's arm as she moved away, still dancing. Ralph stepped forward and reached toward them, almost falling. Unpleasant comments started drifting from the crowd. I decided to step in, arriving at his side at the same time Lynn did.

I approached cautiously. You never know how a drunk is going to react. "Hey, Ralph," I said with a big fake smile. "How are you doing?"

He looked up at me with unfocused eyes. "Hey! I know you." I couldn't tell if he thought that was a good thing or a bad one. He slowly turned his head to Lynn who stood at his other arm.

"Ralph, honey, you might have had a little too much.

Let's go home," she said, gently taking his arm.

Ralph frowned. "What the hell do you care?" he said, slurring his words. He waved his arms at the room, almost tipping himself over. "You go have fun with your friends, bitch." Lynn turned white and stepped back.

"Okay, time to go." I put an arm around his shoulder and pulled him none too gently through the bar. Willie launched into *Your Cheatin' Heart,* and the Hernandez girls retook the dance floor. As Lynn went to get her purse from the table, I maneuvered Ralph through the door and onto the street. Around the corner from the entrance, I stopped and leaned him against the wall.

"That was nasty what you just said to your wife," I told him. He stared at me as if not understanding what I was talking about. A strange look came over his face. I recognized the expression and jumped back just as he suddenly bent over and heaved up all of the tequila and beer that was in his stomach. Then he leaned back against the wall and slowly slid down until he was sitting on the ground.

While this was going on, Lynn walked up and stood beside me. "I'm so sorry," she said softly.

I gave her a reassuring smile. "It's no big deal. I've had people drink too much in my bar before, trust me." I could tell this was not the first time she had seen her husband in this condition.

She knelt down next to Ralph. "Honey, you sit here. I'm going to get us a cab."

As she stood, I told her the bad news. "No, that's not going to work. You'll have to walk down to Tenth Avenue to find a taxi this time of night, and he won't make it that far." I nodded at Ralph who had stopped vomiting and was now catching his breath. "I'll drive you guys back to the resort." She tried to protest, but I wouldn't listen. "It's the only way you're going to get him to your room in one piece."

We both looked at Ralph. "Yes," she sighed, "you're probably right."

She helped me load Ralph into the back of my jeep, which was parked curbside. She took the front passenger seat and turned halfway around to keep an eye on her husband as I drove. I just hoped he wouldn't puke in my car. It was a short ride out to the main highway and on up to their resort. Nobody said anything, but Ralph kept making little *urp* noises that had me worried.

We pulled up to the resort's security gate where Lynn's plastic wristband identified her as a guest, and they let us in. I drove down a long driveway through a fake, manicured version of the jungle to the chrome and glass front of a building that would have been at home on the Vegas strip. The bellman out front started for the car, but when he got near enough to see Ralph's condition, he turned and waved for reinforcements.

Another hotel employee came down the steps, and between us, we pulled the semi-comatose Ralph from the jeep's back seat. The two men each hoisted one of Ralph's arms and carried—more like dragged—him through the lobby, his feet trailing on the floor behind. They were practiced at the move. They had been dealing with drunken gringos for a long time.

Lynn told them the room number, and they headed for the elevators. She turned to me and asked, "Can you wait a minute until I get him settled?" Of course I could.

I sat on one of the couches in the skating rink-sized lobby and waited 20 minutes or so until she returned. I was almost nodding off when she sat down beside me.

"Everything okay?"

"Yes," she said, but she didn't look like it was. "The gentlemen from the hotel helped me get him into bed. He grumbled and moaned for a while but then fell asleep."

Passed out was more like it, I thought.

"I gave them each fifty pesos for helping me. Was that enough, do you think?"

I assured her it was.

She looked somewhat sheepish as she reached for her purse. "Can I offer you … ?"

"Don't even try it," I said, sounding gruff but making sure to smile. She nodded as if half hearing me. She sat very still and seemed to be staring into space. "Would you like to get a drink or something?" I asked. "Or coffee? I'm sure the hotel has a bar or lounge still open."

She shook her head. "Would you mind just sitting here with me for a while? I'm not sure I want to go back up there. Sometimes when he wakes up in the middle of these episodes, he can be a bit unpleasant."

There was no way in hell I would leave her now. "Of course I'll stay. So, this has happened before?"

"Yes. It's not … " She paused and seemed to be trying to figure out a nice way to say her husband was a mean drunk. "It's … it has happened before."

We sat there silently for a while when it suddenly began to pour out of her. He hadn't always been like this. He really could be very sweet. He was under a lot of pressure where he worked. "And I'm not always the best of company. I'm not the easiest person to live with."

She said she had always planned to go back to work after

their son was grown, but now he was heading off to college and she still couldn't seem to find something that meant anything to her. That made her frustrated and sad. She had once had so many plans, so many dreams. She worried she would be betraying those dreams if she ended up simply being a mom and a salesperson at the mall. "Ralph says I am just acting lazy and spoiled and I should get off my butt and do something. He's probably right."

"No," I said, "he's not."

Then I told her of my own dreams and some of my own regrets. I told her how I lost my way and how I ended up on Paradise Beach. I told her things no one else had heard. About San Francisco. I don't know why. Maybe it was those wide eyes that didn't judge. Maybe I was just tired. Maybe I needed to unburden myself as much as she did.

We sat on that uncomfortable modern-style couch in the middle of the hotel lobby for hours. We took turns baring our souls and offering each other understanding—or at least sympathy. By the time 3 a.m. rolled around, we were both talked out. After a short silence, I said I needed to go home.

We both stood up. "I should check on Ralph," she said and held out her hand. I gently pushed it away and gave her a hug. She was a little stiff and cautious but then relaxed and returned it. She even gave me a peck on the cheek. "Thank you," she whispered.

When she headed for the elevators, I went home to my little apartment above the bar.

I slept until almost noon the next morning, waking to the sounds of glasses clinking and music from the satellite radio. The midday sun lit up my room even with the shutters closed. I took a quick shower, pulled on some shorts and a t-shirt with the name of a New Orleans bar on it, and went downstairs. There were a few people at one of the tables, and Jorge was behind the bar.

"Your lady friend is here," he said, as I poured myself some coffee.

My lady friend? As far as I knew, I had been single for a while. For too long in fact. "What? Who?"

"That Lynn lady from last night." His hands were full as he washed out a glass, so he nodded with his head toward the beach. "I think she was hoping to see you," he said with a grin. I walked onto the deck and looked out over the sand. She had pulled one of our lounge chairs halfway down to the water.

I went back to the bar. "She drinking anything?" I asked Jorge without taking my eyes off her.

"Margarita," he said.

"Make another one, please."

When Jorge finished, I took the glass and a small plastic stool and walked down the stairs and across the sand toward her. The breeze coming off the ocean carried the coconut smell of her suntan lotion to me. She wore a big straw hat, pink-rimmed sunglasses, and a little white bikini. It was a good look for her.

She smiled when I got to her chair. "Good morning," she said. I put the stool down and the drink on top of it.

"Compliments of the house. May I join you?"

"I would like that," she replied. I sat cross-legged in the sand next to her chair. There was a short, awkward silence until she said, "Thank you. For last night."

"It was nothing."

"It was something to me. It has been a long time since

anyone tried to help. Or listen. I had forgotten what that felt like." A tear appeared from underneath her sunglasses, rolling down her cheek.

"And today?" I asked. "How are you feeling?"

"Better." She laughed a little, wiping the tear with the back of a hand. "Certainly better than Ralph."

I grimaced, thinking of Ralph's stomach and head after last night's indulgence. "Rough one for him, huh?"

She reached for her margarita and took a sip. "Oh yes. He woke up sick and miserable and hasn't gotten any better. In fact, things got worse when I told him I was coming here to get some sun. And to see you again and thank you for your help."

I made a dismissive motion with my hand to let her know whatever I had done was not a big thing, at least to me. "How much worse?" Now I was a little worried for her.

"He said I couldn't come here because we were leaving to go home." She deepened her voice in an imitation of Ralph. "I'm not staying a minute more than I have to in this crappy country." She laughed at her own performance. "I told him I wasn't about to sit around while he acted like a horse's ass. When I left, he was on the phone to the airlines arranging for a flight home this afternoon." She sighed and took another sip of margarita.

I was beginning to really like this woman. "So this is it?"

She looked at me quizzically. "This is what?"

"This is your last day." I was a bit surprised at my own emotion. "I'll be sorry to see you go."

"Me? Oh no. Ralph's leaving today. I'm not. I said if he wanted to be an idiot and leave early, he could go by himself. He said he would."

"Is that what you want?"

She gazed out at the horizon before giving me a sad smile. "I'm not sure, but I'm going to find out. Besides, I looked forward to this vacation for a long time, and I am not going to cut it short because he tells me to." Almost as if speaking to herself she quietly added, "I've had to do that too many times."

I suddenly felt much better. It was going to be a great day. "How long are you going to hang around?" I asked.

A smile played across her lips. "Just until my skin turns brown."

"Joni Mitchell. The Blue Album," I said and got a huge grin as a reward for knowing that. "So, do you need some time alone, or could we work on that tan together?" We both knew the answer even before I finished my question.

We spent most of the morning on the beach in front of my place, sipping margaritas and watching the waves. That afternoon, I took her down to a little seaside grill where they serve up the day's catch with beans and rice. We were still there when the sun went down. The bartender put an old Stones cassette in an ancient boom box and cranked up the volume. We danced barefoot in the sand until very late. When I took her back to the resort, we made plans to meet in the morning and explore some of the coast. Before she got out of the jeep, she leaned over and gave me a quick kiss goodnight.

The next evening, the goodnight kiss lasted longer. Much longer. A few days after that, she spent the night at my place.

"Are you sure?" I asked, as we settled next to each other in my bed. She looked ten years younger, the candlelight making her fresh sunburn glow.

"No," she answered and kissed me. "But that's not going

to change things." She leaned over and blew out the candle.

We started slowly. She felt guilty and awkward. I was no better, trying too hard to make sure she was all right. We were both in unchartered territory, but eventually we began to find each other's rhythms. The second time was easier. It was perfect.

I don't know when her original flight home had been scheduled, but whenever it was, the day came and went without notice. By then, she had already left the resort and moved into my place. There were no promises. We were making it up as we went along.

As the weeks rolled by, her skin got darker, her laugh got stronger, and some of the lines on her face faded. We would go snorkeling on the reef, or swimming in a quiet lagoon, or spend an afternoon on the beach talking music, books, and personal history. Sometimes we would just lie side by side and say nothing. Then at night we would make love, whisper secrets, and make love some more. She was no longer awkward in bed but had given herself over to a passion that hadn't been fed in a while.

When I had to work or check on the bar, she would hang out on one of the stools. Some of the regulars gave me a questioning look a few times, but that was all. They quickly accepted Lynn without requiring explanations. It was the expat way. On the other hand, Jorge gave me constant sly grins.

I didn't ask about Ralph, and Lynn didn't volunteer anything. Looking back now, I realize we were both living out a dream, and neither wanted to be the one to wake us up. We were playing house like a couple of kids. The only problem was that we weren't kids.

One bright day, we went down to one of the bay's deserted southern beaches. She stretched out on a towel, nude beneath the harsh Mexican sun. She had stopped wearing a bikini days before and was beginning to turn a warm brown all over. I noticed for the umpteenth time the only thing she never took off was a small gold sand dollar pendant that hung from a chain around her neck. I always assumed Ralph had given it to her.

I picked the sand dollar off her skin for a moment. "Something special?" I said, letting it drop back.

She smiled without opening her eyes. "Yes. Very special." She turned onto her side to face me. "I bought it in Key West. I was 21 and on spring break. It was the best time of my life." She gave a wistful sigh. "Ever." She lay back down, talking to herself as much as me now, drifting into the memory. "I felt free and strong, and I was surrounded by beautiful deep blue water. I knew I wanted to remember that feeling for the rest of my life." She placed her fingers against the pendant. "So when I saw this on a street artist's table on Duval Street, I had to have it. It has been my touchstone ever since. It pulls me back to the sea. Even if I can't go, with this I can hear it calling. It lets me know where home really is so I can find my way back."

I watched her lying there, the breeze and the sun and the sound of the waves washing over her. She was right. She was home. I could see it clearly. She belonged here. Naked to the world. Maybe forever. But that wasn't my decision to make for her. It might not even be hers. Sometimes we just can't say no to the demands the world makes.

A week later while lying in bed after making love, she told me she was going back to Ralph. She was leaving the next day. I can't say I was surprised. I knew in my head if not my heart she wasn't staying forever. I had been aware of the phone calls over the past few days that I carefully didn't ask about and she carefully didn't explain.

I had known this time was coming. Even given that, it was strange how sad it made me feel now that it was here. I was used to seeing people come and go. It was part of life on the Margarita Road. The nomad's code was never to get too attached to any place or anyone, because you don't know when you might be moving on. For some reason, I seemed to have forgotten that lately.

She rested her head in the crook of my arm and tried to explain. "You need to know this is all new to me. I never planned this. I never even dreamed this." I started to say I understood and it was all too fast, but she stopped me. "Please don't interrupt. Just let me finish." I shut my mouth.

She had tears in her eyes. "I've never done this before. I don't get into bed with people other than my husband. I have never cheated on Ralph, even after we drifted apart and he seemed to forget me. Even when I knew he was screwing around." She wiped the tears gathering in her eyes. "I made this life, and I was willing to live it out the way it was." She looked around as if searching for something. "But now you, and this and here … " She was struggling like she wasn't sure how to explain it. "It's just … I don't know … that I haven't enjoyed being alive in quite a while. Not like this. Not like, you know … nothing like love … for a very long time. That makes this very special to me."

I wiped a tear off her cheek. "It's new to me, too. And yeah, it is very special." I kissed her. "You don't have to go. I don't want you to go." I really didn't.

She laughed hollowly. "Do you think I want to go? I don't have a life I can walk away from. Even for you."

"I'm not saying leave Ralph for me or move here for me. Do it for you. But if you do it, I'll be here."

She looked up at me. "You've been down here too long. In the real world, people have real lives with real responsibilities."

"Maybe that's why I don't live in that world," I said.

"Well, I do. I have an 18-year-old son who won't understand why his mother ran off to live on some beach without saying goodbye. I have 21 years of a marriage. I owe something to that. Ralph didn't screw this up by himself. He at least deserves an explanation to his face."

"And a second chance?" I held my breath for her answer.

"Maybe. I don't know. I do know that my family deserves more than a postcard saying goodbye. I owe them more than that. I owe me more than that. I have to see what's back there." She started to cry again, and I held her until she slept.

In the morning, we said goodbye. We kissed a lot. She cried some more. She said she would write or call as soon as she was back in Chicago. And she promised that no matter what, I would see her again.

I doubted it. Once she was gone, there was nothing to call her back here. She wasn't leaving anything behind. I didn't tell her that, though. I just kissed her.

We whispered a last goodbye, and then I went out and got into my jeep while she went to pack. She said I needed to go or she wouldn't be able to leave. I drove down the coast and spent the day snorkeling on the reef. I took a spear sling with me, and even though I saw plenty of fish, I never did load it. My heart just wasn't in it.

It was late in the day when I got back. The place was empty, and Jorge was behind the bar. I nodded hello to him.

I asked, "Is she gone?"

"Yes," he said. "I called her a taxi right after you left. She flew out of Cancun a couple of hours ago."

I walked outside to the deck and looked at the sea. The sky was purple out in the distance, and the water was beginning to stir. The whitecaps made me think there was heavy weather beyond the horizon somewhere.

I heard Jorge walking up behind me. "Here, Poppa," he said. "I thought you might need this." I took the glass of rum he was holding out to me. "And this," he said extending his other hand, which held a small, plain brown paper bag.

"What's that?" I asked, taking it.

"I don't know, but she left it for you."

I set the glass on the planks of the deck and held the bag in both hands. I reached inside and took out something wrapped in tissue paper. I unfolded the flimsy covering to reveal the gold sand dollar medallion and chain.

10
Letting Go

I was beginning to see that the Margarita Road was not a place of forever. There is no sense of permanence to be found in shifting tides and drifting sands. Sooner or later, whatever the waves throw up onto the shore will eventually be carried away once more. There is little to be gained in fighting for constancy in an ever-changing world. About all you can do is enjoy the moment you have right now.

Paradise Beach tended to be empty in the early hours of the day. Even as the town began to fill up over the years with new hotels and high-end beach clubs—unlike my funky bar—the early morning hours were still quiet. As the beach comes awake, most tourists are still in their hotel rooms, sleeping off a night spent drinking tequila shots in a vain attempt to recapture a youth they never had.

That's too bad. Those folks miss quite a show. When the sun peeks over the Caribbean Sea's distant horizon, the ink-black night sky slowly gives way to a coral- and purple-colored light display. As daylight begins to illuminate the shallows, pelicans and other birds looking for breakfast skim low over the water, with a grace that manmade flight will never achieve. If you are real lucky, you might even see an exhausted sea turtle hauling herself back home. After spending the night laying her eggs on the beach, she bulldozes a path to the water with a steadiness of purpose most people never find.

After Lynn left town to rejoin her husband, it became my habit to rise early and watch nature's sunrise performance from my deck with a cup of coffee in hand. The solitude of the empty beach was both comforting and unsettling. I enjoyed the chance to spend some time with my own thoughts, soaking in the wordless beauty of the dawn. I realized Lynn had left me in a state I had never really experienced before. I was lonely. For the first time since leaving California, I began to wonder if in all my travels I might have lost something important.

Lynn had sent a few emails and one long letter over the several months since leaving. Her son was off at college. Her husband had agreed to couples counseling, but it didn't seem to be making much of a difference. From the tone of her correspondence, I could tell she was confused as ever about the state of her marriage—and about us. This left me with little to do but drink my coffee, watch the sunrise, and wait to hear from her. Every morning as I did these things, I also kept an eye out for my friend Roy.

Roy was a creature of habit, and that habit included heading down to the beach in the half-light of the hour before dawn. While I greeted the day from the comfort of my deck, Roy started with a dip in the ocean. The water would have to be filled with whitecaps and the beach dotted with red warning flags before he would skip his swim out to the reef. As part of that daily routine, more often than not he would wander over to my place afterwards, looking like a big soaking-wet bear as he lumbered up the beach.

I would have his drink ready by the time he took a seat at the bar and nodded hello. 'Roy's Breakfast Special' was something I concocted just for him: hot coffee with tequila cream (think Baileys with tequila instead of Irish whiskey) and a splash of Havana Club Especial rum from Cuba. Roy said it helped him mellow out enough to greet the day with a smile. After taking a taste, he would always swivel on the seat to look out the open front of my bar at the blue water and finally speak. "Poppa, it's gonna be a damned fine day." Regardless of the weather, he always said that.

I didn't know Roy's story. Not the real one, anyway. At least not all of it. I doubt if anybody in Paradise Beach did. Roy might have even forgotten it himself after enough years here in Mexico. That's one of the nice things about running away to the tropics. You can ignore those parts of your life that didn't work so well in the past and instead become whomever you want.

Life down here is kind of a permanent Halloween where you choose a costume more fitting for your self-image than reality could ever offer. Do you want to be a captain or a cowboy? No problem. People will call you by whatever title or name you choose. You say you're a reincarnated pirate queen or the abandoned love child of a famous entertainer? That's fine with me. We believe each other's stories about who we were and who we are. Being an expat means you can have a whole new life. It's a little like being in the Witness Relocation Program only with flip flops and margaritas.

Of course, if you are slow in creating your cover story, the other expats will gladly do it for you. That's sort of what happened with Roy, even though people's stories about him didn't always agree.

"He used to be a strong-arm enforcer for the Mob. That's how he got that scar over his eye. The big bosses sent him down here when things got too hot for him up in Jersey."

"I heard he was some kind of war hero. Maybe in 'Nam, I dunno. He got a medal for single-handedly attacking a tank. That's how he got that scar."

"He was a billionaire back in the States. Ran some giant company. Then his wife caught him with his secretary and hit him with one of his own golf clubs. That's what I was told by somebody who knows."

It got to a point there were so many outrageous stories about Roy I decided to do something I almost never do: ask a customer about his past. One morning while he sat dripping water on my bar stool and I stood there wiping out some beer glasses, I finally just blurted it out. "Roy, how the hell did you end up with that nasty scar?" I tapped my finger above my left eye.

He laughed a big, guffawing, from-the-belly laugh. A Roy laugh. He ran his fingertips over the faded white line over his eyebrow. "This thing? It's a beauty, ain't it?" He laughed some more. "My kid brother gave it to me when I was eleven or twelve. He was tossing balls in the air and trying to smack them with a bat before they hit the ground." He made a motion as if he were swinging a bat. "Like kids do, you know?"

I nodded.

"Well, I was standing there watching and kind of teasing him because he hadn't hit a one. He would toss those balls and then swing like hell, but he missed every time." Roy paused for a moment and smiled at the memory. "Anyway, I guess he got frustrated and decided to really smash the hell out of the next ball. Of course, he missed that one too, but he swung so hard the bat slipped out of his hands." Roy lightly patted himself on the forehead. "Bam! That bat hit me right in the face. Split my head open and darn near knocked me cold. I was lucky it didn't kill me."

He raised his now empty cup. "Say, Poppa, can I get one more of these?"

I never repeated that story to anyone. South of the border, we like a good legend better than the facts most of the time.

Even without the wild stories of his past, Roy stood out in our little town. For starters, he was a fairly big guy. He wasn't fat, but he was tall with the bulk and spread that often accompanies age. In his younger days, he had probably been in good shape. However, his younger days were long gone. The little hair he had left was gray, and the mustache he wore was salt and pepper in color. If I had to guess, I would say Roy was in his late fifties, maybe even early sixties, when he first showed up on the sand. He was certainly older than most of the gringos here. Regardless, his age didn't seem to matter to him or to the people he crossed paths with on the beach or in the bars.

Roy could throw down with the best of them, drinking frat boy tourists under the table and flirting with their girlfriends until the wee hours. He could commiserate with the middle-aged businessmen who went fishing for marlin but came up empty-handed or charm a busload of blue-haired teachers from the Midwest on a tour of the Mayan ruins.

It wasn't just the tourists who liked Roy, either. The locals did, too. He was known around town as a guy who could offer a sympathetic shoulder or a small loan when it was needed, and most expats needed one or the other at some point. Still, he wasn't a pushover. It would be a mistake to think that. One night I saw him reach out fast as lightning to grab Dirty Jimmy's grubby hand as it was about to close on somebody else's change sitting on the bar.

"That's not yours," was all Roy said. The way he said it brought Jimmy up short with a scared look on his pinched, weasel-like face.

"My mistake," Jimmy said, as he backed away and headed for the door.

Most of the time, Roy was all smiles. He would dance with either or both of the Hernandez twins until he was ready to drop. "Poppa, these girls are killing me!" he would yell from the dance floor. Other times he would share the microphone with our local troubadour, Wet Willie, singing a duet of *Folsom Prison Blues* while the crowd hooted, hollered, and urged them on.

Everyone liked Roy. That in and of itself was a bit unusual. Living in a world of changing tides, any group of expats has its fair share of conflict. Gossip, backstabbing, and infighting are daily activities in any tropical tourist town, but somehow Roy managed to stay above the usual fray. He refused to join in the never-ending dramas that unfolded nightly in the bars. He didn't play favorites and didn't take sides. Everyone along the shore received his attention in equal measure. That is, until Sadie arrived in Paradise Beach.

It was a Friday night, and my place was packed. Roy was in his regular seat, and as I served his drink, I noticed a young woman I hadn't seen before standing near him looking lost. She was trying to hold her spot at the bar as the crowd moved around her, ordering and grabbing drinks from Jorge or me.

"What do you need?" I asked her above the noise.

She dug in the pocket of her cutoffs and pulled out a bunch of Mexican coins. She held her open hand over the bar top. "I'm still confused about the money. Can I get a margarita for this?" It seemed like she might cry if I said no.

Before I could answer, Roy leaned over and took her small hand in his big calloused ones, folding her fingers over the money she held. "Sweetheart," he said in a gentle voice, "if a girl as cute as you can't get a free drink in this bar, we'll get out of here and I'll help you find one where you can." He turned to me and said, "Poppa, make this young lady a margarita, please." Looking back at her, he asked, "What's your name, honey?"

"I'm Sadie," she said with a smile.

That's how it started.

Just like Roy, Sadie stood out as different from the start. She wasn't a typical drifting wanderer running away from home like the rest of us ne'er-do-wells on the Margarita Road. She was the type of girl you would expect to be head cheerleader or homecoming queen before becoming an SUV-driving soccer mom in the suburbs somewhere.

Did you ever see that old movie *Roman Holiday?* Audrey Hepburn plays a princess who runs away to discover the world outside her cocoon of privilege. That was how I saw Sadie. I was never quite certain what she was doing. I wondered if she might be slumming for a time before settling down to a normal life. Or maybe she was fighting against the tide of other people's expectations. I'm not sure Sadie knew herself.

Eventually, she did offer some clues about her past. She mentioned an overbearing mother who wanted a trophy daughter to show off at the country club. And apparently, there had been a boy. In fact, she had been engaged to him.

Looking back, Sadie had told me her fiancé wasn't a bad guy. Ronnie was nice-looking and smart, she said. He had a good heart, and she knew he adored her. However, in moments of reflection or times of too many tequilas, she would confess aloud that as her wedding date neared, she worried her folks liked her fiancé more than she did. Even worse, she sometimes wondered if she picked him to make them happy instead of herself.

It was her best friend Dolores who came to the rescue, suggesting Sadie join her on vacation and take some time to think things over. Dolores told her she was probably going to realize that getting married was the right move, but this way she would know she had given it some real thought and could relax. Sadie said yes and told Ronnie she was going away with her friend.

To her surprise, Ronnie was all for it. Sadie had seemed rather stressed to him lately, and in his opinion getting some rest before the big wedding was a great idea. "Where are you girls going?" he had asked.

"Some place in Mexico that Dolores picked out," Sadie said. "It's called Paradise Beach."

Ten days later, Sadie still wasn't sure how she felt about Ronnie, but she knew she was in love with Mexico. What wasn't to love? It had beautiful beaches and water warm enough to melt the ice that can sometimes accumulate around the edges of the heart. Best of all, not one person she met told her what to do or how to live her life.

She decided on the return flight not to marry Ronnie after all. She wasn't going to take the teacher's aide job her

mother had arranged at a private school. She wasn't going
to do anything that anyone else wanted. She was moving to
Paradise Beach.

Once back home, her news was received exactly as she
expected. "Why don't you just grow up?" was her father's
angry reaction. It was almost easier with her mother, who
broke down in hysterics, took to her bed, and refused to
speak to Sadie. After them came Ronnie. Telling him was the
toughest thing she ever did.

To her amazement, Ronnie wasn't as upset as she expected
him to be. The way he figured it, Sadie was having some pre-
adult-life jitters and needed to go a little crazy before settling
down. "You'll be back," he said, not without a little smugness.
"And soon."

Sadie wondered if he might be right. She hoped not.

A few weeks later, she landed in Paradise Beach with her
suitcase and not a friend in sight. She stayed at a small hotel for
a few nights before moving into a closet-sized studio on a dirt
road a block from the sea. With the little money she had saved
and with some hard budgeting, she could make a year, maybe
longer. Still, it was going to be tough being alone. She knew
she should be terrified, but she wasn't. For the first time, Sadie
felt like she was doing what *she* wanted.

She needn't have worried about being alone for very long.
The expat beach crowd had a 'fresh meat' radar that quickly
picked out the newcomers. A short probationary period
proved Sadie was not psychotic—which in and of itself would
not have meant exclusion from the group—or a non-drinker,
which would have.

Paradise Beach's hard-partying gringos soon welcomed
her with open arms. Sadie was quickly pulled into the nightly

bar circuit and just as quickly became everyone's favorite cruise director. She naturally took to beach life and soon was starting each evening by climbing on the bar to dance or to call out, "Let's do shots!"

In the quiet times following a particularly raucous night, she would sometimes admit to wondering if maybe her father had been right. Maybe this was all about refusing to grow up. Even if that were true, she didn't care. She was young and having the time of her life in this Mexican version of Neverland. Growing up would just have to wait for a while.

With an attitude like that, it wasn't long before everyone fell in love with Sadie. Roy was no exception. In fact, he quickly became the president of her fan club. The feeling was mutual for Sadie. After that first night at my place, the two of them became the best of friends and almost inseparable. At some point on most evenings, they would hook up at a bar where Roy would buy the drinks and Sadie would drag him out onto the dance floor.

For expats, a 'friend' is what you call someone you drink with night after night. Buy a person enough booze in the tropics and they become your best pal. However, for Sadie and Roy, there was something more. Something special. They acted as if they actually liked each other.

Sadie would bring Roy her homemade cookies in little boxes tied with ribbons. They were terrible things that were usually half raw and half-burned. "I'm sorry," she would say. "The little oven in my apartment has no thermostat."

He would open the box and wolf them down, all the time insisting, "These are the best ever!"

In turn, whenever he saw her counting pennies, Roy would take her to dinner or throw a party at his place and insist she take home all the leftovers at the end of the night. "What am I gonna do with all this food? It'll spoil before I ever get to it," he would say, filling her arms with plastic-wrapped bowls of enchiladas and rice.

It was obvious to me that Roy gave Sadie something she never had before—someone who cared but didn't judge. What she gave Roy was harder to figure out.

Of course, Roy wasn't the only one in town to notice Sadie. Sadly, some of the others weren't as nice as he was.

You don't have to live in paradise very long to discover it has its fair share of dangerous creatures. Remember, even Eden had a snake. The Caribbean Sea is no different.

For example, experienced divers here will tell you never to swim where fishing boats have been dumping bait and fish guts, as the Caribbean bull shark gets nasty when there is blood in the water. You should also avoid any large school of fish when there is a group of blacktip reef sharks around. The feeding frenzy can get dangerously out of control. And there are barracudas, sea snakes, and stinging jellyfish.

Still, none of these seagoing marauders holds a candle to the top predator to be found along Mexico's coast. On any given day, a pretty girl in a bikini lying on the sand or dancing on a bar in a short skirt will quickly be pursued and cornered by the most notorious of local creatures: the Tropical Beach Resort Land Shark. Poor Sadie was being circled from the start and didn't know how to swim to safety.

"Most of them are okay, you know, polite enough when I say I'm not interested. But some of them make me wish I had a can of mace or something." Sadie frowned. "What is their problem anyway? It's not like I'm the only girl in town."

Sadie had been jogging on the beach one morning when

she saw Roy emerging from the sea heading for my bar and ran up to join him. The three of us sat on the deck enjoying the early breezes while Sadie expressed her confusion about the male population's attitude toward her.

I tried to clear things up without being too blunt or crude. "It's just that most people here assume that everyone else has a sense of ... " I searched for a phrase. "Personal freedom."

Roy threw his head back and gave a roaring laugh. "What Poppa means," he said to Sadie, "is that everybody here is constantly on the make, and they assume everyone else is, too."

She looked surprised. "Is that true?" she asked me.

I nodded. "I'm afraid so."

Now she looked shocked. "What is *that* all about?"

Roy explained. "Hell, it's not hard to figure out." He counted on his fingers. "One, everybody runs around half-naked most of the time because we're on the beach and it's so damned hot. Two, everybody drinks hard every day. And three, most people moved here because they didn't like all the rules back home."

He put his hand down. "So, drunk, naked people with no restraints add up to a whole lot of folks changing beds all the time." Roy didn't look like he thought that was a bad thing.

Sadie shook her head. "That's fine for whoever wants it. I don't, and I wish some of them would just back off."

I stood up to head for the bar. It was time to start my workday. "That ain't gonna happen, I'm afraid," I told Sadie. "A single, good-looking girl like you is always going to be a target. Unless you settle down with one guy, they figure they still have a chance and will keep asking."

Sadie seemed outraged. "It's idiotic. All I want is some

fun and a little time alone to figure out my life. How am I supposed to deal with this shit?"

As I walked away, I could just barely hear Roy say, "You know, I have an idea that may help you."

A few nights later, I saw Sadie again. She was sitting at my bar enjoying her favorite drink: a sugar-rimmed margarita made with pomegranate-infused tequila. It's a house specialty. There were a fair number of people in the place, and it didn't take long for somebody to hit on her.

I could see Patricio coming from across the room. He was a young Italian who worked off the books and under the immigration radar at a dive shop in town. With his shaved head and six pack abs—always on display as he refused to ever wear a shirt—Patricio was certain he was God's gift to every woman. I knew several women around town who agreed with him.

He stopped next to Sadie and pushed himself against her for full body contact. I moved down the bar ready to shoo him away. As it turned out, I wasn't needed. "No thanks," she replied loudly to his whispered suggestion that they go somewhere together. "I'm here with my boyfriend, and he wouldn't like that."

Patricio was surprised to hear this. So was I. He asked in his heavily accented English, "Boyfriend? When did you get a boyfriend?" He looked around the room in disbelief. "What boyfriend? Who?"

Sadie smiled at someone across the room and waved. "Him," she said sweetly. With a big grin, Roy stepped into the bar from out on the deck and made his way to where Sadie was sitting.

"Hi, baby," she said.

"Hi, sweetie," Roy replied and bent over to give her a kiss.

You could have knocked poor Patricio over with a feather and then used the same one to lay me out. Roy wagged a finger at Patricio and said, "Don't be bothering my girl, now." He laughed as if joking around, but there was an unmistakable edge. Then he looked down at Sadie. "Do you want to blow this pop stand? I'll take you home and make you some pasta primavera."

Sadie grabbed her purse from the bar and jumped off the stool. "Absolutely," she said. Roy gave me a nod and a smile, and the two of them walked out holding hands.

By the next morning, the news of Roy and Sadie had burned through the expat community. The story was passed along over early morning eye-opener coffee in cafes and hangover-easing tequila shots on the beach. Did you hear? *Roy and Sadie. Roy and Sadie? Roy and Sadie!* There were some expressions of amazement and disbelief, along with a bit of snickering and a few dirty jokes. However, since most expats have their own closets full of skeletons, there was generally a feeling of live and let live.

Still, there remained a persistent undertone that was best expressed as *What the hell?* I had those thoughts myself. I told Sadie so, one day at lunch.

I ran into her walking to the beach as I was heading to El Diablo on the other side of town for a bite. The place has the best tacos al pastor around. Slabs of pork marinated in chilies, spices, and pineapple, stacked on an upright rotisserie spit and slow cooked. Fill a tortilla with the pork and add raw onions, cilantro, and hot salsa. Wash it down with a cold beer, and you have a bit of heaven.

When I told Sadie where I was going, she didn't hesitate

to abandon her beach plans and invite herself along. I didn't mind. Having a pretty girl across the table always helps my digestion. Over our meal, I voiced my thoughts about her and Roy. "You have to admit," I said, "you make an unusual couple."

She wiped a bit of hot sauce from her chin before responding. "Maybe. So we are different. So what?"

I proceeded cautiously. "You are both good people. Both friends of mine. I know you two are taking some heat from the gossips in town, and I would hate to see anyone hurt in the end."

Sadie laughed. "You worry too much, Poppa. Everything is just fine. I don't care at all about what a bunch of losers are saying behind my back." She leaned in a little and lowered her voice conspiratorially. "Roy and I know what we are doing. Remember that day Roy said he had an idea for me to avoid being hassled by every guy in town?"

I nodded. Sadie smiled reassuringly. "This was his idea. This was the plan he came up with."

I wasn't sure I understood. In fact, I was sure I didn't. "I don't get it," I said.

Sadie held up a finger for me to wait while she finished a mouthful of taco. She took a moment to swallow and then said, "The plan is me and Roy." I guess my confusion showed, so she continued. "Having Roy as my boyfriend keeps all the jerks away. Nobody wants to be on Roy's bad side. So I am completely protected." She grinned at how clever this idea was.

"So," I said, "you and Roy aren't really together?"

The smile disappeared, and she frowned. "I didn't say that. It's complicated. I love Roy. Everybody loves Roy. He is my dearest friend in the world. He is as special as it gets. I've never felt as close to anyone before. So yeah, right now I would say we are together in a way."

"Right now? In a way?" I quoted back to her. That seemed like hedging on the whole togetherness thing to me.

Sadie nodded, sipping at her beer. "Yes. Right now. We both understand we are free to be with anyone we want if someone nice comes along. There are no claims or holds on anybody here. What matters most to us is the friendship." She brightened up. "Nothing lasts forever, Poppa. Isn't that what you always say? Well, Roy and I understand that. In the meantime, as far as anyone else is concerned, we are an exclusive couple. That's Roy's idea to keep the a-holes at bay."

I knew I should have stopped there. But I didn't. I blundered ahead. "So you and Roy aren't ... I mean ... do you two ... that is, are you guys ... ?"

Her blue eyes went steely gray. "What do you want to know, Poppa? Spit it out. Are Roy and I what?"

I scrambled back over the line I had just crossed. "Never mind," I said. "None of my business."

"That's right," Sadie said, visibly relaxing. "That's what I think, too."

Even though I had thoroughly embarrassed myself and broken my own rule about staying out of other people's lives, I felt better after lunch. Sadie had reassured me that my friends had a good grip on the situation and that it was working fine for them. That feeling lasted for a day or two, until the morning Roy decided to bend my ear.

I hadn't seen Roy as much since he and Sadie had become an official couple. He had been missing his morning après-swim coffee at the bar more often than not, and I had been missing his company. I told him so as he sat down at the bar not long after my lunch with Sadie.

He grinned and looked a little embarrassed. "Yeah, I'm sorry about that, Poppa." He chuckled. "It's just that when you have the demands of a gorgeous young girl in your life, you need your beauty rest." He took a sip of his special breakfast coffee. He looked tired, and for the first time, he looked his age.

"Gorgeous girl or no, maybe you're pushing yourself too hard," I suggested. "Sadie can take care of herself for a few days."

"No, she can't," he said empathically. "She needs me around." Roy looked down at the coffee cup in his hands as if speaking to it rather than me. "That's just fine. She's worth losing sleep over. I haven't been this happy in years." He seemed to remember where he was and looked up at me with a big goofy grin. "I'm in love, Poppa. That's for damn sure."

I made Roy another drink and tried to think of something to say, but I couldn't come up with a thing.

Roy and Sadie's arrangement continued, and after a while, it seemed like they had always been together and always would. But Sadie had been right on target when she quoted me quoting the Buddha. Nothing lasts forever.

It was the late May surge. People were getting in some time on the beach before the summer storm season started, and I was staying busy. Early one evening as I was pouring drinks, I noticed a newcomer walk in. He was young with rugged good looks. The deep mocha color of his skin had been given a reddish glow by a fresh sunburn, and his tight black hair was cut close to his head. He took a seat by himself at the end of the bar furthest from the door and ordered a beer.

He wasn't by himself for long. I swear, in the space of an hour I saw half a dozen women come up to the guy and offer to buy him a drink or show him around town. He politely turned them all down. After one particularly aggressive girl had been rebuffed, he saw me watching and rolled his eyes. I grinned and walked over to introduce myself. "Do you always have this effect on women?" I asked, half joking.

"Hell, no!" he exclaimed with a grin. "You guys must put something in the water down here." We laughed about his predicament. He said his name was Aaron, and he was a fireman from upstate New York.

"Well, no wonder," I said. "You fire guys always get the girls."

That brought a touch of sadness to his face. "Not always." It turned out he had hit a spell of bad luck with a failed marriage. When the final papers were signed, he decided to treat himself to a vacation in paradise for some alone time to recharge his batteries. So here he was in my bar on the second night of his trip. I wished him luck and bought him a beer. We chatted some more before I went back to work and he went back to fending off admiring women. *Nice kid,* I thought to myself.

Sadie wandered in a bit later and sat at a spot near the door, ordering her usual pomegranate margarita. "No Roy tonight?" I asked, as I made her drink.

"No," she said. "He is worn out today. We partied until late last night, so he's taking it easy."

It was then that the light bulb went on, and I decided to steal a page from Roy's playbook. Maybe Sadie and I could help this guy Aaron out. "Babe, can you do me a favor?" I asked, setting her drink down. She nodded yes and took a sip as I told her about the poor guy at the end of the bar being

hassled. I suggested she could ride shotgun for a while to dis-
courage the stream of women hitting on him. "You know," I
said, "just sit with him a bit. Having you there may keep the
barracudas away."

Sadie looked down the bar at Aaron. "No problem," she
said. "He's cute."

"It might cause some gossip," I warned.

She gave a little snort. "Screw that. Like I care." She picked
up her drink and walked down the bar to take the seat next to
Aaron, as I went over and explained our plan to him. "Sadie's
your bodyguard tonight."

He laughed, shook her hand, and thanked her for vol-
unteering for such a lousy mission. She smiled in return and
assured him it was no problem. Having done my good deed, I
left the two of them alone while I went to fill the drink orders
that were beginning to back up.

The place got even more crowded as the night went
on, and I was wishing I hadn't given Jorge the night off. I
looked down at Sadie and Aaron every once in a while. They
seemed to be getting along fine, talking with their heads close
together. Then at some point in the evening, I glanced their
way and saw they were gone. They probably went for dinner
and would wander back later.

They still had not returned when I closed things up at
2 a.m. After sending everybody on their way, I washed out
the last of the glasses and stepped out onto the deck for a
smoke. I knew I shouldn't, but I never could resist the Romeo
and Julieta Cuban cigarettes sold in Mexico. As I stood there
puffing away, I could see a couple walking hand in hand further down the beach. It was hard to tell at that distance in
the dark, but when they were framed against the moonlight

bouncing off the water, it looked like they stopped and were kissing. I had no idea who it was. Or maybe I just didn't want to know. I finished my cigarette and went to bed.

As it happened, I wasn't the only one to see the shoreline lovers that night, and other people weren't as unsure about their identity. A local lady of leisure, whose only pastime was inserting herself into other people's business, apparently saw Aaron escorting Sadie home in the dawn light. According to the tale she told anyone who would listen, their public display of intertwined affection was so intense as to make walking difficult.

Over the next week, the story spread as quickly as only the flu or good gossip can. Sadie and Aaron were spotted together all over town acting like honeymooners, and their every move became subject to review and judgment. The general theme was that Sadie was a whore, Aaron was a loser who stole other guys' women, and Roy was going to kill somebody. Funny thing, the people most upset with Sadie and Aaron were those who had been most upset about Sadie and Roy.

By the time a red-eyed, sad-faced Sadie walked in alone a few days later, I had heard the same gossip—with new elaborations each time—from several different people. One of my regulars tentatively got up and started toward her. When I held up a hand and shook my head no, he sat back down. I poured a shot of Herradura Añejo and then quietly walked down to her spot at the bar, placing the drink in front of her.

She looked up at me through tear-filled eyes. "Thanks, Poppa," she said with a little sniffle. I stood there for a moment waiting to see if she wanted company or not. She picked up the drink, took a taste, and set it back down. Just as I was about to walk away, she looked up again.

"I guess you heard. I guess everybody has heard."

"Fuck everybody," I said. "Want to talk about it?"

She sighed and gave a half-hearted smile. "It's your fault, you know. You introduced me to Aaron."

"He seemed like a nice guy."

She nodded. "Yes, he is. A really nice guy. He asked me to come to see him in New York as soon as I can."

I didn't say anything. I just stood there mentally kicking my own butt for starting this mess. Suddenly the tears began to roll down Sadie's face.

"I never, ever meant to hurt Roy. I really thought it would be fine with him. When I told him, I thought he would be happy for me. I never imagined for a moment he would be so angry. He said I was too young to see how foolish I was being and that I should listen to someone with more experience about these things. He told me I was acting like a child." She picked up a paper napkin from off the bar and pressed it to her nose.

"Roy always used to say that when someone perfect for me came along, I would know it. He said he was just saving the place in my life for that guy. Then when I told him I might have found someone, he got crazy on me. Was he lying to me all this time, Poppa?"

"No, honey," I said, "he was lying to himself."

I ambushed Roy the next morning. The last few days I had seen him on the beach for his daily swim, but he headed home right after. Today while he was still in the water, I made one of his coffees and headed out to the deck. As he came out of the sea, I shouted to him. "Roy!" I held the cup over my head and shouted again. "Hey, Roy!"

I saw him hesitate, standing up to his knees in the surf and trying to keep his balance as he decided what to do. Finally, he pushed himself out of the water and headed up the beach toward me. I walked down the steps from my deck and sat on one just as he arrived. I held out the coffee. "I thought you might need this."

He sat next to me and took the cup from my hand. "Thanks." He took a sip.

We both just hung out there silently for a while. I figured he would speak up if he had anything to say. Eventually he did. "She says this guy is special." He went back to his drink. I waited. After a few minutes, he started up again. "Special. How the hell does she know he's special when she just met him?"

"Sometimes that's all it takes," I said. When he didn't respond, I continued. "Sometimes the attraction for someone is there from the first moment." Again, no response from Roy. "So what happens next?" I asked.

He slouched over his drink while he spoke, as if not wanting to see the world around him. "She says she's going to New York in a few weeks to visit him. Says she wants to see if this might be the real thing. What the hell is that? The real thing? I don't know what that means. I asked her: what did we have, she and I? The fake thing?" His voice was rising, and I could imagine his anger when he posed that question to her. "She's making a huge mistake, and I can't get her to see it."

"You must love her a lot to care this much about what happens to her."

Roy gave me a glance to see if I was joking. I wasn't and hoped he saw that.

"Yeah."

"Have you ever loved anyone that much before?"

He gave me a sharp look of surprise, as if I knew something about him he thought was a secret. "Not since Elizabeth died," he said quietly.

"Your wife?"

He nodded again. We watched the waves some more.

"Forty-four years. Forty-four wonderful years. No cheating, no messing around, just us together forever. We knew what love was back then. We knew what it meant. She helped me build up my construction business. She kept the books, managed the office, and raised two kids. I still don't know how she did it."

"What would she have thought about you and Sadie?"

It took him a moment to answer. "When I look back now, it's almost like she knew I would meet Sadie. At the end … " He swallowed hard a few times before continuing. "At the end, she told me not to waste my life mourning. She said I should follow my dreams. Maybe find a tropical island to live on. When she decided to stop all the drugs and just let it happen … she said she was letting me go so I could get on with the rest of my life."

He wiped at his eyes with one big hand. "So, I did. After Lizzie passed, I moved down here. She knew I always wanted to live near the water."

He gave a half laugh. "I think she would have liked Sadie. I know my Lizzie. She would have told me to let go of the past and to try and find something that made me happy before it was too late."

"Good advice," I said. "Did that happen? Have you been happy?"

"Well, yeah at first. Until this shit with the kid from New York."

"That's good," I said. "That's real good that she made you happy for a while. But you knew it wasn't going to last forever. For chrissakes, Roy, you are old enough to be her grandfather. Did you really see the two of you together five years from now? Ten years?"

Roy scowled at me, but I could tell he was listening. "Maybe it's your turn now to say to Sadie what Elizabeth said to you. Tell her to go and find her happiness before it's too late. That girl came down here needing someone to love her unconditionally, with no ulterior motives and no strings attached. You did that for her. You made her heart strong enough to go on without you. Now get out of the way so she can use it."

We sat silently for a while, listening to the waves and the cry of a solitary sea bird cruising the shoreline. Then Roy said, "I knew this was never going to be her home. Not forever."

"Yeah," I agreed. "All of us are just passing through in one way or another." We didn't say anything more.

Roy finished his coffee, put the cup on the step he had been sitting on, and stood up. "Thanks for the drink, Poppa."

"Roy ... "

"I'll think about it," he said and left, walking slowly down the beach.

Not long after, Sadie went to New York and returned with stars in her eyes. She had decided Aaron was *The One* and was moving north to live with him. A few months later, we threw her a going-away party. Roy didn't show. I didn't really expect him to. Sadie told me that when she went by his place to say goodbye, he hugged her and wished her well. He even told her to keep in touch. That made her happy. It made me happy, too.

Life went on as usual in Paradise Beach after Sadie left. Tourists came and went, I served drinks, and Wet Willie sang. Roy eventually settled back into his pre-Sadie life. He didn't party quite as much and often declined when a girl would try to pull him onto the dance floor. I kidded him about it one day, and he said he was just getting old. He finally confessed to being 75. I expressed my admiration and told him I hoped to have as good a life when I got to be that age.

"Sheer dumb luck is all it is," he said. "Besides, I know age is getting to me. I feel it every morning." When I started to protest, saying how he was in better shape than most of the people I saw around, he held up a hand to stop me. "Don't bullshit a bullshitter, Poppa." He laughed. One of his old Roy laughs. It was good to hear. "It's okay though," he said. "Getting old, I mean. I've had a good run. And it's still a great life. I've been luckier than most. I found paradise. Just look at this place." His face beamed as he gazed around at my bar, the beach, and the ocean. "Best of all, I got a second chance to be young for a while with that little girl." He got a faraway look in his eyes. "Not many people ever get that. I'll always be grateful to her."

I didn't have to ask who 'that little girl' was.

A year or so later, Roy began losing weight, and his morning swim left him exhausted and out of breath. They discovered the tumors not long after. Roy moved up north to live with his son while he underwent a series of operations. "I'll be back," he promised me and himself. I don't think either of us believed him.

When his son called to say Roy had passed, we held a wake. It was a somber affair. I know Roy would have wanted everybody laughing and having a great old time, but we just couldn't pull it off. There were quiet conversations broken by occasional chuckles or tears, as different people remembered a special Roy moment.

Wet Willie played some nice tunes, but when he tried *Folsom Prison Blues,* he broke up and set the guitar aside. The Hernandez twins sat in the corner and sobbed.

Sadie's second pregnancy kept her from coming, but she sent the biggest bouquet of flowers I had ever seen. Before the evening started, I set them on the bar along with a photo of Roy, and after everyone had gone home, I placed Roy's picture on the back shelf next to the bottles.

I couldn't sleep much that night and was up and dressed just as the first signs of the pink sky began to show out over the ocean. I went down to the bar and made a pot of coffee. When it was done, I poured some in a cup and added a good slug of Cuban rum and tequila cream before carrying it down to the beach.

Standing on the sand looking out at the ocean, I thought about Roy and Sadie and me and Lynn. The old questions about life and love in a world where nothing ever stays the same came flooding back. When I failed to come up with any new answers, I kicked off my sandals and stepped into the water.

The waves were gentle and gray in the early morning light. A few gulls circled and moved on. I waded out until I was waist deep and then raised the coffee to my lips to take a swallow. "It's going to be a damned fine day," I said aloud. Then I tossed the cup into the sea and headed back to shore.

11
Jackie Boy
Starts a New Life

Any expat will tell you that the Margarita Road never disappoints. It leads to a world where everything is exactly as hoped for. The journey always ends beneath a palm tree on a white sand beach near clear, sapphire-colored water. In paradise, the sun always shines, the drinks are always cold and strong, and the companionship is always warm and friendly. And if on occasion that turns out not to be true, one can just pretend.

Another Shitty Day in Paradise. That's what the sign said. It hung from a shelf on the back wall of my bar, right beneath a stuffed toy iguana and above a poster that declared mermaids could drink free. It was meant to amuse tourists coming down to vacation on a beautiful tropical beach. Only sometimes it wasn't so funny. Today was one of those times.

A strong breeze blowing off the ocean through an open window had been my unplanned wake-up call. The humid wind pushing into my room carried with it the smell of salt and a fair amount of sand whipped up off the beach. I felt the grit beneath my feet, as I rolled out of bed and went to close the storm shutters.

Unless I received a better offer, I usually slept in the apartment above the bar. This meant I would often start my day looking out on the Caribbean's palette of blues. Only today, the sky was gray and the sea was dark.

The first couple of raindrops were falling by the time I was dressed and heading for the door. Out on the sea, huge white-capped waves looked like snow-covered hills. They rolled toward the beach in a seemingly never-ending queue of mountainous water, each waiting its turn to strike the shore with careless force.

I had decided on breakfast at Handsome Harry's Café. As I walked up to the restaurant, I noticed that the plastic tables on the sand out front were empty, and the brightly colored beach umbrellas were closed and tied shut. The place would usually be packed by this hour, with tourists sipping breakfast Bloody Marys. However, on this morning it appeared most of them were still hunkered down in bed waiting for sunshine that wouldn't show.

Harry's manager, Alejandro, saw me coming and stepped out of the shelter of the small, enclosed restaurant to wave at me. "Good morning, Mr. Poppa. You want some breakfast?" I told him I did, and he opened the sliding glass door into the dining room for me.

The small café was dark and warm. Slowly moving ceiling fans kept it from being unbearably stuffy. Inside were a few tables covered in bright, multi-colored cloths and set with salt and pepper shakers in the shape of cactuses. In the back was an open grill, and off to the side in a small alcove was the bar.

There were only a few other customers. A middle-aged tourist couple sat at one table, and over in the corner I saw Gary Anderson, another local guy, having coffee. He and I nodded at each other, as I took a seat facing the beach.

"I know what I want, Alex," I said, waving the offered menu away. I ordered coffee and Huevos Divorciado. Divorced Eggs are two fried eggs, one smothered in red sauce and the other in milder green salsa. The eggs are separated by a wall of Chilaquiles: tortilla chips soaked in a spicy sauce and then topped with heavy cream, shredded cheese, raw onions, and avocado. When done right, it's simply delicious. You can keep your local greasy spoon's all-American lumberjack specials of pancakes and bacon. I'll start the day with a Mexican divorce every time.

While I waited for my food, I listened to a couple at a nearby table piss and moan about the weather. "Maybe it will clear up," she said.

Her husband was having none of it. "Look at this shit." He pointed at the rain hitting against the sliding glass door. "There's no way in hell this is going to stop enough to go fishing."

The woman looked down at her plate as if she had nothing left to say. I was thinking the trip had been her idea. "Hell," he said, "we can't even lie out on the beach. What's the point of a vacation in Mexico if you can't even go to the goddamned beach?"

She tried again in a low voice. "We can stay in the room and relax. Read or something. We can spend some time together. You know, just the two of us."

He gave a heavy sigh of defeat. "We could have done that back in St. Louis."

I had seen it before. Folks buy into the dream of a trip to paradise only to find their vacations drowned by weather or ruined by Third World realities. I felt a little guilty. After all, I sell people that dream of a perfect trip to the Caribbean. Of course, I wasn't alone. Most of the expats living in Paradise Beach hustled the tourists with some version of that tropical fantasy. It's how we make our living.

Guess what? We're liars. The truth is we lie so the snow-birds will return. It's the only way we can support our flip flop lifestyle. Margaritas aren't free, you know. So we pretend that every day on our beach looks exactly like a travel brochure photo. It's a weird, symbiotic relationship. If tourists keep coming down south on vacation and spending their cash, we get to stay here a little longer.

I know it sounds harsh, but don't feel too betrayed. We expats also lie to ourselves. Sure, we may live in what looks like paradise to you, but the truth is we're here because we don't have any place else left to go. This is the end of the line for a lot of us. So we sip our rum, sit on the beach, and try to convince ourselves this is as good as it gets—no matter how strong the winds blow.

A few minutes after the unhappy couple left to head back to their hotel room, Alejandro brought me over some traditional Mexican coffee—a cup of hot water, a jar of Nescafé, and a small can of evaporated milk. As I was spooning the powder into the cup, Gary Anderson came up to my table. "May I join you for a moment, Poppa?"

Gary and his wife Jane owned a dive shop in Paradise Beach. They had moved down to Mexico from Dallas a few years back. Gary was near 40, with thinning, sun-bleached hair, constant sunburn, and a perpetual smile. He had the sort of speedy enthusiasm most commonly found among used car salesmen—which had been his profession in Texas.

Jane was tall with an athletic build and toned muscle. She was the quieter one in public; however, her sharp, hazel eyes seemed never to miss anything. I always figured she was the smarter of the two. It appeared to me he was the front man while she was the one who did the thinking.

Like most expats in Paradise Beach, they carried some baggage. Hardly anyone hits the Margarita Road free of weighty history tinged with regret or shame. I had heard stories of a drinking problem and a marriage that needed saving. I didn't know if they were true or not, and I didn't know the Andersons well enough to care. Still, we expats stick together, and if he needed to talk to me this morning, I wasn't going to turn him away. I said of course he could join me and motioned him to sit down.

Gary settled in the seat across from me. He started out with a deep sigh. "I want you to know how sorry I am about the way things turned out with Jackie Boy. I want everyone to know how bad I feel." His normal smiling countenance had been replaced by a hangdog look of weary sadness. "I had no idea this would happen."

"No apology necessary," I said. "You shouldn't be so hard on yourself. You gave him a chance. That's more than most people around here were willing to do. Nobody blames you. If they are pissed at anybody, it's at him."

That seemed to make Gary sadder. "I don't want that. If anybody should be angry at him, it's me. Or Jane. Jane is the one he really let down. But we're not mad. We're just disappointed. And surprised. Boy, were we ever surprised. I sure never expected things to turn out this way."

I didn't know what to say to that. Maybe Gary had been surprised by Jackie Boy, but I wasn't. He had been a disaster in the making ever since he showed up in Paradise Beach.

I don't know who first called him Jackie Boy, but it was the perfect name for an aging adolescent. He was a 30-something kid—good looking, tall, and slender with longish-black hair that he wore in ratty dreadlocks. I suspected the permanent grin on his unshaven face was most likely chemically induced. He was unreliable, careless, and on the hunt for the never-ending good time.

I do have to admit, though, the boy did have a strange, mellow, Zen-type quality about him. He seemed to live for the moment, even if that moment was often at someone else's expense. He did some real work from time to time—the standard beachfront jobs like bartender and scuba instructor. However, his tenure at any one place would last only until he got bored or was caught 'borrowing' money from the till. Mostly, he supported himself by sleeping with tourists.

The term gigolo is out of fashion in these days of casual hook ups and sexual freedom, but that's what Jackie Boy was. I saw it more than a few times in my bar. A lady of a certain age would hesitate while looking over the drink menu when he would make his move.

"You should try one of the margaritas. Poppa has the best margaritas in Mexico. Trust me, I know." He would slide onto the stool next to her. Not too close. Not like he was hitting on her. She would give him a glance. A nice-looking boy, she might think, but a woman traveling alone has to be careful.

"Are you an expert, then?" she would say in a standoffish way. It would be best to put this youngster in his place.

Jackie Boy would meet the slight chill with a beaming

smile. "Do you mean an expert in margaritas or in Mexico? Because I qualify as both."

She couldn't help but laugh then.

He would take his time, ignoring her when she ordered a margarita and sipped it for a while. Eventually, she would say he had been right. "This *is* a great margarita."

They would make small talk about the beach, the weather, and where she was from. By the third margarita, she would explain the solitary vacation. "I knew as soon as the divorce was final he regretted it, but it was too late. I wasn't having him back after that."

Later they would take themselves and their drinks down to the sand to watch the moon reflect on the water. She would sit cuddled up next to him while he softly sang Spanish love songs. Then, if Jackie Boy had played things right, it was off to his newfound friend's hotel room for a night of passion. The next morning would come his tearful confession that he was too poor even to take her to breakfast. No matter, she would reassure him. It would be her treat—and could she help him out with just a little something? He usually walked away with his pockets full enough to last another couple of days.

I should also say it wasn't a one-sided deal. It seemed to be a mutually beneficial situation. As far as anyone could tell, any lady who spent some time with Jackie Boy usually went away satisfied. Her tropical fling might have cost a few dollars, but I never heard any complaints. The kid made people feel good. Even among the expats who knew his boyish attractiveness was all veneer, there were a few local women who succumbed to his flattery. He had a natural charm, that's for sure.

Given his reputation, none of Jackie Boy's various escapades around town had ever shocked me. However, I will admit I was taken by surprise when Gary and Jane hired him to work in their dive shop. I said as much to Gary, as I started in on the eggs Alejandro set before me.

Gary nodded thoughtfully, as if deciding whether I could grasp what he was about to say. "Well, Jane was actually the one who came up with that idea. She's the one who saw his potential. She realized that bringing Jackie Boy into our life was part of our mission."

"What mission is that?"

I could see Gary was amused at how clueless I was. "Our mission as Christians," he said.

The Andersons' faith was one of the reasons we had never been close. Gary and Jane were born-again fundamentalists who regularly announced their beliefs in every possible social situation. Any conversation with them was peppered with references to "God's will" and expressions of gratitude for "the Lord's blessings," and as a result, I tended to stay away.

Now, don't get me wrong. I have no problem with anyone's religion. Pray to whoever or whatever you want. Personally, I was raised Catholic, read Watts and Castaneda in my college days, and even spent some time in a Zen temple back in California. In the end, I guess you could say I was a follower of Saint John Lennon who said, "Whatever gets you through the night is all right."

It's just that I have found people who insist on constant public expressions of piety to be a little boring after a while. Regardless, I had to admit that if anybody needed some kind of saving, it was Jackie Boy.

I wasn't alone in being shocked when the Andersons hired him. There was much head scratching in town. It did seem to be a marriage of opposites: the local beach bum hustler working for people who kept their satellite TV turned to FOX News and never missed a Sunday at church. Yet despite their differences, things seemed to work out. If Jackie Boy stayed longer at this job than the previous ones, and maybe even cleaned up a little, that was just fine as far as Paradise Beach was concerned. Local folks figured it was one less hustler they needed to keep an eye on.

Gary and Jane seemed to take Jackie Boy to their hearts. He ended up moving into a spare room behind their shop and more often than not would be seen having dinner with them in different places around town.

Gary continued reminiscing. "Oh yeah, Jackie Boy became part of the family. Jane even took him out and bought him some new clothes so he looked less ragged in the store. She really cared about him. In fact, I began to worry about it. I didn't want her hurt or disappointed. I think I was more realistic about how much we could change him."

He assumed a smug, world-wise look to show his own knowledge of screw-ups and sinners. "I figured he would eventually just drift away from us." Then he frowned. "However, the Lord works in mysterious ways."

I guessed Gary was referring to Jackie Boy's near-fatal accident. While speeding down a lonely stretch of jungle highway, he missed a turn, crashed though a stand of banana trees, and smashed into the stone wall of a long-forgotten and half-buried Mayan temple. Luckily no one else was involved, as he was alone in his beat up junker of a car at the time. His only companions were a nearly empty bottle of cheap tequila and a plastic bag full of tranquilizers.

I figured the booze and pills were probably more responsible than the Lord's hand in the accident, but to each his own opinion. Whatever the cause, the car was totaled, and Jackie Boy was almost as badly damaged.

He broke his nose, a few ribs, and an arm. One of his lungs collapsed, and he dislocated a shoulder. A kneecap was cracked. Worst of all, his head had bounced off the steering wheel, leaving him in a semi-coma. Add in the bumps, bruises, and blood from various lesser injuries, and it was obvious the boy was in a critical state. As it turned out, the crash was just the beginning of his troubles.

In Mexico, two things happen when you end up in a hospital after an auto accident. First, the police come and arrest you. They handcuff you to the bed until your degree of fault or liability for any damages is established or until your freedom is purchased from the arresting officer. In short, it's money first, treatment second.

Once you are cleared of wrongdoing, the doctors then decide whether or not you have insurance or money and provide a level of care accordingly. Since Jackie Boy's monetary assets consisted of roughly thirteen dollars worth of pesos in his pockets, things did not look good for him.

The few beds in the hospital were already occupied, so he was left on a gurney in the hallway. A doctor confirmed he was breathing and promised to check back before he went off duty later. Meanwhile, a cop came, secured Jackie Boy's limp arm to the side of the gurney, and went for coffee.

Yet in one sense, he was lucky. He was an expat. Being a fellow stranger among strangers trumps almost any fuck-up or failure. The lousiest drunk, the biggest whore, the most untrustworthy rip-off artist—it doesn't matter. You are family to your fellow expats when the chips are down. So when word spread about the accident, people charged into action. Jane was at the center of the activity. In fact, she became the force behind it. She called me first.

"Poppa, can you talk to the cops about Jackie Boy? Your Spanish is better than mine or Gary's, and you have experience with this sort of thing."

'This sort of thing' was bailing expats out of jail, an expertise I didn't particularly enjoy possessing. I would just as soon avoid any contact with local law enforcement, but Jane was insistent.

I headed down to the hospital and found the arresting officer watching over Jackie Boy's still form as he simultaneously flirted with passing nurses. I introduced myself and explained that Jackie hadn't hurt anyone but himself, so there was no reason to arrest him. "Él estaba solo," I emphasized. He was the only person involved. I also tried to tell the officer that Jackie Boy was like a son to a local businessman and his wife. Couldn't he please waive the charges for the family? They would be most grateful.

The cop was not impressed. He gave me the silent *I don't understand your Spanglish* look.

I finally gave up and reached into my pocket, mentioning a regalo. A gift.

The policeman's eyes lit up. Looking around to make sure no one was watching, I counted out a thousand pesos, folded them into a small square and extended my hand. The cop suddenly spoke perfect English.

"Señor," he said, taking the money, "I am so sorry this terrible accident has happened to your friend's son. Tell the family I will pray for him." Shortly after that, the handcuffs came off.

Meanwhile, Jane took the hospital like an invading army.

She started at the front desk but was soon roaming the halls, loudly buttonholing any doctor she could find. It wasn't long before Jackie Boy had a real bed, and a neurosurgeon was brought in from Cancun to look him over. Next, Jane spread the word by phone and internet that a lot of money was needed. She announced that cash donations for his medical expenses could be made at the dive shop or through a PayPal account she set up, and she would not accept no for an answer.

Gary and Jane made it clear they personally would supervise the donations. Jackie Boy was not getting a windfall. All of the money donated would be going into the bank to pay his medical and rehabilitation bills. Their word was good enough for those of us living in Paradise Beach at the time, and the money began to roll in. The sums donated by expats, tourists, and even some local businesses eventually reached over $15,000 U.S. Praise the Lord.

Jane also organized a schedule so that someone was sitting at Jackie Boy's bedside every day during visiting hours. "When he comes to, he should see a familiar face," she kept telling people.

Most everyone I knew took a turn sitting next to the comatose Jackie Boy. Hell, I'll admit I even did it myself. Jane was very persuasive. It was hard to say no to her when she was doing more than anyone else. It seemed like she lived at the hospital during those days.

Jackie Boy finally did wake up, and the doctors said that with proper care, he would make a full recovery from his injuries. As time passed, fewer people were needed to babysit him in the hospital, but Jane remained there throughout the ordeal, holding his hand and talking softly to him.

It didn't seem fair for Jane to carry the whole burden of

Jackie's recovery, so I telephoned to see if she needed anything. "If you want help, just call me. I can take a turn babysitting, if you need a break."

"Thank you, Poppa, but I've got it under control. I think he's still a little fuzzy about what's going on, so it's probably best if he sees me around as much as possible. I think it calms him down."

Eventually, Jackie was released. He was limping, moving slowly, talking even slower, and still black and blue, but he was alive. Gary and Jane took him to their house and moved him into an extra bedroom. After that, Jane insisted on staying home most of the time to care for him. You could tell Gary was proud of her. I'm sure he felt it was part of the 'mission.'

"She gets him up and dressed in the morning, feeds him, then drives him to physical therapy. She is a saint," Gary would tell anyone who asked how things were going. "Heck, most nights she sleeps in a chair next to his bed in case he needs her."

If anybody thought the Andersons' arrangement strange, they kept it to themselves. "Those are good people," folks would say while throwing back a few shots. "Good people."

One day after Jackie had been released from the hospital, I noticed Jane leading him across the sand. She had an arm around his waist to steady him as they walked toward the lounge chairs I keep on the beach in front of my place. I headed down the stairs to see if I could do anything for them. By the time I reached where they had stopped, Jane had helped Jackie Boy out of his shirt and settled him on a lounger. She sat on a towel spread on the sand and unpacked a shoulder bag, laying out various tubes and pill bottles.

"Hi guys. How is it going?" I knelt beside them. "You're

looking good, Jackie." That wasn't exactly the truth. He looked thin and pale with more than a few ugly, red scars around his body. Still, he was alive and seemed to be on the mend.

Jackie Boy opened his eyes and took a moment to focus. "I feel good, Poppa. It's all thanks to my angel here." He nodded in Jane's direction. "You start to see how good life is with someone like her by your side." He gave her a big smile.

She blushed. "Be quiet, Jackie. Poppa doesn't want to hear your silliness."

Jackie Boy settled his head back on the chair with a grin and closed his eyes again. I glanced over at Jane. "Can I bring you guys anything? Something to eat or drink?"

She shook her head. "No thanks, Poppa. We're good for now. Is it okay if we just rest here for a while?" I told her they were welcome to use the chairs as long as they needed and to just wave if they wanted anything. I headed back to the bar, as Jane began carefully rubbing sun block over Jackie Boy's scarred body.

As the months of Jackie's recovery went by, I kept hearing reports from people around town about how much better he was doing. He and Jane were always out at the beach or taking slow walks around the town square. It seemed everyone had a Jackie and Jane sighting to talk about, and they were all happy he was getting better.

At some point, he must have recovered enough to be his old self again, because Jackie Boy was able to get out of bed on his own without anyone knowing. He apparently headed over to the bank where he emptied out what was left of the account set up for his medical expenses. As best as could be figured out, he then grabbed a taxi up to the Cancun airport and took the first available flight to Florida.

No one heard from him again.

"I just never thought he could do anything like that. I thought he had changed." Gary sat across from me in the café looking like he was going to cry. "I feel like he slapped us in the face."

"How did it happen? How did he get the money?" I wasn't the only one who wondered about that.

Gary shrugged his shoulders. "Who knows? The only person who could sign on the account was Jane, because she's the one who set it up, and she has no idea what took place. Not a clue. My guess is that he sweet-talked someone at the bank into letting him have it. You know how persuasive he can be. I try not to worry too much about it. What's done is done. I only pray he is using the money wisely to start a new life that has some meaning to it."

Despite Gary's prayers, the hot rumor around town had Jackie Boy back in the States rehabilitating himself with blow and hookers in Miami. Maybe that was true and maybe not. The only thing anyone knew for sure was that he and the money were gone. How or why exactly that came to pass, no one was willing to guess. At least not out loud. Not in public.

"What does Jane think about all this?"

Gary gave a slight frown. "She blames herself. She thinks it's because she got pregnant."

I didn't say anything, and Gary kept talking. "It was a big surprise for us. We had been trying for years to have a baby without any luck. The doctors said there was no hope. When I heard the news, I had never been so happy."

He paused, as if reliving the moment in his head. "The truth is Jackie Boy didn't seem all that thrilled for us when

I told him. In fact, he seemed sort of shocked. It wasn't long after that he took off. Maybe he saw the writing on the wall, figuring that Jane wouldn't have as much time for him with a baby on the way. That's what Jane thinks. Whatever the reason, I guess he figured it was time to move on. I just wish he had said goodbye instead of sneaking off into the night like he had something to hide."

"So you aren't angry at him?"

Gary made eye contact with a look of sincerity on his face that must have sold quite a few cars in his old life. "No, I'm not angry with him. How could I be? This is all God's doing. It's a miracle."

I said I wasn't quite sure how this could be divine benevolence. Gary tried to explain. "I think God gave Jane and me this baby as his way of rewarding us for all we did to save Jackie Boy. It's so clear to me now. God decided to test us to see if we were able to help someone that needy. He gave us a baby after seeing how much Jane could love Jackie. He's the reason Jane got pregnant."

Gary suddenly leaned in toward me and lowered his voice. I moved forward to hear him. "I do have to admit I'm a little worried, though, Poppa. I'm worried people might not understand. They could be upset about the money disappearing and Jackie Boy taking off or, you know, about anything." He paused for a moment as if searching for the right word or phrase. "This place is such a small town, and the gossip can be vicious. I know you hear a lot at the bar. Have you heard people saying anything? About Jackie Boy? Or about Jane or me?"

"Not a word," I assured him. "You know how things are down here. Folks don't pay much attention past what happened at the bar last night or on the beach this morning. Everyone has moved on. Nobody really cares about Jackie Boy or the money. They are just happy for you two. About the baby, I mean."

I was telling him the truth. Mostly. As for myself, I certainly was in no place to judge anyone else's love life. And as I said before, we expats take care of our own.

Gary relaxed back into his chair and gave me a big smile. "That's good. That's very good." He gazed out the door. The rain had finally arrived in full force. It covered the beach in sheets, washing away the accumulated crap and debris the winds had blown in.

After a moment, he stood. "Well, I guess I'll be getting home. It doesn't look like anybody will be diving today in this choppy water, so I can spend some time with the mother-to-be. Thanks for listening, Poppa." I told him it was no problem. We wished each other well, and he headed out, seemingly oblivious to the downpour that soon soaked him.

Alejandro came over. "Do you want anything else, Mr. Poppa?" I thought for a moment, listening to the wind and rain smack against the door.

"A Bloody Mary, por favor," I said to Alex. Why not? I had no place to go, and after all, it was another perfect day in paradise.

12
The Old Man In the Sea

We expats tend to think of ourselves as being free from all those old conventions we left up north. We don't worry about the past, and we have no plans for the future. We believe our destiny is guided by the stars and our dreams. Then again, there are times when I wonder if the truth might be a little less glamorous. What if we are all simply lost souls blown off course, just trying to get home?

"Don't bother. You can't see shit out there."

I was headed for the water when I saw the two of them. They were American teenagers—skinny, pale, and cocksure the world was theirs for the taking. They had probably come down with their folks from Dallas for the weekend. More and more tourist families from Texas and Florida were dropping by these days for short stays. Mexico's Paradise Beach was becoming a backyard getaway for those in America's south.

The kids were walking up the beach, still dripping wet from the ocean, when they stopped to talk to me. They each carried a snorkel, mask, and fins.

"It's murky as hell," continued the kid who had first spoken. "We couldn't see more than a foot in front of us." He sounded disgusted, as if the weather had personally decided to mess up his day. The other one nodded in agreement.

"How far out did you go?" I asked.

The kid shrugged his shoulders and looked out into the bay as if expecting to see a marker on the surface showing where they had been. "I dunno. Almost to the reef, I think."

I doubted that, but I thanked him and told them I would try it anyway. "Once you get past the reef, things tend to be clearer," I said.

The kids exchanged a glance and a smirk before wishing me luck and walking on. I know they were thinking *this old guy has no clue.* I didn't feel a need to explain I had been diving and swimming in this bay for a decade.

The storm had passed through quickly during the night. That's the pattern for this time of year. Every few days, a thunderstorm builds just off the coast of the Caribbean. It gathers strength until ready to pop and then roars ashore, dumping sheets of rain and stirring up the sea bottom, before heading inland to drench the jungle and blow itself out.

As usual, the rain had left the air moist and warm. Coconut trees danced in the remaining winds, shaking water from their palm fronds onto the beach below. The sand sparkled, blown clean of any trash. Things always seem brighter after a storm. Beneath the waves, I knew it would be a different story.

I was sure the loose bottom of the bay's flat, sandy slope had been tossed around by the storm's force. Seaweed, rotting driftwood, and flotsam floated in the tide and added to the swirling mix. Long after the rain and wind were gone, the sea always needed a few days to settle down again. It would be a mess out there. I didn't care. I needed to get into the water. Now.

The summer had been an especially busy one. Paradise Beach was becoming increasingly popular, and all season long, the town had been packed. The place was filling up, and not just with tourists. It was becoming harder and harder to find an open stretch of shoreline. Every day seemed to bring new construction of a condo hotel or upscale restaurant.

No one seemed to drift in on the Margarita Road anymore. Now people arrived by airline charters or cruise ships, coming with a sense of entitlement instead of adventure. At the same time, the old guard was disappearing. Jen Langston had moved to Spain a few years ago. Big Tom had sold the Mermaid after his second heart attack and was keeping a low profile. Even Wet Willie moved on after scoring a steady gig playing down in Belize.

I saw fewer and fewer familiar faces in my bar these days. In their place were college kids from Mexico City with too much money and too little sense. They were joined by middle-aged American businessmen willing to spend a fortune to buy a timeshare where they might stay for a week every other year. Worst of all, hard-faced predators from around the world came looking for a quick rip off.

At least things had finally quieted down with the coming of fall, and I wanted to relax a little. I decided to close the bar for a few days and told Jorge he should take the trip to see his parents in central Mexico he had been planning. Then, with nothing left to do, I took the jeep down the coast to spend some time at Bahía de Pirata. Pirate Bay. According to legend, pirates like Jean Lafitte had once come ashore here to find food and fresh water. Hence the name.

The bay has one of those photo-perfect beaches you see on postcards. Only this view isn't touched up. It's a small semicircle of white sand bordering an expanse of blue water breaking over a stretch of coral reef. Best of all, it was still wonderfully undeveloped and generally free from hordes of people.

Who knew how long it would remain that way? Just that morning, as I drove down the narrow lane that cut through the jungle to the ocean, I passed a sign that sent a chill down my spine. It read *Future Home of the Azul Condominium Community. One-Bedroom Pre-Construction Sales Starting at $250,000 U.S.*, with a Miami phone number. It looked like a different sort of thief was eyeing the bay these days. I crossed my fingers that it would stay quiet and undisturbed for a little longer.

The two kids I met on the way to the water were the only people in sight, which was just as I wanted. I sat on the deserted beach and put on my fins. I spit-cleaned my mask and then frog-walked a few yards into the water until it was deep enough to lie down.

By the time summer ends, the Caribbean is as warm as bathwater, so there is no system-shocking adjustment when you submerge yourself. In fact, there is a womb-like feeling to the water that demands you relax. A primeval part of me hidden somewhere inside was feeling as if I had finally come home.

The teenagers on the beach had been right, though. Despite the blazing sun overhead, it was difficult to see. Muddy water whirled around me, creating an impenetrable wall keeping me from staring deeper into the bay.

It's hard to see underwater in the best of conditions. The

play of light and shadows, the constant movements of the sea foliage, and the quick darting of small creatures all make focusing difficult. When the sea bottom is whipped up, it can be much worse. You are never sure if you are seeing something real or not.

I'll be honest and say that swimming through the muck of all that dirty water was a bit freaky. It's part of our human nature to rely on our vision, and we feel vulnerable when it is impaired. It's one of the reasons we're afraid of the dark.

I wasn't too worried. I reassured myself there was little in the sea that could or would actually threaten me. Sure, I might brush against a jellyfish or scrape against some coral in my near blindness, but that was unlikely. Still, my mind insisted on playing games.

At first I saw a shadow in the periphery of the tunnel vision created by my swim mask—a slight movement that could have been the reflection of a passing cloud or the swirl of some floating garbage. I turned my head but saw nothing more. I pushed forward with my fins.

Again I thought I saw something directly in front of me. What was that? Was it anything? A school of fish, maybe. I stopped and floated in place, watching.

I moved my head side to side but couldn't see a thing. I swam on, mentally berating myself for letting a few shadows bother me.

Suddenly there he was, swimming out of the murkiness just to my right. I didn't even see him until he was a foot or two away. I think he was as surprised as I was.

It was a black grouper. He was big, even for a fish known for its size. The biggest I had ever seen. He was an easy five feet long, probably more. His massive body looked prehistoric, with its shiny scales and long, sloping head. He had a broad face and a large lower jaw that extended out past its upper counterpart, like a seagoing bulldog.

I felt a little flood of relief. This guy was no threat to me. He was a gentle giant who preyed on smaller fish. In this case, *I* was the dangerous predator.

The black grouper is prized as a game fish who will give quite a fight at the end of a line. Its heavy body structure also offers enough meat to make it a favorite target of commercial fisheries. Thanks to humans, this species is already pushing the red zone of extinction and may disappear before too long. I might have been looking at the last of a dying breed swimming silently past me that day.

He wasn't supposed to be there. A fish his size wouldn't last long in the bay's shallow waters. There wouldn't be enough food, and he would be too conspicuous to the boaters and divers. That's not to say he didn't come from around the neighborhood, though. He had almost certainly been born as a young female on the nearby reef decades before. All groupers start life as females and later turn into males as the need of the species demands. Mother Nature isn't as hung up on issues of gender as many people are. She just sees it as part of the natural order of being what you need to be.

Still, as this grouper grew and changed, he moved to the far side of the reef. He needed the deep waters to hide from sharks and to find larger schools of small fish to eat. The bay hadn't been his home for many years, and I wondered what he was doing back here.

It's possible that the previous night's storm had caught him feeding at the surface and pushed him near shore. He may have wandered in to gorge himself on fish trapped in the bay by the strong waves. Or he might be ill with some parasite, causing him to lose his sense of direction. Maybe he was just homesick for the old stomping grounds. Who knows?

I've seen people behave the same way. When they least expect it, they get all turned around. Folks will be swimming along happy with how things are going when something knocks them off their chosen path. A bad storm of debt or divorce or a loved one's passing can cause an out-of-control tailspin. Sometimes a longing for something new and different will send people off in an unknown direction. For others, it's just the opposite—it's wanting to find a way back to where things were once familiar and comforting. A lot of the time, we don't even really know why we choose to head a particular way but end up just floating where life takes us.

At least that's what I have seen over the years with the souls drifting through Paradise Beach. I can't imagine it's much different for the rest of the world's creatures.

Whatever the reason for his being here, I expected the giant beside me to quickly push away, leaving me in his wake. He could outdistance me in the water with no trouble, yet he didn't. We swam in tandem for a few moments. It's possible he saw I was no threat. Or perhaps he just wanted some company.

Our short time together gave me a chance to look him over. He was an old guy. I knew this because he wouldn't have gotten that big except by living a long time. He could have easily been thirty years old, maybe more. He had probably lived longer than most of the people now alive in the United States.

Imagine, three decades swimming along this coast, never knowing of the world far beyond. As he spent years floating over sand bars, through brightly colored coral and over deep-water kelp beds, he had been blissfully unaware of O.J. Simpson's slo-mo getaway, the fall of the Berlin Wall, and the launch of MTV. He knew nothing of *Star Wars* or *Star Trek*. He missed the birth of the internet and the death of Elvis.

Still, he must have seen a lot in his world, even with his limited view from the bottom of the Caribbean Sea. I noticed he bore the marks of a life lived to the fullest. Literally. A small section of his dorsal fin was notched from either a boat propeller or a chance meeting with a shark. Along his left side were several inches of silvery scar tissue. It looked as if he had once been gaffed by a fisherman trying to pull him into a boat but had fought enough to tear loose.

I suspect if we could have talked, he would have told quite a few tales of life in the sea—not just about close calls with sharks and fisherman, but of the changes he had seen in thirty years.

He might have recalled the first time he felt the vibrations from speakers on a party catamaran as they blasted a pounding beat at full volume, the sound waves moving through the water and giving flight to schools of frightened fish. Looking up from the depths at the source of the noise, he might have seen the sun glinting through yard-long plastic margarita glasses of bright neon colors floating on the surface of the sea.

The grouper might have told of the day when his world was enveloped in shadow and a great crash of crunching and scraping echoed through the water. The fish wouldn't have known that an inattentive pilot had let an 85,000 ton cruise ship drift over part of the reef, cracking it into pieces and destroying it forever.

Or he might have recalled that beautiful day when the sun was so bright and the sea so still that the rays of light shot sixty feet down. That was the day he saw the man floating in the water. He was not yet bloated, and the smaller fish had not yet done much damage to his skin and face. He still looked like a man—a man who smuggled drugs up the coast from Belize for delivery in Cancun. A man who chose his partners for the trip unwisely and who was beaten and tossed overboard mid-ocean to drown so that his attackers could take his share of the drugs.

Had the grouper words, there are certainly stories he could tell. He might tell of seas turned black for days by hurricanes or small fish dying while trapped in the plastic bags that more and more often drifted through the water. Possibly, he would remember shrieking teenagers trying to ride on the backs of terrified sea turtles, or the growing emptiness of the reef. Most importantly, his stories might tell of the loneliness of finding no mate for the last two years.

But he didn't speak, and I could only imagine his life and his world.

After a few moments, he swam ahead. I tried to catch up, but it was like a puppy trying to run after a train. I wanted to keep him in sight, but his large, dark form soon blended into the dirty water of the bay, and he was gone.

I continued on, swimming through a break in the coral. Sure enough, the water was clearer on the other side. I moved up and down the outer edge of the reef for a while. Here and there, I would startle a school of fish huddled in the shelter of a coral cave, but there was no sign of the giant grouper. I figured he had made for deep water. When I began to tire, I headed back into the bay and swam for shore.

Stumbling onto the beach, I sat down, setting my fins and mask beside me while I tried to catch my breath. Looking out over the horizon, I saw clouds from another storm already gathering in the distance. I let the waves wash up over my legs, tugging at me to go along as they pulled back to the sea.

As I rested, I began to hear voices. Looking around, I saw two men heading toward me. They were in their mid-40s, with white tourist skin and desk-bound paunches. They both wore brand new, brightly colored board shorts their wives had most likely bought for them. Possibly the fathers of the boys I had seen earlier.

As they neared, I could see they each carried snorkeling gear and swim vests. The taller of the two also held a fancy spear gun. He wasn't supposed to have that on this reef, but I doubt he cared.

When they were close enough to hear me, I stood up. "Pretty bad out there today, guys," I said.

"Really?" said the one with the spear gun. "It looks all right to me," he said glancing out to the bay as they walked over.

"How bad?" asked the other one.

I made a face to show how sad I was about the miserable conditions of the water. "It's as bad as I have ever seen, and I've lived here for twelve years."

They looked at each other as if wondering whether they should pack it in. Then they turned back to me. "That sounds awful," said the second one.

"Oh yeah," I confirmed. "You can't see bottom. You can't even see your hand in front of your face. And the current … " I let that hang for a moment.

"What about the current?" It was the shorter one again.

"It's too strong for me, I tell you." I had their attention now. "I had to fight to make it back to shore, and I'm a fairly good swimmer. I assume you two are both strong swimmers."

"Well, I'm not," said the worried one. "Maybe this isn't such a good idea."

His friend still looked undeterred. "I really wanted to bring in a fish. Something big," he said, lifting his spear. "I paid a lot for this contraption."

"Not much chance of that today. I didn't see anything out there," I lied. "All the big ones have gone deep because of that storm last night." I gestured to the darkening horizon. "Besides, we will be getting more rain soon, guaranteed. Trust me, you don't want to be out there in a storm. You can be swept out to sea in a flash."

That did the trick. Captain Ahab lowered his spear as the wind left his sails. "So," he said sadly, partially to his friend and partially to me, "what do we do with our day?"

I pointed to a thatched-roof building a mile or so away at the far end of the beach. "See that place down there?" They both nodded. "That's Pepe's. Cold beer and great shrimp tacos. Not a better way to spend an afternoon, even in the rain."

The grins spread slowly over their faces. "Sounds perfect to me," said the one who didn't swim all that well.

"Let's do it. We'll come back for the fish another day," said his buddy.

They were friendly enough and invited me to join them, but I begged off, saying I had to get to town for some reason or another. I watched them walk down the beach before turning my gaze back to the bay.

I stood there for a while, looking out on the waves and feeling the breeze begin to strengthen. I imagined the aged grouper swimming into the darkening water beyond where the whitecaps were breaking on the top of the reef.

In my mind's eye, I could see him diving deep as the daylight faded above him. Looking out on the rolling surface of the sea, I silently wished him luck. I wished him lots of babies, plenty of food, and a safe haven. Mostly I wished him a good journey wherever he was headed. I had the same wish for myself.

I bent down to the water's edge and washed the sand off my gear. As I straightened up, I saw a flash of lightning far out over the Caribbean. Thunderheads were gathering again above the vast expanse of empty water between Mexico and Cuba. They would be moving this way soon. I turned and headed back up to where my jeep was parked. I hoped I would get home before the storm hit.

13
Storm Warnings

The Margarita Road leads to hidden places the real world doesn't know of yet. However, it may be that as we expats drift along, we leave enough breadcrumbs in our wake to allow civilization to follow. Suddenly the secret places aren't so secret anymore. Then we have to ask ourselves: what do we do when the world comes roaring in to paradise? Who's to blame when that happens?

"What do you mean you're closing?" The woman was outraged. "Why? For how long?"

She and her husband had wandered in an hour or so before. Her jewelry was gold and too heavy for the beach. The spray tan she received a week before was already fading.

I figured they had come into town for some local 'color' before heading back to the resort down the highway. After claiming some loungers on my deck, they proceeded to race through several margaritas each. When her spouse reached the comatose stage, she left him snoring and moved inside to order another drink for herself. When I told her I couldn't serve her since we were closing up, she got pissed off.

I gave her a reassuring smile. "We're getting ready for the storm. Just in case."

She turned to look at the sea, which was calm and beautifully blue. "Just in case of what? What are you talking about? It's gorgeous out there."

"It is now," I said. "But in the next day or so, a big hurricane is either going to land here or pass close enough to make a mess out of things."

When I saw the shock in her eyes, I realized she had no clue. "I'm surprised your resort didn't say anything. They'll probably be evacuating all of the guests soon."

This news made her even angrier. "Evacuating? Motherfucker! How can they do this to me? I wait all year for a vacation and then this shit happens to me. Unbelievable." She set her glass down on the bar and hopped off her stool. "Fucking Mexico!"

She headed back out onto the deck to rouse her sleeping husband. "Harold. Harold! Wake up. We need to call the travel agent. We're having a hurricane!" As she dragged Harold off down the beach, I wondered if she knew the storm was going to pass over countless islands and screw with the lives of thousands of people before getting here. I decided if she did know, she didn't care.

For those of us living in paradise, this was not unusual. Most of the time, Mother Nature simply drenches us with countless rainstorms through the summer months. However, every once in a while we get something a little bigger, a little stronger. Sometimes we have a hurricane to deal with.

Hurricanes come with a number attached, one to five. After living through a couple, you get a sense of what that means. A Category 1 will bring enough rain to cause the roof to start leaking but usually won't keep you from enjoying your happy hour margaritas. A Cat 2 is a little rougher with downed power lines and flooded streets. It's best to stay inside until things blow over. When a storm reaches Cat 3, most people know to get off the beach and head for shelter far away from the rising tide. When a Cat 4 or 5 show up, it's crunch time. Those can be life-changers. Or life-enders. Adding to the unpredictability, a hurricane may suddenly get stronger just as it lands right on top of you.

Like most of its kind, the storm now approaching the coast started as a big pile of hot air drifting out over the Atlantic from Africa's Sahara desert. The winds moved westward and began to suck all the heat out of the water. As the whole mess slowly moved across the ocean, all that warm, wet air turned into thunderstorms that got bigger and angrier each day. By the time the thunderheads rolled past the Leeward Islands and into the Caribbean, the storm had doubled in size. The next day it doubled again. Then all of a sudden, that line of thunderstorms began to dance in a circular motion.

The weather folks named her Bertha. Bad-Ass Bertha, the local bar crowd called her. She was big, nasty, and looking for a fight. All the experts said our tiny beach town was likely to be her opponent.

I don't usually listen to weather predictions. It always seems like a lot of guesswork to me. When I do watch weather shows south of the border, it's mostly just to check out what the ladies giving the forecasts aren't wearing on camera. The tiny bit of cloth that passes for a skirt on TV in Mexico is something to see.

Still, this particular storm warning was getting more of my attention than the cute meteorologists. If the forecasters were correct, a Category 4 hurricane was going to wade ashore on my beach with 150-mph winds and 20-foot waves. My little thatched-roofed bar wouldn't stand much of a chance against that. I figured I should shut things down and prepare as best I could.

For the rest of the day, Jorge and I packed the glasses in boxes and put them in the storage room alongside the stools, tables, and beach umbrellas. We tied the lounge chairs to the railing of the deck and wheeled our big oil drum grill into the men's room. By the time we were done, anything that could move, blow away, or be broken from flying debris was secured or locked away. We even took down the poster of Brooke Burke wearing nothing but gold paint.

Then I went upstairs to my room above the bar. Some might call it small, even tiny. I called it cozy. As for the furnishings, there wasn't much to show for the last twelve years and not much that I would care about losing.

There was the little Buddha statue, a few books, my laptop, and some CDs. I popped the copy of Paul Butterfield's *East-West* out of the computer and put it back in its case. Then I bundled up my clothes and personal papers from the dresser drawers. Finally, I took my framed photo of Lynn playing in the surf near Tulum from off the wall. There wasn't anything that couldn't be quickly zipped up in a duffel bag and carted off some place that would hopefully stay dry through the storm. So that's what I did.

"Of course you can store your stuff with me. You can stay yourself, if you want. Lots of people are planning on riding things out here."

I had driven over to see if I could find shelter from the storm with my friend Chaz. Once there, I saw I wasn't the only one with that thought. Chaz gestured at the floor of his living room, which was piled with backpacks and a few sleeping bags. "Most of the group from the condos down on 38th will be here, and that bartender from Harry's is coming with some girlfriends. It's shaping up to be quite a party. You have to bring your own booze, though."

My semi-pirate Irish friend had recently moved inland and rented a large concrete block house on a dirt road in the jungle outside of town. Chaz said he needed to get away from the tourists and the noise of the never-ending hustle of life on the beach. I gave him some friendly grief about getting old, but I did understand his feelings.

The beachfront had become a nonstop party over the last few years. The blaring of electronic music put an end to seaside siestas. Twilight rum drinks and slow walks along the water's edge had given way to late night drunks vomiting in the sand and coke deals in the shadows. It was wearing thin for those of us who had moved to Paradise Beach to find a little peace and quiet.

Chaz's place now offered a different kind of refuge. Hopefully, it was far enough from the water to avoid the storm surge and strong enough to withstand the wind. "Sounds good," I said. "I'm in. Let me make sure Jorge is taken care of, and then I'll be back. Save me a spot on the floor."

As I left, Chaz raised his beer toward the sky, which was beginning to darken. "Just make sure you're here before the storm makes landfall," he shouted after me. "You don't want to be wandering around when it starts. And bring back more beer!"

I had promised Jorge I would help him put some plywood on the windows of his house before the storm hit. We took my jeep and drove out of the hotel zone, heading down the dirt roads that made up the large neighborhood where Jorge lived. He said he knew a place near his house to buy wood.

We were driving down the street, scattering kids and dogs, when Jorge told me to pull over and park. "What's going on?" I asked.

"You need to get out here and wait for me. I'll take the jeep and get the wood. It's just down the block."

"Why don't I just go with you?"

"Because they will double the price if they see you," he explained with an embarrassed look on his face. "If I go alone, I will pay the locals' price."

I handed Jorge the keys to the jeep and got out, and he headed down the street alone. About fifteen minutes later, he came back with a stack of plywood tied to the top of the jeep. I climbed in. Neither of us said anything as we drove away.

Before we got to his house, Jorge suddenly said, "Things are changing."

"Changing how?" I asked, although I already knew the answer.

"The Americans coming to town now, they don't want to fit in like before. Not like you. Not like the others who first came here. The ones coming now have lots of money. That's not a bad thing, but they think it can buy anything they want. The gringos want the best of everything in a place that's not theirs. It's beginning to make some Mexicans resentful. And greedy."

We pulled up in front of his house and unloaded the wood. It took us a couple of hours to nail the boards over the windows. By the time we were done it was getting dark, and the first raindrops were beginning to fall.

"Why not stay here with us tonight, Jefe?"

I thanked him for the offer but told him I already had a place lined up.

"Do you want me to go out to the beach later and check on the bar?"

"No. I want you to stay here with your family until the storm passes. There is nothing we can do until that happens." As I left, his wife was gathering the children to light a candle in front of a statue of the Virgin de Guadalupe.

By the time I made it back to Chaz's place, the rain was coming in sheets, and winds were sending trash blowing down the street. The electricity was already out, and Chaz had set candles around a makeshift bar in the living room, giving the place a warm glow. A good-sized group had settled in to wait out the storm. Like most gatherings in Paradise Beach, it had an international flavor.

As promised, I saw the voluptuous young barmaid from Handsome Harry's. She had brought some others—kids from the States on summer break from college was my guess. They were already cracking the top on a bottle of tequila. Any reason to party. There were also two or three couples, ranging from aging adolescents to nearly retired middle aged, all staying in the new condos near the beach. They were smiling, but I could tell they were nervous about the storm.

Over in a corner, I saw Tomas, the young Italian dive instructor from a shop near my bar. He was snuggling up to a frightened-looking Argentinean girl who supported herself by giving massages on the beach. Sitting alone out in the kitchen was a local named Paco who seemed to be several drinks ahead of everyone else. Beer and tequila bottles were piled up on the table in front of him.

I took Chaz aside and asked about Paco's condition. He shook his head sadly. "The best I can tell, he's been on a binge for a day or two. I found him just after they tossed him out of the Mermaid Café. He refused to go home, but everybody is closing down, so I brought him here. I figure what the hell, what's one more stray in this mix?"

"So why is he getting so drunk?"

Chaz shrugged. "Who knows? He's in a Mexican mood tonight. Somebody said he lost his job, but I don't know for sure."

"Shit," I said. "This is not good." I looked at Paco's head beginning to droop. Mexican men have a tradition about booze: once the drinking starts, it keeps going until the last one passes out. *Go Big or Go Home* is the slogan down here.

While Chaz went to help the college girls with their tequila bottle, I walked over to offer Paco some solace. "Hey, buddy," I said. As I sat down across the table, another storm wave hit. That's the way of hurricanes: wind and rain pass through, followed by calm, followed by another wave. I wondered how strong the storm would get.

Paco looked up from his beer with a frown on his face. "Pinche gringos."

He was a good-looking kid, probably in his late twenties. He spoke perfect English, sold timeshares in town, and had lived for a while in Los Angeles. He was as Americanized as Mom's apple pie. Except when he drank.

"That means fucking gringos."

"I know," I said. "I speak enough Spanish to figure out when I am being insulted."

Paco glared at me and took another swig of beer before setting it down carefully and then picking up a full one. I knew this could get a bit rough. While a drunken binge south of the border may have times of unrestrained laughter and camaraderie that only alcohol can sustain ("I love you man!"), it may also have a dark side. The underlying sense of Norte Americanos as an invading army is always just beneath the surface.

From past experience, I recognized I had better tread carefully. Despite years of friendship with Paco, I understood I wasn't part of his definition of 'one of us' when he was drunk. He liked me well enough but didn't care for my skin color at the moment.

It's not exactly racial prejudice. It's more like self-defense. Some Mexicans see their country as the world's unwanted stepchild. They are not quite Spanish and not quite Indian, a mixture that leaves them confused about their roots and heritage. The wonderful Mexican poet Octavio Paz said that Mexicans see themselves as the fruit of an Indian maiden violated by a Spanish invader. They are hijos de la chingada—the children of raped mothers.

A self-image like that can instill some serious cultural resentment. Given this history, some Mexicans wonder why anyone not born here would want to assimilate into a society full of corruption, poverty, pain, abuse, and confusion. Those foreigners who say they do are viewed as having ulterior motives. Even gringos who come to embrace Mexico may still be suspected of trying to rip her off.

I sat down and picked up a beer. "Yeah, the tourists can be a pain in the ass," I said.

Paco shook his head violently in disagreement. "It's not just the tourists. At least they spend all those Yankee dollars." He slammed his palm on the tabletop for emphasis, knocking over some of the empty bottles. "The ones I really can't stand are the ones who come here to stay. The ... the ... " He searched for the word lost in his booze-addled brain.

"The expats," I offered helpfully.

"Yes!" he exploded. "Them! The pinche expats. That means ... "

"I know what it means." I took advantage of his taking another swallow of beer to try to lower the intensity a little. "What's wrong with expats? They aren't all bad. Look at me," I said with an exaggerated smile.

Paco did as instructed, trying to focus on my face. "Yeah," he said finally, "you're all right. You at least remember you are in Mexico. Those other putas don't belong here." He swung his arm around as if to include a crowd that was there only in his mind. "They treat my home like it's a fucking suburb of Dallas." He threw up his hands in disgust. "Chinga sus madres!"

As the howl of the wind began to deepen, he settled back in his chair and let out his breath. I thought it was over, but he was just taking a break before starting in again. "I hate them all. I hate their fucking Starbucks, and I hate their fucking Haagen Dazs. You ever see a local kid in one of those Haagen Dazs stores?" I gave a noncommittal shrug.

Paco answered for me. "Of course not. They don't put those places out in the barrio because Mexicans can't afford them. They're only by the big hotels. Tell me, why is this Mexican town full of places Mexicans can't afford?" He shook his head sadly. "Lemme ask you something else," he said, the words beginning to slur. "You know how many gringo charities there are around town to help stray dogs and cats?" He pronounced it *shhtray*.

"No, I don't." I knew that several folks from the States funded some animal shelters a few years back and pitched the tourists for donations on a regular basis. The owners get a tax break, and the tourists feel good about themselves. It didn't seem like a bad thing to me.

Paco laughed, but it wasn't a happy laugh. "Four." He looked disgusted. "Boy, you gringos love our fucking puppies and kittens. You can't walk down the street without somebody asking for a handout for the damned dogs. 'Rescue animals' they call them. Why doesn't anybody want to rescue the people who live here? Huh?"

He shook his finger in my face. "Tell me, how many U.S. dollars are given to the mother with three kids who works six days a week changing dirty sheets in some resort?" He was practically shouting now. "Who helps her when her kid needs an operation—but the only doctor available for Mexicans is 300 kilometers away and there is no money for a bus ticket? How many gringos step forward to rescue that woman? None!" he shouted before I could answer.

He regained some composure. "You people love our street dogs, but our kids are nothing to you. You don't care about them until they are old enough to wait on your table at the beach club."

I couldn't say he was wrong.

Paco picked up another beer and took a long swig before setting it down. He let out a heavy sigh. "The ones like you, Poppa, and people like Chaz—you're okay. You came down to live in Mexico. That's cool. But these other pendejo mothers just want us to be Miami with better prices."

I thought for a moment he might cry.

"Too many of you want Mexico without the Mexicans. I

know there are good Norte Americanos, but sometimes I pray to the Virgin that someday one of these hurricanes will be strong enough to blow all you gringos back north across the border. Maybe then we could have our country back."

He folded his arms on the table in front of him and laid his head on them. In a few minutes, I heard him softly snoring. The evening was finally over for Paco. For me, too. I was beat.

I got up and wandered back into the living room to pour myself a shot of tequila. One of the couples from the condos, their fear of the weather now drowned in alcohol, was dancing to a Jimmy Buffett CD on Chaz's battery-operated boom box.

The woman paused in her dancing to reach out and grab my hand as I passed her. "What's his problem?" she asked, nodding toward Paco in the kitchen.

"Nothing," I said, slipping loose of her grasp. "Just a little too much to drink."

She frowned and rolled her eyes. "I heard some of what he said. I don't get it. These people never had it so good until we all started coming here from the States to spend money." She shook her head in disgust and went back to dancing with her husband.

I took my tequila and one of the candles and headed upstairs. I paused at one door and heard the unmistakable sounds of expat ecstasy. I moved further down the hall, found an unoccupied room, and settled in on the floor, leaning my back against the wall to get some rest.

The house suddenly shook, as the force of another storm wave passed over. I heard the rain pounding against the boards that covered the windows and wondered if Paco just might get his prayer answered tonight. From downstairs, I could faintly hear the sound of drunken laughter and people singing along with the music.

"Wasted away again in Margaritaville ... "

14
Heading Out

Scientists and astronomers call them black holes. They are stars that have shone too brightly for too long. They use themselves up and burn themselves out, eventually leaving a darkness so dense that no light can penetrate it. When that happens, the brilliant place that once filled up a part of the sky can no longer be found.

It had been a few weeks since Bad-Ass Bertha passed through Paradise Beach. Before going on her way, the hurricane had decimated the town and taken down all the electrical lines along the coast. The plan issued by the Palacio Municipal was to have power restored to the big resort hotels first and then later concentrate on the neighborhoods.

Someone obviously decided that turning the resort lights back on would keep the tourist money flowing. Or maybe somebody in the government had been slipped some pesos to do it this way. Regardless, after the sun went down, the beach was pitch black. As I walked onto the sand, the only lights to be seen were from passing ships out in deep water.

I had brought along a candle and managed to find an

unbroken glass while rummaging around in the ruins of my bar. I put the candle inside, lit it, and sat down on the sand where Poppa's Bar and Grill had once stood. The small flame didn't help a lot, but I wouldn't need any light to say goodbye.

There wasn't much left of my place but a few scattered boards here and there. About half of the roof remained, supported by a beam that would fall with the first good push. Most of the deck had been buried in the sand. The rest of the building was strewn over the beach and carried inland. Out in the surf, one of my beer coolers floated with the tide.

In the old days, I could have built another bar in a few weeks without any problem. That's how it was done when I first washed ashore on Paradise Beach. A few local guys would construct some cinder block walls and cover the whole thing with woven palm leaves. Life was simple back then. Not anymore. Things had changed.

The storm had barely passed out to sea when the government started arranging to bulldoze over any memory of my place. By the time I was able to get down to the beach and assess the damage, I found a city inspector already posting a sign on the wreckage declaring my business abandoned.

"Señor, I haven't abandoned anything," I said. "This is my place, and I have had this spot on the beach for the last 12 years."

He was short and stocky with a stomach that hung well out over the belt pushed low on his hips. His face was covered in perspiration from the effort of walking on the beach. With a bored expression, he looked up from his clipboard to glance at what was left of my bar after the storm had knocked it down like one of the three little pigs' straw houses.

"There is nothing here now. If you want to start another

business, you must apply for a construction permit." He handed me my official notice and headed down the beach toward where Handsome Harry's Café once stood.

I had worried about this moment for some time. Even before the storm, the local authorities began enforcing new rules for building on the beach. Construction could only be done by pre-authorized companies, the owners of which were generally connected by family ties to local politicians. The prices they were charging were way beyond what I could pay to rebuild. Even with whatever the insurance company would pay, I just wasn't wealthy enough to get back on the sand.

It didn't matter. Even if I could afford to build a new bar, the city was never going to give me a business permit. I wasn't wanted anymore. Guys in suits were calling the shots now.

Drug cartel lawyers and foreign investment bankers had begun taking notice of Paradise Beach long ago. Those types are always on the lookout for a place where money can be laundered and hidden in plain sight. This little slice of heaven looked pretty good to them.

It started quietly with the funneling of cash to local officials, cops, and hotel syndicates. Bit by bit, the bad boys had been laying claim to the town. Nobody seemed to notice. The Mexicans knew better than to say anything, and the tourists didn't care who owned the beach as long as the margaritas were cold. As for the expats, well, there was always another beach out there somewhere.

The hurricane had finally given the big-money folks a real chance to dig in on a large scale. Once the local politicians were paid off, the devastated beachfront was up for grabs, and plans for the transformation of Paradise Beach into another Cancun went into high gear.

Little places like Poppa's Bar and Grill would eventually be replaced by steel-and-chrome monstrosities complete with stone pizza ovens and giant-screen TVs. Multi-story condo hotels would keep the tourists close by to sip drinks out of a spigot and swim inside a roped-off 'private' section of the ocean.

I figured Paradise Beach had a glorious future as a world-class resort town for the beautiful and rich, and it was clear I was not invited to be part of it. The people who ran things now had decided riffraff like me should be cleared off the new beach.

Oh sure, I might be able to find a job as a bartender somewhere in town. I could probably find work at one of the big hotels. I'd end up wearing a white shirt and bow tie while serving overpriced pre-mixed margaritas to dot com millionaires. "Would you like salt on the rim, Mr. Smith? That will be another fifteen dollars, please."

Or maybe I could start over. I could set up shop back on the side streets of one of the outlying neighborhoods where rent was still affordable, hoping my old customers would search me out. But why bother? Even that wouldn't last long.

It wasn't my town anymore. Civilization had come to Paradise Beach, and like a young Huck Finn, I knew from experience I wouldn't fit in. It was time to get back on the Margarita Road.

As it turned out, I wasn't alone either in the choice to go or in deciding to spend my last evening sitting on the sand. My friend Chaz had similar ideas.

Chaz had been swimming against the tide for a while. A few years back, he had grown bored with sailing boats down from Florida for other people to enjoy. Later, the steady work of piloting party catamarans up and down the beach had allowed him to stay in Mexico on a permanent basis. Eventually he grew frustrated with trying to live off of shitty wages and a few tips.

Unfortunately, with Paradise Beach's growing status as an upscale vacation destination, there wasn't a real need for a sailor with Chaz's skills. Tourists didn't want much more than a sunset cruise just offshore for an hour or two. Even inexperienced local boys could handle that chore with a little training. Chaz told me he could have made some decent money if he was willing to run boats up from Belize at night with no questions asked, but that wasn't his style. "I'm desperate, not crazy," he said.

It had become clear that Chaz wasn't going to make a living on the water in Paradise Beach anymore. When I suggested he find something other than boats to make money, he dismissed it out of hand. "Sailing is what I do. I'd go crazy if I had to give it up for long. Besides, even if I could find work, it's time to go somewhere else. This place belongs to other people now."

I understood. Even before the hurricane had wiped the beach out, the wanderers who first settled in on this edge of the Caribbean were leaving. Those who stayed on were slowly being overwhelmed by new arrivals.

The beach had been filling up with North American retirees and upscale tourists for a while. They were joined by kids with too much money and attitude from Paris, Buenos Aires, and Mexico City. Crowding the beach clubs during the day and packing the bars at night, they were well off, rude, and demanding. This was their town now. It wouldn't be long before the taco stands and fishing boats were crowded out by Diesel stores and Sunglass Huts. Strolling mariachis would soon be replaced by recorded hip-hop blaring through gigantic speakers.

People like Chaz and I were dinosaurs. Things were changing, and if we couldn't accept that, we needed to move on. Since neither of us was very good at adapting to the world we once left behind, we had each decided it was time to go. When we discovered the other was also leaving, we agreed to meet on the beach in the wee hours of the morning to say our goodbyes to the little bay that had been our home.

"Over here!" I yelled to Chaz when I saw him coming down the dark beach with a flashlight in hand. He made his way to where I sat and plopped down beside me. He had not come empty-handed. From his backpack, he pulled a bottle of very pricey, very old Cuban rum.

"Figured we ought to celebrate ... or something," he said as he twisted the cap off the bottle. He took a swallow and handed it to me.

I hesitated. "Are you sure you want to drink this tonight? Shouldn't you save it for a special occasion?"

"Well, I had been planning on keeping it until the day Heidi Klum showed up and wanted a private sailing lesson." Chaz grinned. "Since she never did, this seems as good a time as any."

I tilted the bottle, and the rum flowed into my mouth. The taste was sharp at first, followed by a soft memory. Thank goodness the folks back in the U.S. had been saved from this insidious caribe-communist plot for decades. Maybe someday that would change. Maybe not.

Chaz took out a cigarette and lit it from the candle. He looked sad as he glanced around at the broken boards sticking out of the sand. It was all that was left of my bar. "Man," he said morosely. There wasn't much else to say.

"So tell me, where are you headed?" I asked, handing him back the rum bottle.

Chaz smiled again. "Querencia," he said.

"Where the hell is that?" I'd never heard of it.

Instead of answering, he asked me a question. "Have you ever seen a bullfight?"

I said I had, many years ago, and didn't care much for it.

"Yeah, you Americans like your beef killed in secret so that it magically appears in plastic at the grocery."

I ignored that. "What does that have to do with where you're going next?"

He didn't seem to hear my question but went on about bullfighting. "When the bull first goes into the bullring, he is the king of everything he sees. He is the most powerful and skillful creature there. The bull knows this, the horses in the ring know this, and the men in those funny clothes certainly know it. They are all afraid of the bull. As well they should be. Then the attack begins. First, it's just guys waving brightly colored capes and flags. The bull charges again and again. He knows he can catch these puny little things, except it turns out he can't. Those fluttering pieces of color somehow stay just beyond his reach. He can never quite get to them."

Chaz stretched out his hand toward the sea and quickly closed it on nothing, as if he had missed whatever he was reaching for.

"Now the bull really starts to hurt. Men stick him with spear points from up high on horses. Others throw sharp darts into his back. It's all pain, blood, and confusion. Then the matador comes out. For an instant, the bull begins to feel better. He should be able to kill this one guy, but he can't. He's too tired by now. He has lost too much blood. To the bull's amazement, he finds the man has become his equal. He is uncertain, maybe even fearful, for the first time in his life. He needs to get away—to find a safe spot so he can get his strength back."

I was beginning to see what all this had to do with Chaz and me. "The bull wants to go home," I said.

Chaz nodded in agreement. "Just for the moment. Just to catch his breath."

"But he can't," I said. "He is stuck in the bullring."

"Yes, he is. And he is not leaving there alive. By now, even the bull instinctively knows this. That doesn't mean he's giving up. He just needs to find a spot where he can feel safe for a minute. Maybe it's back up against the wall of the ring where he feels protected. Maybe it's the point furthest from the matador. It's different for every bull. Wherever it is, it's the place where he can gather strength before heading back into the fight. That spot is called his querencia."

Chaz and I sat quietly for a moment.

"So where is it?" I looked and saw him smiling in the glow of the candlelight. "Where's your querencia?"

"France," he said.

I was surprised. Over the decade I had known Chaz, I had heard him tell wild stories of sailing throughout the Caribbean and of years spent in Australia, the South Pacific, and a dozen other places. I had never heard him mention France. He told me about it now.

"When I was sixteen, I ran away from Belfast. I was tired of it all. Tired of the British soldiers, tired of the IRA drumbeat, and tired of being poor and hopeless. And I was really tired of being smacked around by my old man. I lied about my age and got a job on the first freighter heading away from Ireland. It took me over to Le Havre in France. I was seasick as hell and puked my guts out the whole way." He chuckled at the mental image of his younger self.

"When we docked, I headed inland. I didn't have a clue. I spoke no French and only had a few coins in my pocket. I was just trying to get as far away as possible from my miserable life. I started hitchhiking south. I would beg for food and sleep on the side of the road and then every day stand next to the highway with my thumb out. After a couple of days of hitching rides, a bloke dropped me off at the seaside in Nice. I had never seen a beach like that. There wasn't any sand. It was all rocks. Little round, smooth stones. Out in front was the Mediterranean, all blue and dark and just the most beautiful thing I had ever seen. It was sunset when I got there, and I stretched out on those little stones and fell asleep. I guess I must have been tired. I woke up with the sunrise and started my new life."

He sighed softly at the memory. "That's where I got my first job on a sailboat. That's where I was really born. I'm going back there."

"Do you think you're going to find that 16-year-old kid again?"

He leaned back and looked up at the stars. "No. That boy is long gone. There's no use in even looking for him. But it was my starting point once for a new life. I figure, why not try it again? Maybe I'll get just as lucky the second time around."

I lifted the rum bottle in a salute to him. "Querencia," I said.

Chaz nodded in return. "And you? Where's your safe

place?"

I was afraid he was going to ask me that.

"I don't know. I don't even know what's next. Cuba's possible. I know a guy who says he can arrange something for me. There's a beach club in Thailand where I can work if I want. And there's always New Orleans. I love the French Quarter. Maybe none of them. Maybe all of them. I do know I'm starting in Key West. Then I'll see what happens."

"Key West? What's in Key West?" Chaz asked.

I reached under my shirt and picked the gold sand dollar off my chest where it hung from a chain around my neck. I rubbed it between my fingers "Somebody special."

Chaz raised his eyebrows. "Really? The woman from Chicago? What's her name? Lynn?"

"Yeah, that's the one. We've been in touch. She called me a few days ago. She filed for divorce and put her house up for sale. She is ready to start her new life, she says. We are going to meet up in Florida and see what happens next. I think the Keys are her querencia."

"Are they yours?"

I shrugged. "I haven't figured that out yet."

"There's no place you call home?"

"I don't know. Maybe I'm still just chasing colored flags."

We sat silently on the beach for a time, finishing off the rum and listening to the sea's night sounds. Eventually, the first rays of the rising sun showed in the eastern sky.

Chaz stretched his arms out as if embracing the whole scene. "Time for me to go, amigo. I have a plane to catch this morning. What about you?"

"I still have a few hours," I said. "I'm heading out tonight."

He looked me in the eye. "Stay in touch. Drop an e-mail

or something from time to time. Maybe we'll cross paths again."

"For sure."

We stood and hugged. Chaz stepped away and looked around the beach, its sand now glowing pink in the dawn. "It was fun, wasn't it?"

Then he was gone.

Sitting back down to finish watching the sunrise, I saw the small birds begin to run on the sand. In a short time, groups of pelicans began to fly low over the shallows, looking for breakfast. They had been good company for many years, and I hoped their new neighbors would treat them well.

I thought of how Chaz had asked me about finding a home. I wasn't sure I knew what home was, let alone how to go about finding one. Once, back in the hills north of San Francisco, a bald, robe-wearing Buddhist monk named Harold told me that understanding life started with the knowledge that nothing lasts forever. "It's always changing," he said. "Time is a stream rushing by. You can never stop it. All you have is this exact moment."

It's the same lesson that living on the beach has taught me. I've watched driftwood get stuck in the sand, only to be pulled back out to sea and carried by the currents to another beach or island. I often wondered: where does the idea of home fit in with all that?

One thing I knew for certain: I had always been drawn to the edge of the world—near an ocean where the sun rises or disappears, where the rules are a lot less rigid, and where the open water and endless sky can make a person feel free. For a long time, Paradise Beach had been like that, and if I had to keep traveling to find another place as special, it was a journey

I was willing to take. Having the company of somebody I loved on that journey just might make it the closest thing to home I'd ever know. I hoped to find out.

A short time later, I heard the sound of trucks pulling up on the beach behind me. Out of the corner of my eye, I saw a bulldozer roll onto the sand. I stood and slowly walked up to the frontage road where my jeep was parked next to a recently created sand dune.

I was giving my jeep to Jorge as a farewell gift. It wasn't in great shape or worth very much, but if he could keep it running, it would be a help to his family. I was heading for his house, and he would drive me to the airport later that afternoon.

I stood for a moment, looking back out over the beach. The water was as calm and motionless as I had ever seen it. It must have been mornings like this that made the first sailors want to set out to sea to find something more. "Vaya con Dios," I whispered to the birds in flight above me. After a final glance out to the horizon, I stamped my feet to knock the sand off, climbed in the jeep, and drove away. I was back on the Margarita Road.

Acknowledgments

Writers tell themselves that theirs is a lonely task done best in isolation. Well, that's a load of crap. Writing a book requires a tremendous amount of help. I found myself in a constant state of needing assistance with everything from proofreading to finding plot holes to recovering pages stolen by the gremlins that live in my computer.

Luckily, I was blessed to have the unwavering support and patience of family and friends in my endeavors as an author. To each and every one of them, I offer this woefully inadequate expression of gratitude. I couldn't have done it without them.

There are a few people whose contributions were so unique and transformative as to require special recognition:

My friend Melanie Dusseau-Ray is a poet, author, and teacher. The truest of friends, she assumed the roles of muse, taskmaster, and critic early on. Without her suggestions and strong belief in my work, this book would never have come to be.

Bestselling author Cyra McFadden took my collection of papers and edited them into something readable. For me, this was a gift from the gods, as working with Cyra was an advanced education in writing. She made me a better writer and along the way became the dearest of friends.

My Dharma brother Peter Coyote is one of the most giving human beings I have ever known. He generously took time from his normally insane schedule as an author, activist, actor, and Zen Buddhist priest to read drafts of this book and offer some truly creative approaches to my work.

Of course, there would be no book at all but for the lovely and loving people I met in my ten years south of the border. The locals, expats, tourists, and drifters who shared their lives and dreams with me were the inspiration for these tales. I cannot ever adequately express my love for Mexico and the people who embraced me there.

Finally, my greatest appreciation goes to my wife, Cheri. She is on every page. She proofread, typed, spell-checked, corrected my grammar, offered suggestions, and brainstormed ideas. She held my hand through the entire writing of this novel and never doubted its value, even when I did. Her love is what sustains me in writing and in living. This is her book as much as mine.

The Author

Before running away from home, Anthony Lee Head was a trial lawyer, history teacher, and martial arts instructor living in San Francisco. In a fit of middle-aged madness, Tony and his wife Cheri drove 3500 miles to begin a new life in Playa del Carmen, Mexico. There they bought a run-down hostel near the Caribbean Sea, which they transformed into an award-winning hotel and bar.

Living in a white sand and blue water paradise, they rented rooms, poured drinks, ate tacos, blogged about their unconventional life, practiced their Spanglish, and navigated the endless challenges of living and working in a foreign land.

After a decade of inhabiting the wonderfully strange world of expats, they returned to California, bringing with them a pack of rescue animals—four dogs and six cats. After settling just north of the Golden Gate Bridge, Tony began formal practice as an ordained lay Zen Buddhist, while beginning to indulge his inner storyteller.

Driftwood: Stories from the Margarita Road is his first book. He is currently working on both a new novel and a memoir based on his adventures in Mexico.

www.anthonyleehead.com
tony@anthonyleehead.com
www.facebook.com/anthonyleehead

Made in the USA
Coppell, TX
04 June 2021

56897103R00151